W9-ASH-736

DISCARDED

MYS

Death
Without
Tenure

Books by Joanne Dobson

Quieter Than Sleep
The Northbury Papers
The Raven and the Nightingale
Cold and Pure and Very Dead
The Maltese Manuscript
Death Without Tenure

Death Without Tenure

Joanne Dobson

Poisoned Pen Press

First Edition 2010

10 9 8 7 6 5 4 3 2 1

Library of Congress Catalog Card Number: 2009931424

ISBN: 978-1-59058-585-6 Hardcover
       978-1-59058-709-6 Trade Paperback

Poisoned Pen Press
6962 E. First Ave., Ste. 103
Scottsdale, AZ 85251
www.poisonedpenpress.com
info@poisonedpenpress.com

Printed in the United States of America

For Serena Dobson

Acknowledgments

My thanks to the following people who have helped inspire, clarify, and provide information for this story: Harold Bonacquist, Frank Couvares, David M. Dobson, Ayesha Khan, and Barbara Strauss. I want to especially thank those at Oberlin College who went out of their way to make my visit so enjoyable and informative, among them Professors Wendy Kozol, Eve Sandberg, and Sandy Zagarell—and to their wonderful students.

And to my manuscript readers, who keep me on track and in control: Marie-Laure Degener, Diana Healy, Kate Lombardi, Eve Sandberg, Sandy Zagarell, and, especially, Bev Myers.

And, as always, to Dave Dobson, who supports me at every turn.

Chapter One

Friday 10/2

I was in my English Department office grading papers at a red-hot pace, a red pencil clutched in my fist, when the door crashed open and Professor Miles Jewell came storming in. He fit the red color motif: his face was crimson, maybe even darker, maybe the color of his buttoned-up burgundy cardigan.

I'd been grading fast. As soon as I was done with the papers, I planned to put finishing touches on a new scholarly article to submit along with my petition for tenure. Tenure in the Enfield College English Department would cap my long journey from hardscrabble New-England single mom to academic woman with a secure professional future. Almost, almost, I could feel the long weight of my scholarly preparation begin to lift from my shoulders.

But now, here was my elderly colleague, breathing heavily, staring at me pop-eyed. I jumped up from my desk chair. "Miles!" What had I done this time to tick him off?

Miles was attempting to speak. *Ah hee, ah hee.* His thick white hair stuck up on one side. I feared he was going to drop dead right then and there on the antediluvian Oriental rug in front of my desk.

I rushed over to Miles, took him by the arm and led him to the green vinyl chair. "What can I get you? A glass of water? Some bourbon?"

An ambulance?

He plopped into the chair, and the cushion made its customary *ffffrrrttt*. "No, no. I'll be all right. Just give me a minute." He began tugging at his black knit tie.

I went for water from the cooler in the department office. I knew where the bourbon was if I needed it—in the bottom drawer of Monica's desk, next to her emergency stash of sanitary napkins.

By the time I got back to Miles with the water, he looked more composed. He took the flimsy paper cup. "Close the door," he said.

Miles Jewell was chairman emeritus of the English Department. In some ways it was too bad he no longer headed it; he'd had a death grip on the position for so long that his outmoded style of scholarship was coming back in again. Miles and I had squabbled off and on over my penchant for teaching literary texts other than his precious Great Tradition: Chaucer, Shakespeare, Milton, and their hordes of dead white sons. But he'd been fighting a losing battle: by now the writing of women and other too-long dispossessed social groups had been thoroughly integrated into the curriculum of literary studies. He'd learned a few things from me, I think. I know I'd learned from him: to read texts closely, to respect the language as well as the message, even to consider the possible benefits of Tradition. But, while no longer kneejerk intellectual antagonists, we weren't exactly pals.

Therefore I was dumbfounded when he said, "Close the door," which in Enfield College protocol suggests either secrets to be shared or a dressing down to be administered. I closed the door. Pulling up the black captain's chair, I sat down across from him. What could have driven Professor Miles Jewell to such an agitated state? Since Miles was no longer in a position to tell me off, he must have some dire secret to share with me.

"Karen," he said, "I've just come from a meeting of the senior faculty...."

Oh, God: this was about tenure. My heart flipped. Then it flopped. The protracted silence and the look of...could it be *compassion?...*in Miles' beady eyes derailed whatever composure I might have summoned. I picked up the red pencil and began rolling it between numb fingers. "What?" I exclaimed. "What?"

"...and I'm furious. You and I have had our differences through the years..." he began, sonorously.

The phone rang. I ignored it. It would go to voice-mail. A little popping noise from my computer let me know I had a new e-mail message. It would keep.

"...but I've always had respect for your scholarly integrity, and your popularity with the students is indicative of excellent teaching."

"And...?" I urged, hoping I shouldn't be saying "But..."

"But...given the sloppy and doctrinaire thinking of the new department leadership, I'm afraid there's a possibility that your tenure petition might be in jeopardy."

The red pencil snapped in two. I let the pieces fall to the floor, along with my heart. "What did I do?"

"Nothing. Absolutely nothing. Of course you know that faculty meetings are strictly confidential."

I nodded. *Then what the hell was he doing here? It must be apocalyptic, for him to be breaking The Code.*

With his elbows on his knees Miles leaned close, keeping his voice down. "I have always strictly adhered to the rules of confidentiality, but when the department to which I have devoted my entire professional life is being led by its nincompoop of a chairman to commit an egregious wrong, I'll step up to the plate one last time. I'm on the verge of a much deserved retirement. What can they do to me? Snatch away my emeritus rank? And I think it's only right that you know what you're up against."

He took a drink of water. My throat was dry, too.

Placing the cup on a side table, Miles stroked the white beard he had recently cultivated. It wasn't the full, mustachioed type of beard that would have made him look like Santa Claus, but rather a chin-line growth, affording him the appearance of an sagacious old sea captain. He continued, "Given the growing vulgarity that passes for academic discourse these days, I shouldn't be astounded at our new chairman's tactics, but, frankly, I am."

A tentative knock on the door startled me. I checked my watch. It was the beginning of office hours. "Come back later," I croaked to whichever student was seeking my counsel. Then I took a deep breath—might as well get it over with. "What's Ned done?"

"Ahem. You do know, don't you, that the college administration announced this semester that only one person in each department could be granted tenure this year."

"Yes." Words had become knives; little bloody cuts scored my psyche. "To avoid a skewed tenured-to-untenured ratio in the faculty, right?"

"Yes, ahem. A very problematic move, in my opinion—could very well leave us open to litigation. And now, at that lame excuse for a senior-faculty department meeting, Herr Professor Doktor Hilton announced that if we're only allowed to tenure one candidate, it should be Joe Lone Wolf rather than you."

I felt as if my heart were pumping cold red ink. *Joe Lone Wolf!* As far as I knew, my colleague Joe hadn't published a book. In fact, rumor said he hadn't even finished his dissertation.

And I had published a lot—two scholarly books, several articles in academic journals, one in a much-lauded book of essays—plus I had another book manuscript under contract.

And there they sat, my scholarly works, piled in modest heaps across the shiny surface of the long oak conference table. It was late afternoon and the sun slanted through the russet leaves of the maple tree outside the window, casting a golden patina over my desk, chairs, and bookcases, positively sanctifying the manuscripts, books, and scholarly journals awaiting evaluation by my colleagues.

And then there was the box. Next to the table. Waiting.

I hate to think about how much time and energy I had put into choosing the box in which I would submit to the Enfield College English Department the scholarly material upon which I would be judged worthy of tenure. Or not. I'd given in to magical thinking; if I had just the right box—size, shape, color, political correctness (*recycled* cardboard)—serious but accessible, dignified but modest, a box that spoke volumes about my intellectual capacities, collegial usefulness and pedagogical skill—then surely I would unanimously and enthusiastically be granted tenure. But now...

"Why Joe?" I croaked.

"Reparations for the atrocities of history." Miles looked as if he'd just eaten prunes. "Joe is Native American. According to Hilton, because Joe Wolf is a member of a native tradition where, from prehistory, knowledge has been transmitted orally, he should not be judged on his writings, but on his 'speakings.' Evidently it would perpetuate hegemonic oppression to expect him to complete a written dissertation. In his case we must practice radical equalitarianism."

"Oh, God." I dropped my head into my hands. My fingers were cold against my burning cheeks. I was doomed. Radical equalitarianism? *Speakings*?

Joe and I had been hired during the same year, but we'd never been friends. Any overtures I'd made to my Native colleague, he'd spurned right from the start. As far as I could tell, he'd never had even a single pal among the other professors. He'd kept such a low profile in the department, sitting in the back of the room during department meetings, never speaking up or volunteering for committees, that eventually I'd almost forgotten about him. Joe Lone Wolf was a loner by name and a loner by nature.

Miles continued. "And then Ned brought out Wolf's teaching evaluations, which, I must say, have been consistently enthusiastic over the years. Hilton called them 'evidence of tenurable excellence in teaching.'" Miles found a blue-edged white handkerchief somewhere in his sweater, and wiped sweat from his forehead. "He says that tenuring Joe Lone Wolf, despite an incomplete dissertation and even though he's never published a word, 'would constitute a bold challenge to print-dominated Western culture, thus striking a radical and visionary blow for intellectual reparations to a persecuted race.'"

So, I was right; Joe had no Ph.D. I could feel a minute flame of anger beginning to burn in my chest. I wanted to throw a tantrum, scream, "It's not fair!" I wanted to hit someone. I wanted to slug that pantywaist, Ned Hilton. And I could do it, too—he's such a skinny wimp. "Why is Ned doing this?"

"You know Ned. As far as I can tell, he feels he's on a mission, one so transcendent in importance that it justifies setting aside the customary tenure standards in the interests of social justice."

"So, it's a political mission?"

Miles put his gnarled hand to his chin and thought for a moment. "I think he sees it as even larger than that. He's got grandiose 'polycultural' plans for the makeup of the English faculty—'multicultural' is no longer an adequate descriptor, he says. I truly believe he's deluded himself into thinking that the mere teaching of literature can obviate global injustice."

Like world peace, obviating global injustice is a laudable goal. I just couldn't see how denying me tenure could help achieve either of these worthy objectives. I cleared my throat. "Did anyone take issue with him?"

"I was vociferous, of course."

My champion. I studied him, this ancient academic warrior. For him "vociferous" was as muscular as it got.

"And a few others made stabs at defending your case. But I'm not happy about the makeup of the tenure decision committee."

"Don't tell me—Sally Chennile?" Sally considers herself to be an academic gadfly, a provocateur. She's Enfield's punkish talking-head celebrity, taking the sexiest tenets of cultural theory on the TV talk-show circuit: Oprah, Leno, the View.

"I'm sorry to say." He bowed his head, then looked up and stared me directly in the eye. "And Harriet Person. Harriet suggested that you might well be 'too successful' for the Enfield English Department. That your ambition might better be satisfied at some large research university."

In other words, I had more publications than Harriet, the Director of Women's Studies, did, and she was jealous. I jumped up from my chair and went over to the bookcase where I keep *The Complete Poems of Emily Dickinson.*

"Then Chenille said you were a contentious presence at department meetings."

In other words, I often disagreed with Sally about department policies, and she didn't like it. I opened the Dickinson volume at random.

"And Person added that she suspected you were giving inflated grades, because your classes were always suspiciously full."

In other words, Harriet had the most under-enrolled courses in the school. I glanced down at the book. *A great Hope fell / You heard no noise / The Ruin was within.*

Doomed. Doomed by my hard work. Doomed because I call it as I see it. Good-bye to tenure. Farewell to the lovely green campus of Enfield College and the future I had envisioned for myself there.

"Who are the others on the committee?" I sat down again with the volume of poems in my hand. I'd always have Emily.

"Don't worry—they're on your side." With his hands on its arms he pushed himself up out of the green chair. He walked to the door and grasped the brass knob. Before turning it he looked back over his shoulder. "But, of course, it takes only a couple of negative votes to give the deans pause."

As I watched Miles lumber down the hall, I felt as if I'd been hit in the head with the Oxford English Dictionary, the old-fashioned kind—in print.

For most of my adult life I had been working toward this goal—a secure future doing what I did with skill and passion, teaching literature to college students. I'd come from the narrow houses and narrow lives of working-class Lowell, Massachusetts. I had not taken a college education for granted and had worked against daunting odds to get one. I began pacing back and forth from the door to the windows. From the windows to the door. Graduate school, surprisingly, had been easier, what with scholarships and grants and teaching fellowships. Then I was flabbergasted to find myself teaching not so very far from gritty Lowell, at one of the most exclusive colleges in the nation.

Sometimes democracy works.

Enfield and I had been a good fit. I was crazy about the students, and they appreciated my irreverent take on American literature. When I got back to the windows, I stopped pacing and looked out. On the grassy common a brown boy with green hair sat up against a tree and played a spare, lilting tune on his flute. I loved these kids; I loved this leafy, red-brick campus; I loved the spacious new library; I loved my campus friends, Earlene Johnson, Dean of Students and my Friday-night dinner partner, Greg Samoorian of Political Science, Jill Greenberg of Sociology. I loved my former students still in the area: Sofia Warzak, thriving in the MFA program at the university, Shameka Gilfoyle, returned from culinary school to take over the kitchen at Upper Crust, a trattoria in town, pony-tailed Mike Vitale, still making pottery over in Northampton. I loved my large, light-filled office.

I walked back over to the book shelves to replace the Dickinson. There I picked up a pottery figure, Edgar Allan Poe, given to me by Mike Vitale, who, as a student, hadn't much liked Poe. In this witty little figure, Mike's contempt showed. I caressed the wild ceramic hair and placed Edgar Allan back on the shelf.

All I wanted was to be granted my tenure, well deserved as far as I was concerned, and teach Enfield College's smart, savvy students for the rest of my career. And, now, because a change in departmental leadership had placed a wooly-brained liberal-run-amok in a position to make crucial decisions about my future, everything I hoped for was threatened.

My dream was to leave my rented house in the boondocks, to buy a place in town so I could be within three blocks of the college library, walk to work, and have friends over at the drop of a mortarboard. A home. And maybe Charlie and I…Anyhow, there's a little green house for sale on Elm Street with a deep porch just right for one of those big wooden swings…

What should I do? What *could* I do? I sat down at my desk and hid my face in my hands, waiting for inspiration. When it struck, it was in the form of a single word: *Google*. Spinning my chair around, I grabbed the computer mouse, called up the Internet search engine, and typed in *joe lone wolf.*

Nothing. A couple of bars in Texas called Lone Wolf Saloon, with owners named Joe. One called Lone Star Wolf Cafe.

Oh, here he was: a single mention of Professor Joseph Lone Wolf, English Department faculty, Enfield College. But that was simply *pro forma.* We all had a listing on the Enfield College website. I kept scrolling. A Joe Wolf seemed to be connected to an online gambling site. But otherwise—nothing.

For comparison, I searched my own name. There was more than one Karen Pelletier, but I came up first. I was definitely an Internet presence—conferences attended, talks given, publications cited. And I'd made absolutely no effort to get my name out there. No blog. No website. But here was my colleague, a professor at Enfield at least as long as I had been, with nothing noted on the Web.

It was almost as if he were intentionally underplaying his existence.

I felt as if I were in danger of losing tenure to a ghost.

I closed down the computer, packed up the ungraded papers and walked to the door. Before I opened it, I turned back and stood there, taking it all in: my expansive but cluttered desk, the green vinyl chair in which so many students had sat, the overflowing bookcases, the tall windows that looked out onto the Common, the cushioned window seat. The long oak conference table stacked with books and articles to be submitted for tenure. The box.

I felt as if I were saying goodbye.

Chapter Two

Friday 10/2

Without even leaving a note to cancel my office hours, I drove away from campus, feeling as if all the hounds of academe were at my heels. The exquisite Indian-summer air—golden with sun and leaves—mocked my sudden despair. I don't remember the drive to my little rented house in the woods twenty minutes north of Enfield. One minute I was turning left out of the college parking lot, the next I was in my driveway pulling the key out of the ignition. I sat there in the car staring at the empty house. It was an old one-story farmhouse, a little shabby, centered in a narrow strip of grass that I kept cut with a hand mower. Every once in a while on a walk in the woods—second-growth oaks, maples and birch—I'd come across remnants of the meandering old stone walls of what for a couple of centuries had been rocky New-England farmland. Hay, potatoes, sheep, a few cows, a dozen or so hens, a pig: everything a family would have needed to sustain a frugal life.

Maybe that's what I'd do after Enfield denied my tenure petition, I thought: I'd farm. I'd buy a few hens, build a coop, live off the land, stack up a woodpile, bathe in water from a steel-hooped rain barrel. Reinvent myself: English professor turned dirt farmer. And I already had the grindstone I'd need to put my nose to—er, to which I'd need to put my nose. The one summer I'd tried to grow a vegetable garden in a small, flat patch of ground on the far side of the driveway, my shovel struck something so unyielding three or four inches deep in the sandy soil that I had to dig around it until I discovered its perimeter. When I saw what the impediment was, a huge, tan, hand-chiseled sandstone disk, I asked Charlie to excavate it for me. It's in the living room now, standing against the wall next to the fieldstone fireplace, ready to sharpen any tool I might ever need, except those that would win me tenure.

◇◇◇

Charlie. More than anything else I wanted to talk to Charlie and tell him about Miles' warning, wanted the comfort of his solid, sensible presence, the security of his arms around me when my entire world seemed to be spinning out of control. But there was no way I could call him. For the next ten months, he'd have to call me. For the next ten months Lieutenant Charlie Piotrowski, Bureau of Criminal Investigation, Massachusetts State Police, would be unreachable—in Iraq with the National Guard.

He had to go, he said, when he was called up. He had no choice. It was his duty. And, besides, he said, it would be an adventure, maybe even the adventure of his life.

Adventure. It was a guy thing, I guess. My pleading got me only a promise that he would call or e-mail me every day. If he could.

And he had, for all nine of the days he'd been there so far. Only nine and three-quarter months left to go.

I missed him. I worried about him. Some nights I worried myself sleepless. And, now, when I needed him most…Sighing deeply, I got out of the car. The phone was ringing in the house. Charlie! It was the wrong time of day for him, half-way across the world. He usually called at the end of his day and the beginning of mine. Nonetheless, I sped across the unpaved driveway, house key extended, twisted the doorknob.

The phone stopped ringing.

Damn. But the red light was blinking. I snatched up the receiver. Not Charlie. The message was from Earlene Johnson, my good friend, so—cancel that *damn.*

Karen, remember—we're meeting at Rudolph's at seven. Girl's Night Out.

Thank God, dinner with a rational human being. A friend. Someone I could trust to have my best interests at heart.

Friday evening 10/2

"He's sure not drinking like a man who expects to get tenure," Earlene whispered in my ear. It was shortly after seven, and given the empty glasses in front of him on the bar, Joe Lone Wolf already had two drinks under his belt and was well into the third. Whiskey, it looked like. Double. Neat.

Professor Joe Lone Wolf of the Enfield College English Department, a squat man with a straight dark braid dangling over his left shoulder, sat on the high barstool at Rudolph's Café, hunched over, glaring at nothing, his shoulders preternaturally wide in the fringed deerskin jacket.

I groaned. All I'd wanted in going out with my friend for a burger and a drink was a brief respite from the angst that had hounded me since Miles' dire warning that afternoon. And, here I found myself in the same bar as my nemesis.

Earlene turned to the student host with the menus. "Is there another table free, Winky?" As dean of students, she knew all the kids by name. But "Winky?" With his shaved head, multiply pierced lip, and earlobe plug, this looming young man looked like an ogre escaped from an online fantasy game.

I pulled out the brushed aluminum chair and sat. "That's okay, er, Winky," I said. "This'll be fine."

At Rudolph's Café, the usual weekend hubbub was building. In the refurbished neo-funky lounge, exposed silver-painted pipes and vents stood out against forest-green walls and ceiling. Dim lighting, cast up from embedded bulbs around the floor's perimeter, gave the room a general air of illicit goings-on, as if it were a prohibition-era speakeasy. But Rudolph's was simply your high-end college-town dinner joint, a place to hang out, order pricey food that looked artistic on the plate, and wind down from a brutal week of studying and teaching. Those students who could afford to pay twelve dollars for a basic burger tarted up with ciparelli onions and shitake mushrooms were there already. Faculty members would drift in as the evening grew later, and they'd made at least a few small dents in the mounds of midterm papers on their desks.

Earlene took the opposite seat, back to back with, and almost touching, Joe. "I'll sit here, Karen," she muttered. "Give you at least a little distance from him."

"Thanks," I said. The only problem with the seating arrangement was that now I had a direct view of Joe's brooding visage. Elbows planted on the dented-copper bar-top, he was in the process of ordering another drink.

The first time I'd met my colleague Joe Lone Wolf, I hadn't pegged him as Native. His skin was dark olive rather than brown, but, once I was told his ethnicity I could see the dark Native tint in his eyes and the monumental Native bone in his sculpted high-bridged nose. Some Indian nations insist on a full one-half blood quantum for tribal membership; others are inclusive, requiring only one-sixteenth Native blood among any hodge-podge of European and African ancestry. Joe must be a descendant of one of the more inclusive tribes.

Earlene leaned toward me, her bead-trimmed gray dreadlocks hanging across her forehead. "How many times do I have to tell you," she scolded in a whisper, "you don't have to worry about Joe Lone Wolf. You're a shoo-in for tenure."

"Shoo-in? I don't knooow," I moaned. "After today I wouldn't count on it." I spilled my tale of woe, giving her a stuttering version of what Miles had told me. Then I fussed with the single bamboo shoot in a purple ceramic vase on the table.

Earlene brushed dreadlocks back from one side of her beautiful dark face and regarded me quizzically. "So, he's American Indian. And that brings in the affirmative-action factor, right? And you don't seem comfortable talking to me about it because I'm black. Right"

"Yes, I guess," I said sheepishly. "Affirmative Action Is Important." I sounded like a sixth-grader.

"Yeah, it's damn important, but it's not a mandate for reverse discrimination. What's crucial is stereotype-free perception and advancement. Face it, that tenure-committee meeting wasn't about social justice—it was about Ned. Finally he's in his puny position of power—dogmatic and single-minded, like all petty tyrants. But just how influential is he? Think about all the ways in which you surpass Lone Wolf."

I told her about what Sally Chenille and Harriet Person had said; I was too successful and too popular with students. Earlene chortled. "I know those women—they just want to flex their muscles. Makes them feel good. But they'll vote the right way."

"You think?"

"Listen, you need a little reality therapy. What are the three cardinal points of tenure decisions? Collegiality, scholarship, teaching." She ticked them off on her fingers. "Number one, you get along with your colleagues, don't you?"

"Yes, of course. When they're not being idiots."

"What about Joe? Isn't he notorious for shirking departmental obligations?"

"I don't think he's served on a single committee—not even the new-faculty integration committee, which is a slam dunk."

"Two: you've published two scholarly books, right?"

I sighed. "Yes. They've been well reviewed. And I've got a bunch of nicely placed articles."

"How many books and scholarly articles has Joe published?"

I shrugged. "None, as far as I know."

"Okay. Number three: teaching?"

"That's the most important to me. My teaching evaluations are...gratifying."

"I'm not surprised. The students love you."

"Do they? Miles says the students love Joe, too."

"So that's *one* in his column to your *three*. She spread her hands wide. "So, like I said, you're a shoo-in. But..." Earlene twisted around to grab the waiter, "...where are our drinks?" Catching a glimpse of Joe, she turned back and leaned over the table toward me. "And just look at the guy." She jerked her head in his direction. Her voice was one notch above mute. "He's hammered."

I sighed and responded at the same nonvolume. "Yeah, and if I was looking to get smashed, I sure wouldn't do it a block and a half from campus. Let's forget about Joe Lone Wolf and get on to real life. I'm being paranoid."

Earlene laughed and snatched a thin pretzel from the bowl the waiter delivered with the two glasses of red wine we'd ordered.

Just then a tall, well-built man in jeans and cowboy boots brushed past me, knocking against the table. I grabbed for the pretzels. "Hey!"

He didn't acknowledge me, but strode toward the bar and pulled out the stool next to Joe. He doffed his broad-brimmed hat, and shoulder-length blond-white hair flew loose around a tanned and weathered face.

Joe crooked his arm at the elbow, slowly raised it, peeled back the cuff of his jacket, and checked his watch. He made quite a production of it.

"Late, am I?" the newcomer drawled, slapping Joe on his leather-clad back. "Well, damn, then I'm just gonna hafta drink all the harder to catch up with you. What're you havin', *hombre?*" He threw his arm around Joe's bulky shoulders. "Hey, bartender! Down this way!"

"What do you know?" I said, in a demivoice. "Who would have expected McCutcheon to be buddy-buddy with Joe Lone Wolf, of all people?"

Clark McCutcheon, distinguished visiting professor at Enfield College and superstar in the academic world at large, was a big, hearty Montanan. He was broad-shouldered and rangy, and the kind of outdoorsman garb he favored might have elicited no comment on a rich man's hobby ranch. In this New England college town, however, the Stetson and custom-tooled boots turned heads.

"So *that's* McCutcheon? I've heard about him." Earlene gave him a long once-over and sighed. "You suppose he has a horse tethered to the hitching post out front? I wouldn't mind riding off into the sunset with that cowboy."

"He sure is an eye-catching dude," I responded. "If you like that kind."

"What kind is that? Hot? Or gorgeous?"

"The kind who's full of himself. You should have heard him at the meeting of the comparative American studies faculty last month. We were trying to choose a big-name academic to give an endowed lecture in the spring, but McCutcheon dismissed every scholar mentioned as having an 'inflated reputation.' An inflated *ego* seems to be no problem for him, though; he's hot stuff in academic literary studies, and he doesn't let us forget it. About ten or fifteen years ago he wrote a really knock-out essay. It's called, 'Whaddya Mean, "We," White Man?,' and it revolutionized the field of whiteness studies. The English department is lucky to have him."

Keeping her dark eyes on McCutcheon, she sipped her wine. "Well, he certainly does up the testosterone equation on campus."

I mimed fanning my face with my hand.

She laughed. "But what the heck *is* whiteness studies, anyhow?" McCutcheon was adding so rambunctiously to the growing din in Rudolph's bar that Earlene spoke now in a normal tone of voice. "I'm no literary scholar, but I would have thought that it's all pretty much *been* whiteness studies ever since Enfield College was founded."

"Well, yeah, in a way. But McCutcheon's style of scholarship *critiques* whiteness—it doesn't celebrate it. Whiteness is seen not so much as a skin color, but as an inchoate dominant structure of power, and whiteness theory reads white texts—literature, film, popular culture—to expose white privilege and condemn its consequences."

Earlene snickered. "Yet another bleeding-heart scholarly outlet for white liberal guilt," she said. With the back of her hand to her forehead, she gave a melodramatic, silent-movie, toss of her head. "Oh, the unbearable whiteness of being," she sighed.

I laughed. "Funny lady. But McCutcheon's a good bet to be appointed to the Palaver next year." The Palaver Chair of Literary Studies was an unfortunately monikered but prestigious named chair funded by an Enfield College alum. Extremely well endowed as the chair is, the English Department hadn't fared well with its recent choices for the Palaver. "Ned hopes Clark McCutcheon will bring 'muscle as well as prestige' to the department. He thinks he's hiring an intellectual John Wayne for the job."

I glanced over at the bar. Joe was tilting his head in my direction now. He said something to McCutcheon, who glanced my way, widened his eyes briefly, then responded to Joe *sotto voce*. The men regarded me together, then picked up their drinks and moved to the far end of the bar, completely out of earshot. Immediately they went into a huddle, as if, instead of being new acquaintances, they were old friends with much to talk about.

"What's that all about?" I asked Earlene.

But she was gazing distractedly over my shoulder, in the opposite direction from the bar. "Karen, don't be obvious, but look over toward the door. Who's that stunning woman?" I stretched my neck, as if I were working out a kink, then I turned my head. Just coming through the green plush door curtain was a tall brown-skinned woman with exquisitely molded Native cheekbones and a strong, arched nose. She wore a denim jacket and skin-tight black pants.

"Pocahontas," Earlene breathed, answering her own question. So much for stereotype-free perception.

As the woman stood there peering into the dim room, my two colleagues at the bar continued their conversation, unheeding. Her dark gaze settled on Joe Lone Wolf and stayed there. She took a step in his direction, waited for a waitress with a shoulder-held tray to pass, took another step, pushed a chair aside, and marched toward the two men. When she reached them, she slammed the oblivious Joe between the shoulder blades with the flat of her hand, grabbed his arm, and spun his stool around so he was facing her.

At the sight of her he paled.

She clenched her fist and pulled her arm back. McCutcheon, now off his stool, grabbed for her arm, but missed. Then he stood there, boots planted wide, staring at this wilderness apparition, his blue eyes gleaming.

"You bastard!" the woman screamed at Joe. "You cheating, double-dealing, no-good, two-faced bastard." She hauled off and slugged him. Right in the kisser.

Joe slid off the barstool onto his feet, dazed and shaky. "Graciella—"

McCutcheon lifted his tanned, long-fingered hand to hide his mouth. It looked to me as if he were attempting to hide a grin, as if this face-off were the funniest thing he'd ever seen.

Things like this don't happen at Rudolph's—brute-force confrontations, I mean. Oh, there's lots of one-upmanship, multisyllabic name-calling, maybe even a little genteel tossing of drinks in faces. Or at Maccio's, on the far side of town, a drunk or two will get out of control on the weekend and noses will bleed. But…Rudolph's? Fisticuffs in the house of purple cauliflower and sweet-potato fries? This had to be a first.

I sat there and gaped. Twenty years of advanced literary study, including intensive reading of Shakespeare, Wordsworth, and Dickinson, and what deathless poetry came to my brain in that moment of crisis? From Amanda's childhood I recalled, "Weebles wobble but they don't fall down." And then she hauled off and hit him again, and he did.

Graciella Whoevershewas stalked out, moving easily between aghast and goggle-eyed restaurant patrons, not one of whom made the slightest move to stop her. The door curtains closed behind her, and I turned to look at Joe. He was on the floor, leaning up against the bar, his nose bleeding into a wad of cocktail napkins.

What does it say about me that I didn't even feel sorry for him?

Fri. Night 10/2

From: kpelletier@enfield.edu
To: charles.piotrowski@army.mil.gov
Subject: I Miss You

Charlie, life without you…oh, God! And it doesn't help that Amanda is on the other side of the world, too. I haven't heard a word from her since she arrived in Kathmandu. Okay, okay, I know, she's a grown-up—I should stop worrying about her. But…backpacking in Nepal with a guy I've never met! So, they're seeking spiritual enlightenment? Why can't she do that at the Episcopal Church across the street from campus?

Also, speaking of campus, there seems to be a problem at work, but I'll wait until you call to tell you about that.

Call SOON.

I love you! Karen

Chapter Three

Monday 10/5

"Trickster is a shapeshifter, a mischief-maker. He's tricky, bawdy, obscene, disruptive—and a major culture hero of traditional American Indian narrative. As you can imagine, he makes for some unforgettable stories."

Except for one beautiful, poised brown-skinned girl wearing a *hijab*, my American-literature students sat slouched and twisted in their chairs. They'd dragged themselves out of bed in time to get to this nine o'clock Monday morning class, but they seemed somehow to have forgotten their bones. The Enfield College classroom was a large, high-ceilinged space with tall windows and embrasures so deep students sometimes chose to sit on the sills. We were six long weeks into the fall semester, a low-energy time. No one was on the windowsill today.

I'd come into my office on Sunday afternoon to pack my tenure box. The building had been empty then except for a new janitor, a slender young South American—Peruvian, I thought—who was mopping the hallway floors. His dark-green uniform shirt had "Ricardo" embroidered above the pocket. I stopped and introduced myself, but his English wasn't up to much conversation.

Earlene's pep-talk had calmed my fears—for the moment. I packed the books, journals, offprints of articles, my activity report, and detailed C.V. into the box. Almost done. I still had to put the finishing touches on the manuscript of a quirky essay speculating what Emily Dickinson's poetic "career" might have looked like had she been born into a family of Lowell millworkers rather than that of a prosperous Amherst lawyer. All I had to do now was spend a few hours in the college library checking quotes and citations and I'd be ready to print it out, pack it up, and close the box.

But when was I going to do that? My tenure submission was due a week from this coming Friday, and I had a full week ahead of me, including extended office hours for these AmLit students who were in the midst of writing mid-term papers. The following week wasn't much better, since I had to grade all those papers.

"So, what do you think about this Native Trickster figure?" I asked my students. "Let's speculate on his significance to American literature."

Dead silence. It's odd how individual classes have individual personalities. This one was smart and quirky, and, for the most part, I enjoyed them. Cat Andrews was wearing jeans and pajama tops printed with little red and blue boats. She was eating cornflakes from a plastic bowl, and today her buzzcut was tipped with neon yellow. Hank Brody, tall, thin, and disheveled, with matted straw-colored dreadlocks, was barefoot. His eyes were at half-mast. Garrett Reynolds, a brown-haired suburban kid who seemed to major in Abercrombie & Fitch, was busy reading something on his laptop computer.

I asked my students to turn to the Winnebago tribal story I'd assigned them to read for class. "So, okay," I said, "here's Trickster, starving in the wilderness during a brutal winter. He finds a prosperous village whose chief has a handsome son. By means of a pair of elk's kidneys and an elk's liver, Trickster turns himself into a beautiful woman."

Someone in the class giggled. There was a general clearing of throats.

"Trickster then marries the chief's son and bears him three sons. So, through the use of magic, he takes advantage of the village hierarchy and of the handsome son. Power and sex, right? In the end his magic fails—the supposedly female Trickster jumps over a fire pit and drops 'something very rotten.'"

That musical giggle again. I looked around. I thought I knew where it was coming from.

"And Trickster is revealed as the mischievous, masculine, shapeshifter. What purpose do you think such a tale might serve?"

Blank stares. There's nothing quite like classroom resistance. It has an energy all its own, an impenetrable cloud of negative ions charging the air between the professor and students. Stephanie Hart studiously drew manga characters in the margins of her American literature anthology. She was the class nodder, the student who bobbed her head in affirmation to any point I made. Every class has one. I always fall for them at first, thinking I've found a terrifically brilliant kid. Until about the third day of class. But I wasn't getting much feedback at the moment—even from her.

I cleared my throat, ostentatiously. "Okay, boys and girls, I do understand. A frank discussion of this scene requires vulgar language and images, and you guys are just not used to talking dirty. Right?" Cat Andrews grinned sheepishly and nudged Stephanie. "Well, at least not in the classroom. Is that the problem?" A little smile. Eyebrows raised in inquiry. Hmmmmm?

Garrett Reynolds, the kid with the laptop, was the first to break. "I don't know *what* to think about it," he blurted out. "In fact, I don't even know why we *have* to think about it. This is supposed to be a course in American literature, and there's nothing American or literary about these…tales." His tone was querulous, as if he suspected he wasn't getting sufficient value for his high-end tuition dollar. "They're just primitive and crude." He looked back down at his laptop and typed a few words; I'd distracted him from his e-mail.

Hank Brody, still slumped in his chair, hazel eyes half shut, spoke without sitting up, as I'd known he would. His dreads hung over pale cheeks covered lightly with the scars of past acne. "Of course it's American literature. How could you get any more American than this? These stories go way back, before the arrival of the European invaders." He and Garrett had been feuding since the first day of class, and I suspected his languid, not-worth-the-effort, posture was designed to infuriate his antagonist.

"Colonists," Garrett corrected him. If it was possible for a six-foot-three football player to sound prissy, he did. "Not invaders—colonists."

"Invaders," Hank insisted, almost deigning to open his eyes. "There's a huge body of preconquest Native narrative—mischievous, magical tales like this one, creation stories, heroic epics, historical narratives. It's the real thing—American literature."

"Preconquest? You're way overboard with this political-correctness stuff, Brody. None of these so-called narratives were ever written down until the Europeans came. How can you say they're American? America only began in 1776."

In the classroom, heads turned back and forth to follow the argument. Cat Andrews peeled a banana and let the peel fall next to her sheepskin slipper. Stephanie nodded.

Hank responded to Garrett without raising his hand. "The *United States* began in 1781, Reynolds—that doesn't mean *America* began then."

I seized the opportunity—a teachable moment if I ever saw one. "If you remember, the first day of class I asked you a couple of questions. I said those questions would problematize everything we learned in this course. What were they?"

Garrett paged though his notebook, but Ayesha Ahmed, my one Muslim student, the dignified girl in the head scarf, raised her hand. "The questions were: *'Who is an American?'* and *'What is literature?'*"

"*This* story isn't literature, for sure." Garrett twisted his lips. "I think it's just plain silly. Magic? Hah!"

Ayesha laughed out loud. So she *was* the source of the musical giggle. "Yes, isn't it silly—gloriously, magically silly." The daughter of a Moroccan diplomat to the United Nations, Ayesha looked so modest in the lace-edged *hijab*, stark white against her dark skin, that I sometimes forgot how smart and funny she was. "That's what makes it so brilliant—"

"Brilliant?" Garrett snorted.

Ayesha gave him a stare befitting a queen. "Well, I think this tale is hilarious, low comedy at its best. Very much in the folk tradition. I know African stories like this."

I practically purred at her. "You mean to say, Ayesha, that these American Indian tales connect not only to the concept of 'American,' but to an even more universal literature?"

"Yes, of course. Just think about how complex the story is—it toys with our assumptions—deconstructs them, right, Professor? Nothing is what it seems to be. The categories we think of as being absolutely fixed—man/woman, animal/human—aren't... dependable. An elk's kidneys can become human breasts. A man can have babies. In the next story, Trickster defecates so much he almost suffocates in it. Think about the imagination that went into conceiving that scene!" She giggled. "It makes you laugh from your belly instead of from your brain."

Garrett scowled at her. Then he turned abruptly back to his laptop and began typing in short bursts.

Hank Brody, not one of the computer-privileged, was writing at top speed in his notebook. In fact, this small-town, working-class boy didn't seem to be privileged in any way but in brains, and of those he had plenty; he was the kind of student for whom full scholarships had been invented. Now he ran thin fingers through his mop of cornhusk braids and ventured a glance at Ayesha. He adjusted his posture; when speaking to Ayesha he always sat up straight. "It *is* a unique folk tradition, like you said." In the blatant disregard for style affected by some high-minded students—whose style is to be *beyond* style—Hank wore his matted dreadlocks hanging halfway down his back, and his usual washed-out blue sweatshirt and frayed khaki shorts. "If it problematizes such fundamental categories as who is a man and who is a woman, what is natural and what is magical, why can't it also problematize other categories. *Who is an American? What is literature?*"

"Yes, right—it's the same kind of thing, isn't it?" It was as if the two of them were having a private conversation. Their eyes held a second too long. Then Ayesha turned to me and tittered.

"Trickster even carries his penis in a box! Think of the psychosexual implications of an image like that?" Everyone laughed, and the classroom atmosphere lightened up. My one Muslim student may have been religiously observant, but she was no prude.

Class was almost over. Stephanie's head bobble was beginning to slow. I began to sum up. "Stories are central to all cultures—they meet primal needs. Think about how cruel and meaningless life would be without the stories that offer meaning, purpose, and healing, that provide political and cultural cohesion for the tribe. Any tribe. The kind of physical comedy that characterizes these tales has a long, and literary, tradition, often in the theater. Remember how bawdy Shakespeare can be—and Molière. These Native narratives may not have been written down, but, like European drama, they were performed.

"We are physical beings, the Trickster reminds us, with all the powers and limitations of the physical body. But we can rise above hunger, cold, physical danger, even gender. Like Trickster, we can transform ourselves, only we do it through stories. During the hungry, dark, cold winters in the longhouse, the storyteller would have told this crude comic tale with his whole voice—its pace, rhythms, tones, shouts, and whispers. His body would have taken on different poses as Trickster changed shape. For this story...well, you can imagine the postures."

"Uggh," Garrett said.

"Hmm, *performance*...That's interesting." Ayesha said. "Sounds to me like it's very up-to-date. Sounds like spoken-word poetry—like a poetry slam."

Hank stared at her openly. "That is *so* brilliant. It's *just* like a poetry slam."

She looked at him, then dropped her gaze. What was going on between those two?

"Exactly," I concluded. "*Performance* of the word, not just the reading of it in print. And unlike European drama, the tales were passed orally from one generation to the next. So when we study Native stories in an American literature course..." I turned my attention to Garrett, "it's not as if we depart from the categories of 'American' and 'literature'—we simply broaden and enrich them." The wall clock ticked to nine-fifty and books slammed shut.

Hank Brody zipped up his battered green backpack and grinned as he passed me. "Bye, Doc. Great class."

"Terrific insights, Hank," I replied. I did wish he'd get a decent haircut.

◇◇◇

When I entered my office and caught sight of the black-and-white speckled file box containing my tenure materials, I recalled Miles' warning and felt a brief pang in my heart. Was it possible all that work would be for nothing? What would I do if Enfield College denied me tenure? Where would I go? Would I have to leave Charlie behind?

Then I heard the e-mail click announcing a new message. *Amanda?* But, no, nothing from my daughter. Just another note from an anxious student. Where *was* Amanda? It was a week now since she'd called from the hotel in Kathmandu, and I was becoming more and more concerned by her silence. I fired off an e-mail: CALL ME! Then I checked through the 27 NEW MESSAGES I'd received since last evening: announcements of meetings and deadlines; the inevitable penis-enhancement and work-from-home opportunities. Then there was an e-mail from the mother of one of my freshman students explaining in detail that Melody-Ann was an extraordinarily sensitive young woman who suffered painfully when called upon in class. I responded that I would be mindful of the situation, meaning…virtually nothing. I call on all my students. It's a part of academic life. Get over it.

Now here was a message whose title read: *Catherine Andrews invited you to join Facebook.* After class, Cat must have scuffed in her sheepskin slippers right to her dorm-room computer and sent the message. I didn't have a Facebook account, so I simply deleted the message. Next time I saw her I would explain that it was nothing personal, but, for reasons of privacy and time-management, I avoided any involvement with social networking sites.

Then the phone rang. "Karen?" A woman's voice.

"Yes?" But I knew instantly who it was, and my nerves seemed not to jangle but to congeal. Especially in my stomach. "Connie?" My sister. I hadn't heard from her in weeks.

I walked the receiver on its long cord over to the door, which I closed for privacy. "Is Mom okay?"

For the past five years our mother had been living with Connie in Lowell. It was the best arrangement. Mom was comfortable in a neighborhood she knew. She got confused a lot, our mother did, but she felt at home at Connie's.

"That's why I'm calling, Karen. I need your help." Her voice sounded strained, as if this were a difficult conversation for her.

"Sure," I said, "how much?" I send her five hundred dollars a month for our mother's expenses.

There was a long, cool silence before she said, irritated now, "That is just so like you, Karen."

"What? You asked for help." I sat in the green vinyl chair.

"And, of course, you offer money—Ms. Gottrocks." Connie had worked at WalMart ever since it came to Lowell. A few years earlier she'd been promoted to manager of the electronics department. So she was doing okay financially, for a woman with a community college degree, but she had this perception that because I was teaching at a wealthy school, I must be rich myself.

"I'm so far from being Ms. Gottrocks, Connie, you can't even imagine it. I'm stretching my budget as far as it'll go, sending what I do send. What more do you want?" Why do our conversations always turn into squabbles.

"Well, I'll tell you what I want." She cleared her throat. "You're going to have to take Mom for a couple of weeks."

"What!" My mother was increasingly disoriented. Because Connie lived right in the middle of a familiar town, she could leave Mom alone during the day when she went to work. But out here in the woods? No. Mom would wander off and be eaten by bears. And as for taking her onto campus with me? I shuddered. The academic bears were even fiercer. Especially now.

"Connie, I can't do it. I'm up for tenure. I have to watch every move I make."

"Is that so?" Her tone was dry. "Well, Sister, let me tell you something. You may be up for tenure, but *I've* been invited to Bentonville." She said this with a reverent emphasis on the final word, as if she were announcing that she'd been invited to the White House or the Vatican.

"Oh?" Where the hell was Bentonville? *What* was it?

"Yes, Bentonville, WalMart headquarters in Arkansas. I'm a finalist for store manager. They want me out there for interviews and—if all goes well—training."

"Oh, Connie. That's marvelous! Congratulations! I wish you the best of luck." I was genuinely happy for her. Just because Connie and I have never gotten along doesn't mean I wish her ill.

"Thank you." A pause. "So you'll take her."

"No!" I could imagine the look on Sally Chenille's face if she met my poor, stooped, confused mother in the English Department hallway. "No, I can't possibly. Not now. Maybe later."

"Later's too late."

But what would I do with with Mom when I was teaching? Seat her in the back of the class? "What about Denise?" Our other sister.

"Denise is drinking again."

"Oh. I'm sorry to hear that." Poor Denise. "Well, listen. I'll put money in the mail tomorrow." I did some rapid calculations. How much could I send without bouncing the rent check? "I'll send a thousand. That ought to help you find someone."

She didn't say anything for a long moment.

I heard my mother's querulous voice in the background. "Are you talking to Karen? I want to talk to Karen, too."

Then Connie finally spoke. "Thanks a lot—Sister!" And she slammed the phone down.

I was swamped with guilt; standing there in my sunny office, I was writhing with guilt. Even though there was no good reason I should be.

Twenty years earlier, when my father had refused to shelter me from my abusive husband, my mother and two sisters wouldn't, couldn't, defy him. I remember with traumatic clarity that desperate phone call home: "Come get me. Please." And my mother's anguished whisper, "Karen, you know how he is. I don't even dare tell him you called." Standing there in the cold of a November morning, clutching the receiver of a public telephone on a desolate, wind-swept street in North Adams, Massachusetts, with Amanda crying in her stroller, I'd hit rock bottom. Twenty years old, with a two-year-old daughter and on the far side of the state from anyone I knew, I had nowhere to turn for help but to the Salvation Army. It was thanks to them that I found safe housing, that I got day-care for Amanda, that I'd begun to work my way through college. When I was most needy, my family had abandoned me; I'd sworn then that I'd have nothing to do with them, ever again. I can still feel the cold wind whipping around that western Massachusetts corner and the even colder silence of the cold phone receiver in my hand, and the cold determination in my heart to survive. It was a cold world, and I was on my own.

Then Amanda, when she was in college, made a forbidden pilgrimage to Lowell and brought my mother and sisters back into my life. When my mother first saw me again, the hopeful expression on her much-aged face weakened my resolve, and I had to relent. Not that things were hunky-dory between us now—far from it. Connie and Denise thought I was an elitist intellectual snob, out of touch with the real world. I resented their hostility and chafed at the narrowness of their views. But... my poor destroyed mother...

I started going to Lowell three, four times a year. My sisters and their families came to me only once, for an awkward Fourth of July picnic, where the food was too fancy for them, the company too snooty, and the music was all wrong. After that, Enfield became so far away from Lowell, you'd think it was in Hawaii.

The phone rang again, and I eyed it warily. If it was Connie calling back, I was afraid I'd wind up saying yes. I didn't even look at the phone readout for the number, but grabbed the keys and my bag and scooted out the door, letting it slam shut behind me. A long slow walk would give me time to put that check in the mail. If I walked *very* slowly and took an hour and a half to get to the other side of our compact campus, it would be time for a scheduled lunch meeting of the American Studies Department.

What was I running from? Only the long shadow of my past.

Chapter Four

Monday noon 10/5

"Where's Lone Wolf?" Clark McCutcheon asked. At the sound of my tenure rival's name I choked on a bite of whole-wheat roll, then tried to cover my reaction by coughing into my napkin.

Ten of us sat at the large round table in the Faculty Commons, the remains of lunch scattered around: pizza crusts, half consumed sushi, the congealed remains of arroz con pollo in a bowl. I picked at the few wilted lettuce leaves remaining in my Cobb salad. Fastidiously, Clark stacked his soup bowl on top of his hamburger plate, folded his paper napkin into a neat square, and beckoned to the student worker to clear his dishes. Then he wiped away the few crumbs in front of him and centered the salt and pepper shakers on the table. Rufus Jefferson, the chair of Comparative American Studies, had just called the monthly AmStuds faculty meeting to order.

Since scholars can no longer agree on what it means to be "American," the once seemingly unambiguous and unitary department name, American Studies, has been complicated. *Comparative* American Studies means, in effect, that we're not just studying white folk anymore—which is, of course, a good thing, but makes for awkward language and administration. Sally Chenille was here for Women's and Gender Studies (WAGS), Gay, Lesbian, Bisexual, and Transgender Studies was represented by Tommy Lyndon, Whiteness Studies by McCutcheon, Ethnic Studies—which comprised Latino/a Studies, Asian-American Studies, and Russian Studies—by Ramona Yin. Fatima Narhudi had come for Arab-American Studies, Pablo Suarez for Borderland Studies. As for Native Studies, Joe was usually present, but today he seemed to have absented himself.

In short, the crowd around the table looked exactly like America in the twenty-first century, black and white and brown, which is why I thought the department should go back to its former name, plain old American Studies. To assume that "American" still meant "white," and that all whites are privileged and that therefore scholars had a political and moral obligation to oppose or complicate "American," seemed to me to be an artifact of a previous century—at least a decade ago.

"Where's Lone Wolf?" Rufus echoed. He was dark-skinned and wore a devilish little goatee to compensate for his bald head, which gleamed in the overhead lights. "Who knows? But at least we can get some work done without having to draw pictographs." He gave a dry little laugh which no one echoed.

"Now, just a sec, Jefferson..." McCutcheon's John-Wayne drawl gave the gravitas of an Old-West showdown to his response. "You of all people should know better than to resort to racial slurs."

Rufus' eyes opened wide. "That was no slur. It was just a little joke. What's the matter—white people don't have a sense of humor?" Today he wore a gray wool suit and a denim dress shirt with a yellow tie striped in blue.

McCutcheon's height and his cowpoke's denim jacket lent an air of the outdoor male to the indoor sport of academic one-upmanship. Another woman might have succumbed instantly to Clark's broad shoulders, the rangy height, the perfectly proportioned features, the wide, amused mouth, mobile lips with smile lines around them, but there was something of the poseur about him. I'd been uneasy with Clark right from the start.

"That wasn't humor—just pure and utter anti-Native racism." He didn't have to flex a muscle to appear stronger than any man at the table. Any woman, either.

"Clark, honey," Sally Chenille slid her hand down McCutcheon's arm, lingering at the biceps as if she were claiming territory there. "Rufus couldn't possibly have meant anything defamatory." Her punkish crew-cut matched her lipstick—pumpkin orange. For Halloween, I assumed. She gave him a luminous smile. He was outrageously studly in his denim-jacket and tooled-boot masculinity, a celebrity-academic gadfly's dream come true.

McCutcheon squinted at her. "Are you claiming that as a black man, Rufus *de facto* cannot be racist? Poppycock! Humor is a powerful perpetuant of racist stereotypes."

Sometimes I can't breathe on this campus the air is so clogged with political rhetoric. "Cut it out!" I snapped. Heads swiveled in my direction. "I've had enough of this! We've got a semester's curriculum to plan. Now, let's get to it. What about next fall's freshman seminar?"

McCutcheon's blue eyes focused on me in a long cool lingering assessment. His gaze discomfited me. It seemed to be an extremely practiced gaze, and I knew better than to fall for a ploy like that. He took a sip of water and turned to the group at large. "Whiteness, Cultural Imperialism, and the American Movies," he responded. "That's what we'll do for the fall."

"Oh, no, McCutcheon," Greg protested, scraping his fork over the cheesy crust remaining in his empty lasagna dish. "For the purpose of a campus-wide seminar that's too narrow. At our last meeting we voted to implement a seminar called Interracial America. No reason we couldn't show one or two movies in that course."

"One or *two*?" McCutcheon dabbed at a spot of tomato sauce on the sleeve of his jacket. Being pale of skin he reddened up noticeably when angry. "Movies are the ur-text, the national imago, the dominant representation of the twentieth-century imperialist American zeitgeist...." He went on.

Greg, next to me, whispered, "Great, we can sell popcorn." Then he attempted to interrupt McCutcheon's polemic, for it had become a polemic indeed, involving terms such as *pseudo-praxis* and *indiginist retribution*.

But nobody was listening anyhow, because Fatima Narhudi had jumped into the fray, objecting to "interracial" in the title of the Seminar on the basis that in the United States the word "interracial" was coded language for "Black/White" and thus linguistically eradicated an Arab presence from the freshman curriculum. Then Latisha Moshier, the chair of African-American Studies…

I went for coffee. The Faculty Commons had acquired a neat little machine where you chose a "pod" of gourmet coffee, stuck it in the top of the coffee maker, pushed a button and, *voila*, a cup of fresh-brewed, fair-traded joe from Colombia or Guatemala or Equatorial Africa, coffee choices at least as global as Enfield's curriculum choices. When I got back to the table, the meeting was breaking up, the majority having agreed to submit suggested texts for a syllabus for the Interracial America seminar. Clark McCutcheon walked off with Sally Chenille, his hand possessively centered in the small of her back. *Low* in the small of her back. But for some reason he turned his head and, eyes narrowed, looked back at me.

I was meant to notice that.

Monday afternoon

Autumn was at its New-England apotheosis: leaves still on the trees, flaming red and yellow and orange, the sky aster-blue, the air cool and crisp as apples. In the golden weather a holiday mood had set in across campus. Cat Andrews, my would-be Facebook friend, lounged on a wide, granite library step, still in her pajama tops with the little red and blue boats. She was smoking, one hand on the step behind her, body arched, her head back and to one side, releasing a slow, sinuous, almost sinister stream of cigarette smoke over her shoulder, as if she'd been watching film noir and practicing on the sly. Unfortunately she'd spiked her short neon-yellow hair and pierced her upper lip with a dull black stud, so, along with the kiddie pajama tops, the effect wasn't exactly what I imagined she'd hoped for.

She was staring fixedly at Garrett Reynolds, who held sway in a circle of students seated on the Common. As I cut across the grass, I thought I saw Garrett pass a marijuana roach to Stephanie Hart, the Nodder. She must have seen me glance her way, because suddenly there was no sign of it anywhere. Surely they wouldn't be so stupid as to smoke dope right smack in the middle of campus. Or would they?

President Avery Mitchell strolled past with a copy of the *Boston Globe* tucked elegantly under his arm. Everything about Avery is elegant. He's the only man on campus who can wear a suede-elbow-patched tweed jacket without looking pretentious. Even in this *uber*-elite place, he radiates to-the-manor-born. It has nothing to do with tailoring; it's in the bones.

Avery gave me a nod and a smile. I was quite willing to stop for a chat, but our President didn't miss a beat on his way toward wherever he was going, probably a meeting with Enfield College alums, movers and shakers of American culture and capitalism.

Let me say this about Avery Mitchell. I like men; I'm made that way. But most of them don't ring my bells the way Avery Mitchell does. Probably has something to do with that old saw: *opposites attract*. When I'm in his vicinity, my breath contracts, my skin tingles, and there's a sort of heightened sensitivity to my entire consciousness. That's to say, he sure does get my attention. I'm not saying I love the man—I love Charlie Piotrowski, heart and soul. Am I aware when Avery Mitchell is in the room? You bet.

Rumor had it that Avery was being wooed away from Enfield by the Trustees of the Boston Public Library, who had made him an offer of their directorship. I had no idea how much truth there was to that, but I, for one, would miss Avery if he went. But, then again, maybe I would be gone, too. I sighed; I'd found myself sighing a great deal these past few days.

Not the least of which was because, oddly enough, I hadn't heard from Charlie in response to my last message. In the short while he'd been in Iraq, he'd e-mailed me every day and called me twice a week but, suddenly—nothing. I'd become a devotee of CNN International News. What was going on over there that he couldn't contact me? How much danger was he in?

Then—an e-mail click:

From: charles.piotrowski@army.mil.gov
To: kpelletier@enfield.edu
Subject: Will Call

Got your latest e-mail. I've been out of reach—sorry. What problem at work? Will get to the phone early—around 7 p.m. your time. Love, Charlie

◇◇◇

When Ayesha Ahmed called that afternoon at three, just at the end of office hours, and asked if she could see me around five, I decided to stay on campus and work in the library until then. I was looking forward to an excellent mid-semester paper from Ayesha and was happy to give her whatever assistance she asked for. I assumed it was her paper she wanted to talk about—although she had sounded uncharacteristically solemn on the phone.

Ayesha's bawdy giggle in class this morning had been just another surprise in getting to know the girl. I'd had a few Muslim students in the past; they tended to be hard-working and focused on specific career goals. But I'd never taught one who set herself apart from the American women students quite so radically, wearing the headscarf and traditional modest long-sleeved shirts with her jeans. I'll admit that when I'd first met this "covered" young woman, I'd made a few assumptions; her manner had such gravitas. Then I'd taken a second look. The jeans also told a story: they fit her, and fit her well, and she wore them like a girl who enjoys living in her body.

I wondered what being religiously observant meant to Ayesha. Obviously she didn't believe in total gender separation, as the Saudis did. But what about boyfriends? Young Muslim women were expected to be chaste. Touched by a man outside of marriage, no matter how casually, I'd read, they were ritually "defiled." But Ayesha didn't seem to be stifled, either in body or in mind. She was one of the two most adventurous thinkers in the American literature class, and her clever defense of the Native narrative's earthy humor had tickled me pink.

Evening darkness was beginning to set in as I left the library. In front of Dickinson Hall the bike rack held a sleek, shiny-green racing model that I'd seen Ayesha riding, so I picked up my pace as I headed toward the door. A conversation with a bright student was just what I needed to keep my mind off my tenure problems.

It was cool and dark in the hallway, and I paused for a second just beyond the foyer. The English Department office door was closed. The department seemed deserted. No lights gleamed behind the windows of office doors. But a low murmur of voices from somewhere told me that not everyone was gone. Once my eyes began to adjust to the dimness, I saw a couple of shadowy figures, one small and slight, the other taller and solid, at the far end of the hall; they must be the source of the murmuring voices. I had my hand on my office doorknob before I finally identified the shadowy duo: Ayesha Ahmed and Joe Lone Wolf.

Joe's bulked-up physique dwarfed the petite, slender girl. He'd cornered her between the mailboxes and the staircase, and she shrank away from his looming presence. The broad olive-tan face, the wide-shouldered deerskin jacket, the thick dark braid hanging down his back, all contributed to a sense of physical menace. I was about to announce my presence when Joe spoke up in more strident tones. "You *have* to participate. The project of anti-racist mobilization demands unilateral solidarity—"

"I'm Muslim," she protested. "We don't—"

Joe placed a proprietary hand on Ayesha's arm. She pulled abruptly away from him, but he secured her arm again and bent over her, still lecturing, "…unite to define pristine race as a principle of power in the context of creeping American hybridity—"

"Let go of her," I blurted out, shocking even myself.

His broad, brown hand fell from her arm, the fringe on the sleeves of his jacket swirling as he pivoted toward me.

I strode in their direction— No, I strode in Joe's direction. He was a defiler of vulnerable young womanhood, and I was her righteous champion. Or, at least, that's the way I saw it. "For God's sake, Lone Wolf, don't you understand what it means to be a Muslim woman. She's not supposed to be touched by a man until she's married." I didn't pause for even a moment to consider either the appropriateness of my anger or its true source. For me this innocent girl was being compromised in a manner that as far as I knew could have untold consequences for her. I was in battle mode.

"What business is it of yours, Pelletier?" Joe's expression was a mix of fury and cagey caution. The fury I understood, but not the caution. He didn't give me even a second to figure it out but edged in on me, almost nose to nose. "Can't I talk to a student without being hounded?" He poked me in the chest with a thick finger. His voice rose. "And you…you race- privileged slut! What gives you the right to butt in on a conversation between persons of color? White entitlement?"

"Race has nothing to do with it." I poked him in return—hard. Surprised, he backed away from me. "That's my student you're harassing." My voice rose to compete with his. "I have every right to see that she's not…dishonored by some hot-shot opportunist—"

"What's going on out here?" The English department office door had flown open. We all three twisted toward it. Ned Hilton appeared in the doorway, his expression stony. Joe's face reflected instant horror. I felt mine burning. There we were, two candidates for tenure in the English Department of one of the most prestigious schools in the nation, and we were going at each other like two-year-olds in a tantrum. Ned edged into the hall, as if he feared a more direct approach might place him in peril. A small group of English professors, including Sally Chenille and Harriet Person, followed him. Each wore the controlled expression of a dignified professional facing an Extremely Awkward Situation. Oh, God, no! Not Ned Hilton, Sally Chenille, and Harriet Person…the tenure committee! They must have been conferring in Ned's inner office.

To say that Ned looked strained would be a gross understatement. Pale and skinny, with straight dun-colored hair flopping
over his bulging forehead, Ned had grown weedy in the past year
or so. His shoulders slumped, and a small pot belly had begun
to emerge. He'd taken to wearing tweed jackets that bulged at
the elbows and gray flannel pants that bulged at the rump. This
was Ned's first semester as department chair, a distinction he'd
attained only once it became crystal clear that nobody else on
the senior faculty would agree to do it. Ned, as far as I could
tell, had lacked the courage to say no.

So far, he'd approached the job with diffidence and hesitation.
Because he could never bear to force his colleagues to come to
the point, or to pressure us into a consensus, department meetings were endless. Plus he had an absolute phobia about possible
lawsuits, the department being sued for some inadvertent breach
of the Equal Employment Act or for violation of the College's
sexual harassment policies, or...you name it. It was as if some
vindictive legal/political tribunal resided in his head, and all
potential department decisions had to march past it in review.
When Miles was chair, department meetings had been so boring
I'd taken to bringing books of crossword puzzles, but with Ned
in charge I'd advanced from Monday's puzzles to Wednesday's,
and I was certain that by the end of the semester I'd be ready
for Sunday's.

"Karen! Joseph! What's the problem here?"

"He—" I said

"She—" he said.

And then I remembered Ayesha. Where was she? I couldn't see
her among the cluster of colleagues now witnessing my humili-
ation. How embarrassing this must have been for her—two
professors putting on such a juvenile display and using her as a
pretext. I was beginning to realize that perhaps there might have
been a more diplomatic way for me to handle the situation. I
hadn't been quite rational about my approach to Joe, had I? Now
our spat was public spectacle. Oh, God. What had I done?

And I couldn't see Ayesha anywhere. I stood on my tiptoes and looked over Joe's head. There she was down the dimly lit hall by the open office door with a tall, lean young man who looked familiar to me. Then a ray of late sun shone in through the glass of the door and lit up his matted blond hair.

It was my other brilliant student, Hank Brody, and Ayesha seemed very comfortable in his arms.

Chapter Five

Monday evening

"Oh, Charlie, I don't know what to do. Ned scolded us as if we were naughty schoolchildren. I was so humiliated! And then I saw Ayesha in the arms of a boy, and the whole rationale for... chiding...Joe went right down the drain."

"Sounds like you did a lot more than 'chide' the man, Babe. Sounds like you just about skinned him alive. It's not like you at all to lose your cool in front of colleagues. What was really going on?"

I'd driven home on autopilot again, and the phone started ringing the minute I got in the house. When I heard Charlie's voice, I flopped down on the old overstuffed couch and unburdened myself of the whole embarrassing scene. It had been three days since he'd been able to call, and I hadn't wanted to get into my tenure dilemma by e-mail.

Then he had to go and ask that question: "What was really going on?"

What *was* really doing on? "You just won't believe it, Charlie. Miles Jewell came storming into my office—"

"Jewell? That's the old guy, right? The one who's given you so much grief for being a mushy-eyed liberal?"

Mushy-eyed? "Yes, but even he thinks what's going on is an outrage." I wiped my eyes on the sleeve of my new silk blouse. Was I crying? No. Couldn't be.

"Calm down, Sweetie. Take a deep breath. Blow your nose. Good. Now tell me—what *is* going on?"

And I told him all about it: the probability that, simply because he was Native, Joe Lone Wolf would take my place in the ranks of Enfield's tenured faculty. "I don't know if Ned's support for Joe is because he's terrified of an affirmative-action lawsuit, or if he truly believes I should be sacrificed to the gods of justice to make reparations for the whole sorry past of American history."

"Okay, sweetie. God, I wish I could be there with you! But, listen, I heard you use the word 'probability.' Don't you think 'possibility' might be more like it? After all, not *all* your colleagues are idiots."

"When it comes to racial politics, nobody's quite sane these days. I can't be sure which way the department will jump." The soft couch cushions were beginning to suffocate me. I pushed myself up and went to the window. Seven o'clock and dark already. Winter was coming, and I'd spend it alone. Charlie in Iraq. Amanda in Nepal. Me…

"Babe, now remember, I'm an outsider. I'm not certain how this stuff works. After six years you apply for tenure, right?"

"Right. You present your case, and the senior members of the department—those who already have tenure—vote yes or no."

"Does the department have the last word?"

"Well, no. Their decision goes to the deans, and they look at it. If there's even one or two negative votes, they sit up, take notice, and start asking questions."

"So, the deans have the last word?"

"Well, no. Then it goes to the president." The thought of Avery Mitchell casting the deciding vote made my stomach do flip flops. We had a history, Avery and I. Well, we had a tiny history—a one-kiss history. A long-ago-one-kiss history.

"You're in with him, right, Babe? You've done a lot for the school, and he seems like a reasonable guy."

"Yeah, you're right. Avery's a reasonable guy." That didn't offer me any comfort. He was reasonable—but he was also the consummate political animal. Would he buck the tide if it went against me?

On the phone I heard someone speaking to Charlie, but couldn't make out the words. Then Charlie said, "Listen, Babe. I'm gonna have to get off the phone now. Word is we're headed out into the provinces." I wouldn't say he sounded exactly thrilled, but there was an excited edge to his voice. *Adventure.* "That's what I called to tell you. I may be out of touch for a few days."

"Oh, God. Listen to me kvetching when you're the one who's in danger." It began to occur to me that maybe I was over-reacting to Miles' news; Charlie's safety mattered a hell of a lot more than my tenure.

Someone in the background yelled, "Hey, Piotrowski. On the double!"

"Listen, gotta go. One last thing. Put it all in proportion— what's the worst that could possibly happen? You might lose your job. Happens to thousands of people every day. That's just the way things work. So you'll find another one.

"And, anyhow, Babe," his voice went husky, "if the worst should ever come about, believe me, I would never, ever, let you starve."

"Piotrowski!" the voice bawled.

"Coming! Bye, Babe. I'll call when I can."

◇◇◇

I sat there with loneliness buzzing through the telephone's receiver. I hated it, that abrupt severance: one second Charlie was there, the intelligence, the passion, the unique consciousness of him; the next, nothing but that meaningless electronic tone that spoke only of immutable distance and unwanted separation.

My computer suddenly clicked out an e-mail from Amanda.

From: APelletier@sbcglobal.net
To: KPelletier@enfield.edu
Subject: Don't Worry!

Can't CALL YOU, Mom. Am out in the hills. One small

Internet café in this town. Saw Buddhist funeral procession today winding up into the mountains—saffron and white against greenest green you could ever imagine. So beautiful here, and simple. People very friendly. Love, Amanda.

I wrote back:

Beautiful here, too, high autumn, but not simple. I miss you! Keep in touch!!!! Love, Mom.

Chapter Six

Tuesday 10/6

"Joe Lone Wolf says you attacked him for no reason." The expression on Ned Hilton's narrow face was stern. "He called it an ambush."

Ned sat behind the chairman's desk in a leather chair so large it threatened to engulf him. All three buttons on the beige polo shirt he wore beneath his brown tweed jacket were fastened. It was the next morning, Tuesday. At ten o'clock his east-facing office was flooded with light from the tall, recessed windows behind him, momentarily blinding me. Had he timed it that way?

Ned had called me early—nine a.m. on the nose. He wanted, he said, in a voice so flat he might have gargled with liquid Xanax, to talk with me and "get to the bottom of that disgraceful scene yesterday afternoon between Professor Lone Wolf and yourself."

"When?" I asked. I didn't know it was possible for me to sound so Minnie-mouse meek.

"Now. My office." He hung up. *Masterful.*

Wearing black pants and my favorite denim jacket embroidered on the back with a peace symbol, my hair loosely plaited in a single braid, I sat in the hot seat and tried to defend myself. Motes of dust hung in the air, creating an aura of desiccated light around the chairman's head and shoulders. "Ned, believe me, it wasn't anything like an ambush or an attack. I simply informed Joe that I felt his behavior with a student was inappropriate."

"What behavior was that?" Ned was squeezing a hot-pink stress ball in his right hand.

I felt like a fourth-grade tattle-tale. "He touched Ayesha Ahmed—twice."

"Where did he touch her?"

"By the staircase."

"Karen…"

"On the arm. Okay? He grabbed her by the arm, thus violating Islamic rules of gender separation and college sexual harassment policy—no touching, no hugging, etc. We get a memo about that every year, remember?"

"Joe says he didn't touch her—he simply gestured in her direction."

A brass letter opener in the shape of a dagger lay on the desk within easy reach. I folded my hands in my lap. "He touched her."

"So, it comes down to your word against his. Shall we call Ayesha in to settle this?"

"No! We can't put her through that." As the catalyst for that ridiculous scene, the poor girl had had enough embarrassment.

Ned leaned back in his chair and did something contemplative with his lips. It looked as if he had a bad toothache. "And, in any case, you overreacted, didn't you? A simple touch on the arm?"

"Perhaps." It pained me to have to admit the possibility, but I was determined to continue in my policy of departmental congeniality, unaccustomed as I am to public meekness.

"Perhaps?" The stress ball migrated to his left hand.

I refused to respond to that hostile little nudge. A long, long, looong silence ensued. I sat it out, staring past Ned and through the window. A girl with a shaved head sped past on a bicycle—her clunky bike-lock chain hung around her neck. A guy with a blue backpack and a guitar case strolled by. A yellow Labrador retriever wearing a dark-blue bandana knotted around his collar jumped up and caught a high-flying Frisbee. Every campus has a yellow dog and a Frisbee.

Finally Ned let out a sigh. "Karen, we both know what this is all about, don't we?"

"We do? What?"

He leaned back in the chair and intertwined his fingers. "You are up for tenure—a stressful time for anyone, but you're not handling it well. Making a scene in front of your colleagues. Tarnishing your chances." He fiddled with his polo shirt's top button until it suddenly popped off in his hand. He stared at it, bewildered, then opened his center desk drawer and placed it carefully in what I speculated must be a compartment designed especially for beige shirt buttons. Then he glanced back at me. "But this is a particularly sticky case, involving issues of social equity and racial equality. Some of us must make sacrifices in the name of reparative justice. You do understand, don't you? Not everyone can be tenured everywhere, you know, Karen. Departments have their individual needs and obligations. I'm sure I don't need to say anything more than that."

It's a funny thing about unaccustomed meekness; sometimes it's nothing but a ticking bomb. I stood up, very slowly, and walked around the desk behind which Ned had barricaded himself. "Professor Hilton," I said. My voice was sculpted ice. "You may very well outrank me. You may very well hold the key to my future in your puny hands...."

The stress ball fell to the carpet. He skittered his ball-wheeled desk chair away from me and back toward the windows. I truly think he expected me to slug him.

"...but," I advanced on him, pushed the top of his chair with my finger, hard, and it tilted even further backward. "But, you may not patronize me, and you may not threaten me."

"That wasn't a threat," he squeaked, attempting to right himself.

I stooped to pick up the hot-pink stress ball, gave it a squeeze, tossed it to him. He tried to catch it but missed, and it bounced onto the wide windowsill and came to rest in a terra cotta planter bristling with cacti.

"Have a nice day, Professor Hilton." I was dead, and I knew it. I might as well go straight home and write my letter of resignation.

As I stalked out on Ned and entered the hallway, Joe Lone Wolf's office door opened. I think I gained the sanctuary of the ladies' room before Joe could see me. There I whipped out my cell phone, dialed Earlene, and got voice mail. "Call me as soon as you can," I said to the electronic memory device I'd reached instead of my friend. I called Greg. Ditto. Sometimes modern life offers only cold electronic consolation. My heart was thudding and my face was hot. I stood at the old marble-top sink and splashed cold water on my face until I felt sufficiently recovered to face the world.

When I left Dickinson Hall on my way to lunch, having finally made contact with my friends, I saw Joe Lone Wolf strutting across campus ahead of me. Elmore O'Hara, a black kid with shaved head and a little goatee, was walking toward us. Joe tilted his head at Elmore, as if questioning him. Elmore responded with two thumbs up. Not a word had passed, but something had been agreed upon.

Tuesday Noon

"You said that to him? You actually said 'puny hands'?" Greg Samoorian's expression was properly scandalized, but his brown eyes held an irrepressible glimmer of glee. He sat across the table from Earlene and me in the back booth at the Blue Dolphin diner drinking coffee from a ceramic mug. It was lunchtime and the aroma of hamburger and onion suffused the air.

"I did. And now I'm dead meat. That's why I called you guys."

"What on earth came over you?" Greg asked. He was studying the menu's Specials of the Day.

"Nobody, but nobody gets away with threatening me!" I had no appetite at all.

Earlene set her coffee mug on the table. "Karen, as you know, I come from a background similar to yours, so I do understand the knee-jerk pride—"

"Knee-jerk? He was abusing his power!" I couldn't repress the tears that had been building since I'd left Ned's office.

"You think?" Earlene placed a hand on my arm. "Or was he simply being an insensitive jerk?" She handed me a paper napkin.

I mopped my eyes and sighed. "Could be. My first year at Enfield, Ned was up for tenure himself, and his situation was iffy. I never saw anyone in such a state of despair. You'd think now he'd have empathy for someone in the same position."

The waitress showed up with a red plastic bread basket. She had brassy hair crimped into tousled ringlets and a wide streak of eyeliner above each eye. Her nameplate said SONIA. "Sorry to be so long," she said. "It's a madhouse. What can I get you?"

My companions ordered the special, corn chowder and BLTs. Sonia wrote it on her little green pad, turned to me and raised an inquiring eyebrow.

"Nothing." The thought of food nauseated me.

"She'll have the same," Greg said. "Cup of chowder. B.L.T."

Sonia changed the number 2 to 3. "Listen to your husband," she said, as she walked off, "he knows what's good."

"He's not my—"

Greg laughed and took my hand across the tabletop. "Yes, Doll-baby, listen up. Hubby knows best."

Earlene plucked a bread roll from the basket. "Ned is one of those people who latches onto a perfectly valid and well-meaning set of beliefs and then turns them into stone. It's a kind of character flaw, the inability to live without absolutes." She broke the roll and buttered it.

"God help us," Greg said, "when one of these secular fundamentalists is handed a little power—especially in the academy. Talk about rigid!"

"You know, Karen," Earlene went on, handing me half the buttered roll, "I continue to believe in the fairness of the tenure system here at Enfield. More rational minds than Ned's will prevail. And, if they don't, there's always the appeal process. The college has no reason to want to lose you."

"I'd love to believe that's true."

"But…but one thing I am concerned about…" She glanced over at Greg. He nodded.

"What's that?" I stopped the bread roll halfway to my mouth.

Greg took over. "We're afraid, the way you're going, you're gonna shoot yourself in the foot."

When Greg gets serious, I sit up and listen. "Shoot myself—"

Earlene broke in. "I wouldn't put it quite that way, Karen, but I am concerned about the instability you've shown over the past couple of days—"

"Instability! Me?"

The waitress set a cup of soup in front of me. I pushed it away.

"Maybe that's too strong a word." Earlene had her deanly manner on, which meant she was both sincere and worried. "But you've lost your temper twice now in an extremely impolitic manner. That's not at all like you."

Greg grinned. "'Puny hands,'" he chortled.

"Samoorian! Don't encourage her!"

I pulled the soup toward me and began spooning it into my mouth. That way I didn't have to talk.

Greg still had that smirk on his face. "One absolute necessity for success in the academic world," he intoned, "is the ability to suffer fools—if not gladly, then at least mutely." He took a sandwich plate from the waitress and placed it in front of me. The smell of bacon was almost irresistible. "And speaking of fools, did you see today's *Student Voice*? Ned gave them a long interview."

"I really couldn't care less." A former student of mine with long red hair entered the diner. I gave him a dispirited wave and hoped he wouldn't come over to talk to me. He didn't. Turning back to Greg, I said, "But, okay, I'll bite. About what did he give them the interview?" I sounded like a well-educated foreigner who'd read all the grammar books: *Never end a sentence with a preposition.*

"About the subject of the book he's working on, *Hallucinogenic Ideation in 1960s Counter-culture Poetry.*"

I stared at Greg over my soup. "That's what Ned Hilton's working on? 'Hallucinogenic ideation?'"

Greg shrugged. "I guess he wants the kids to know just exactly how cool he is."

"Cool? Ned?"

"Cool…*Not.*" He laughed. "Supposedly it's about how the imagistic, linguistic, and spiritual manifestations of hallucinogens differ from maryjane to LSD to mescalin to…whatever. There's a chapter for each drug."

The B.L.T. was crispy and flavorful. "So that means he has to do primary research?" I quipped. "Maybe that explains why he's been so strung out this semester—he's got the DEA on his heels."

Earlene frowned. "Given the increased problems we're having on this campus with drugs, it's irresponsible of him to publicize that— But, listen, we've gotten sidelined. We're here to help you get through all this stress. What can we do?" She wasn't about to let me off the hook.

"You've already helped. I hear you—I'm my own worst enemy sometimes."

"So what are you going to do about it?" Two sets of brown eyes were fixed on me. It was a come-to-Jesus-moment.

I sighed. "Apologize. I'm going to apologize to both Joe and Ned."

Greg smiled with sympathy. "It's like you're telling us you've decided to drink the Kool-Aid."

"Do it, Karen." Earlene was looking very sober. "And, listen, I have a question for you." She leaned toward me in a hush-hush manner. "Have you ever considered going into therapy?"

"*Therapy?*" My voice scaled upwards. "Me? Why on earth would *I* want to go into *therapy?*"

◇◇◇

On the way home, I drove six blocks out of my way just so I could pass the little green house that was for sale on Elm Street. If it were mine, I would get rid of those lacy curtains in the large front window and replace them with wooden-slatted interior shutters, one set closed on the bottom for privacy, another set open on the top to let in the light. And on the wide sill, currently dominated by a scraggly spider plant, I'd place a huge Christmas cactus—the kind that blooms three or four times a year.

Chapter Seven

Wednesday 10/7

I knew I had to apologize to Ned and to Joe, and the sooner I got it over with the better. So the next morning before my nine a.m. class I peeked in the department office to see if Ned was in yet. He wasn't, and Monica Cassale, the department secretary had no idea when he would be. "Not that it much matters," she said, pushing her chair back from the desk. Monica, a chunky woman with chopped-off brown hair, wore blue jeans and a turtleneck sweater that would have been better suited to raking leaves in the privacy of her back yard than to staffing the front desk of the English department office.

"Not that it matters?" I echoed. Monica can be honest to the point of insolence, but if you were willing to tolerate the lip you could always count on her to tell it like it was.

"I'm not saying anything the faculty isn't aware of, Karen, and you know it. Either he comes in or he doesn't come in. When he's here, either he works or he doesn't. Most of the time he sits at his desk staring out the window. I'm getting to the point where I miss Professor Jewell. He may have been a crabby old geezer, but he knew how the department was supposed to run. If it wasn't for me…"

This was nothing I was in a position to address, so I ignored the grumbling. "You're telling me I'll see Ned when I see him?"

"Yeah, if he's not too spaced out to talk."

"Spaced out?"

"I'm not sayin' another word. I got a kid to support. I can't afford to lose this job." She pivoted back to the keyboard. In the hall outside the office I paused, listening to her type at her usual preternatural speed. Everyone knew Monica was a witch. I mean that literally. She was a member of a local Wiccan coven. It was no secret; she wore the silver pentagram on a leather thong around her neck for all to see. No wonder she could type so fast.

Back in my own office I gathered up books and notes and headed out to Emerson Hall to meet my class. My apology to Ned would have to wait.

◇◇◇

Ayesha Ahmed's *hijab* was green today, a wonderful celery color that contrasted beautifully with her dark eyes and skin. She had been uncharacteristically quiet during this morning's discussion of our assignment, "The Schooldays of an Indian Girl," by Zitkala Sa, a Sioux Indian. "Schooldays" is an astute and angry narrative by a woman who, "a wild little girl," as she called herself, was lured by white missionaries to the "iron routine" of a missionary boarding school designed to "civilize" native children. There, she says, her "spirit tore itself in struggling for its lost freedom."

My other students, thoroughly versed in the discourse of racial politics, responded with well-educated outrage, tending toward terms such as "assimilationism" and "cultural genocide." Stephanie drew manga. Garret typed on his keyboard. Ayesha seemed preoccupied. Finally she raised her hand, and I called on her immediately.

"None of you know what you're talking about." Her voice was shaky. Something was troubling her. From her first sharp words a breathless silence overcame the other students. "Oh, yes, you're all very glib and politically correct about this memoir, but I'll bet not one of you understands it like I do—with your heart and your blood. And your skin."

Garrett glanced from his laptop, eyes suddenly fixed on the Muslim girl. Hank Brody sat up straight, his expression concerned.

Ayesha jumped up from her seat, and I feared for a second that she was going to rush out of the room. But instead she took her anthology, walked to the blackboard, picked up a piece of chalk and began to copy Zitkala Sa's words out of the book in bold capitals.

"THE THRONGS OF STARING PALEFACES DISTURBED AND TROUBLED US." She underlined it.

Then she began a new line. "I SCARCELY HAD A REAL FRIEND, THOUGH BY THAT TIME SEVERAL OF MY CLASSMATES WERE COURTEOUS TO ME AT A SAFE DISTANCE." She underlined this twice.

The chalk cracked in half as she finished the final line: "I NO LONGER FELT FREE TO BE MYSELF, OR TO VOICE MY OWN FEELINGS." She hesitated, and then plunged ahead, her manner regal. "You Americans! All so smug! So self-righteously outraged about atrocities that occurred a century ago. But you don't recognize yourselves in this narrative, do you? Here and now—today?

"How many of you have been detained at airports by Homeland Security—seven times? How many have had their freshman roommate switch to a room with someone of her own religion and skin color? How many have ever gotten hateful—"

The bell rang. I was baffled. Ayesha had always been extremely composed; she'd seemed to have lots of friends. Something dire must have happened to elicit this bitter indictment. I took a deep breath and opened my mouth, trusting that appropriate words would come out.

"Ayesha," I said, "will you stay a moment, please?" Then I turned to the rest of the students, sitting in their seats embarrassed and stunned. "We'll take up the issue of forms of racism and their consequences in the next class," I said. "See you Friday. And, remember, your mid-semester papers are due."

Cat Andrews cut me off before I could get to Ayesha. "Don't you want to friend me on Facebook, Professor? I asked you because I really admire you, and I want you to be part of my network of friends."

"I'm too old for that social networking stuff," I replied, annoyed by her persistence. I was staring over her shoulder, trying to locate Ayesha.

"Ayesha," I called. But she was out of the room before I could stop her, with Hank right behind her.

I thought maybe I should ask her to come to my office, so I could find out what was behind her outburst, but life caught up with me, and I didn't get around to it.

I e-mailed Amanda. *I miss you! Be careful. Love, Mom.*

◇◇◇

"Joe," I said, "I'm sorry I yelled at you the other day. It was uncalled for, and I hope you'll accept my sincere apologies." I was standing by myself in the women's room speaking to the pale apparition in the mirror. She wore a harvest-gold silk blouse with a longish brown wool skirt, and her dark hair was clasped tightly at the nape of her neck in a large ebony barrette. Her pale lips were tight. Shadowy smudges circled her gray eyes. She looked like hell.

Joe had been in his office with the door open when I walked by on the way back from class, but he was talking to a student and I certainly couldn't interrupt the discussion with my *mea culpa*. In the bathroom combing my hair and applying a red lipstick called "Slash," I rehearsed three or four different apologies, from just plain "Sorry, pal," to the more dramatic, hand-on-the-heart, "*Je suis désolée…*"

Less nauseating than some and more sincere than others, "*I'm sorry*," and "*uncalled for*," sounded like words I might actually be able to get out of my mouth. "I'm sorry I yelled at you…," I rehearsed again, took a deep breath, exited the women's room, turned right in the hall and headed to Joe's office.

The door was shut.

The light was out.

Apology deferred.

Friday 10/9

Friday morning the students looked exhausted, having no doubt stayed up half the night to get their papers done. Also it was the last class before the holiday weekend and their minds were clearly elsewhere. "You can go now," I said, when they'd all given me their mid-semester papers. I was too tired to go through the motions of teaching comatose students. "I'm sure you remember Monday is Columbus Day. No classes. See you Wednesday. We'll be discussing Native American oratory." I hadn't deliberately scheduled Native literature to coincide with Columbus Day, but there was a nice irony to it, Columbus being the prototype of European oppressors who brought about Native genocide. At Enfield College, however, tradition trumps political correctness and, with much professorial protest in the more enlightened classrooms, the holiday survives. No student, as far as I knew, has ever protested; a day off from classes is, after all, a day off.

It wasn't until I was back in my office, checking the mid-semester papers into my grade book, that I realized Ayesha hadn't shown up, hadn't even submitted her essay by proxy. This wasn't like her. In fact, after that blow-up between Joe and me in the hallway, she hadn't come to see me about her mid-semester topic. Then that odd episode in class. And, now, no paper handed in.

I pulled the phone toward me and dialed a number from the college directory.

"Hello?"

"Ayesha, this is Professor Pelletier—"

"Oh, Professor, this is Edie Sosa, Ayesha's roommate. Her brothers picked her up last night. She's gone home for the long weekend. Why don't you try her by e-mail?"

Skipped class to go home early? Without submitting a required assignment? Well, maybe Ayesha was just like an American college kid, but I hadn't expected such lax behavior from my diligent Moroccan student.

I thought about her reaction to the writings of Zitkala Sa, the bitter remarks directed to her classmates, and I picked up the phone again—this time to call the Dean of Students office. Maybe Earlene could help me understand what was going on with Ayesha Ahmed.

To: charles.piotrowski@army.mil.gov
From: kpelletier@enfield.edu

So good to talk to you Monday night. I could say heavenly or fabulous or stupendous, but good covers it. Good. Good. Good.

I know you said you'd be out of touch for a while, but, wherever you are, maybe my love will reach you through the ether.

Karen

Saturday 10/10

The new library is a civilized gathering place for students and faculty—plus books. After decades of cramped reading rooms, echoing stone staircases, and some book stacks still numbered by the Dewey Decimal System, the Enfield library has joined the twenty-first century: five stories high, a bright two-storey lobby with cozy overstuffed chairs, portable ottomans in primary colors, low tables holding half-completed jigsaw puzzles, and hardly a book in sight—just islands of computer tables, three computers each, with sturdy, ball-wheeled office chairs. Off to one side is the jazzy new coffee shop, which was raising faculty and student caffeine levels to unprecedented, jittery heights.

I sat in a red vinyl booth half-hidden behind a raw concrete pillar. A gigantic paper-lantern-like chandelier lighted my hideaway as I paged through the *New York Times*. Across from me, a woman student wearing a fluffy pink scarf was curled up on a banquette, with her iPod in front of her, earbuds in, reading a much thumbed copy of *Lolita*. The rich scent of fresh-ground beans pervaded the bright, spacious room.

I wasn't really here to read the newspaper but to do final checking for the bibliography and footnotes of that one last essay for my tenure file. The research would be tedious, checking page numbers, exact wording of the titles, publication dates, correct spelling of authors' names, etc. I needed to fortify myself with coffee first.

No sooner had I settled down with my steaming "ecotainer" when someone slid onto the seat next to me, bringing with him the scent of high skies and wide open plains and, perhaps, just a hint of something that might be sagebrush—although, to tell the truth, I didn't have a clue what sagebrush smelled like. I glanced over: Clark McCutcheon, Wizard of Whiteness.

"Karen Pelletier," he said. "I've been wanting to get to know you." The toothiness of his smile and the directness of his intense blue gaze signaled that "knowing" me could—possibly—take any form I chose.

"Oh?"

"Oh, yes. Nothing escapes me, you know." He winked. "Beyond all doubt you are the most…intriguing woman on campus." He must have had his teeth enameled, they were so uniformly white.

"Is that so?" I responded. Then I couldn't help myself. "I thought you found Sally Chenille 'intriguing.'"

"Ah." He laughed and shook his head like a wayward stallion. The shoulder-length gray-blond mane spun out around his strong, square jaw. "Funny you should say that. The good Professor Chenille wishes, above all else, to intrigue, but, sad to say, there's nothing substantive there. I find Sally to be totally predictable, an academic construct, a self-created projection of sex, postmodern theory, and celebrity culture. But, you—I think you're the real thing." He paused, then leaned forward, elbows on his knees, his eyes looking straight into mine. "I like that."

I leaned back as far in the booth as I could without going through the wall. "Well, Professor McCutcheon, I'm very flattered, but I don't…what I mean to say is, I'm in a committed relationship."

"That's not a problem for me." The effect of his slitted blue gaze was almost, but not quite, hypnotic. "Is it for you?" His hand was on my knee now, the hand that I had last seen groping Sally Chennile's ass. Then he grinned—Robert Redford as cowboy roué. "And do call me 'Clark.'"

I took a deep breath and stood up abruptly, dumping newspaper all over the floor. "Well, Clark, it's very nice to talk to you, but…I've got work to do."

He chose to remain oblivious to my discomfort. His slow gaze bathed me in the sunlight of his approval. Standing now, towering over me, he gave my arm a strong, meaningful squeeze. I inadvertently checked out his hand: square and workmanlike, with the nails recently polished. He spoke in a considered drawl. "I like women, Karen. It's only natural, right? Give me a call anytime you get tired of commitment. I'll…buy you a drink." He winked again.

I walked out, leaving my much-needed coffee behind. When, on the open, curving staircase to the second floor, I looked back down into the busy lobby, I could just see the back of his denim work jacket disappearing out the library doors. From its cut and quality the "work" jacket must have been a Ralph Lauren.

I went back downstairs to retrieve my coffee. I needed it more than ever now.

◇◇◇

It was midnight when I left the library. The work had proven even more tedious than expected. I wasn't dressed for the autumnal chill, and I quickstepped my way across the well-lit campus with its eerie blue safety lights glowing chimera-like against the solid brick and stone. The faculty parking lot held only a few cars, one of which was Joe Lone Wolf's lime-green Volkswagen bus— nostalgia on wheels. As I clicked open the door of my Subaru, a high-visibility-yellow sports car, low-slung and mean, squealed into the lot. I recognized it as belonging to Sally Chenille, she of the sex-postmodern-theory-celebrity construct. I was in my car by the time Sally's sporty vehicle pulled up to Joe's old bus, barely pausing to let Joe out. Joe slammed the passenger door and the yellow car took off. He glared after it as it peeled out of the lot. Then he shrugged and inserted his key into the VW's door lock. The engine reluctantly turned over, then caught, and the bus rolled slowly toward the exit.

A third car, headlights off, edged out of tree shadows on the street. It was a fairly new compact, maybe dark green, and I didn't recognize it. But as I sat there in the dark, I watched it follow closely behind Joe Lone Wolf's bus as it turned left, heading for home.

What the hell was that all about? Was someone shadowing Joe? Should I call him and make sure he'd gotten home okay?

Chapter Eight

Tuesday 10/13

A windstorm over the weekend had blown down all but the oak leaves, and by Tuesday afternoon when I came on campus after the Monday holiday, autumn had transformed itself from terminal summer to nascent winter. Old brick buildings had taken on chillier facades—straight, stark, Puritan lines without the redemption of nature's green. Groundsmen had run their leaf-blowers over the sidewalks, but the Common itself was buried in fallen leaves. Hank Brody was scuffing across the hidden grass. Other students had donned jeans and wool jackets, but Hank still wore his cargo shorts and sweatshirt. Wasn't he cold?

"Hey, Hank," I said. He was coming toward me from the direction of Dickinson Hall, and I wondered if he'd been looking for me.

Hearing my voice he glanced up, startled. He was pale, his matted corn-husk dreads flopping over the high forehead. "Oh, Professor, do you know where Professor Lone Wolf is?"

"Professor Lone Wolf? No."

"I had an appointment with him for two o'clock—about my paper. I waited a half hour, and he's still not in his office. He didn't make either of his classes this morning, either."

"Did you try the office? Maybe he told Professor Hilton or Monica, the secretary, where he was going."

"Ha!" Hank exclaimed. "That secretary said Professor Hilton was in no fit state to see anyone, and what did I think *she* was anyhow, a babysitter for the faculty? I'm not going back in there—phew! That lady's scary."

"Monica's bark is worse than her...bark," I said, lamely. When Monica was in a bad mood, the entire department tip-toed around as if they were walking in a field of activated hand grenades. Once we were back in the English department, I let him into my office. "You don't have to talk to her again, but let me see what I can find out."

Monica was at her computer, scowling over a game of Mahjong Titans. She didn't shut it down when I walked in, didn't even raise her eyes from the screen. Hank was right—she *was* scary. Then all at once I realized that maybe I'd be better off in the long run if I didn't ask Monica about Joe Lone Wolf; Joe might well be a sore spot for her. For a while he and Monica had been tight. Joe had spent a good deal of time in the office leaning over her desk, laughing and chatting. Monica was the only person I'd ever seen him chummy with. Three or four years ago, I'd even come across them smoking weed late one long summer evening when I was taking a walk on the back campus. Monica had glared at me, but who was I to condemn anyone? I remember thinking what an odd couple they were. Around then, Joe stopped coming into the office, and his friendship with Monica seemed to end.

Discretion being the better part of earning tenure, I turned quietly on my heel and left the office.

Seated behind my desk, I lied to Hank. "Sorry, kid. Monica doesn't have a clue as to Professor Lone Wolf's whereabouts."

"Oh." The lanky boy slumped in the chair. "I really need to talk to him."

"Did you call his home number?"

"He's not answering—home or cell." Hank unfolded his tall body from the armchair and stood there, biting his lower lip. "I don't know what I'm gonna do," he mumbled and turned toward the door.

"Hold on." I stood up and followed him into the hall and out onto the Quad. "Is something wrong? Can I help in any way?"

He stood still, looking down at the leaf-strewn grass. Stress had tightened the muscles of his face so that his lips were thin and his cheekbones protruded.

"Hank?" I prodded. "If you've got a problem, I might be able to get some help for you." He was shivering now, in his summer-weight clothes. Didn't he have anything warmer? I tapped him lightly on the back of his hand. "You're not alone on this campus. There are all sorts of resources for students. Why, Dean Johnson—"

"No. Please, not the Dean. My scholarship…" He turned and began kicking dry leaves as he walked away. I thought I heard him say, "I just have to talk to Joe Lone Wolf," as he headed in the direction of downtown Enfield.

◇◇◇

I glanced up from the screenful of accumulated e-mails on my computer. Cat Andrews, standing in my office doorway. I stifled a groan. I'd thought I might be able to catch up on some work without interruption. "Hi, Cat. Can I help you?"

She gave me a complicated look, pity and compassion. "You're not *really* too old to be on Facebook, no matter what you think. You want to be up on the latest with your students, don't you? Joining is *really* easy. Look, I can set it up for you in just five minutes. And then you can connect to so many *friends*. People from high school. People from college. And people can *poke* you and write on your wall and send you *gifts*." She was leaning over my shoulder now, staring at the screen.

Not only was Cat interrupting my work; she was also castigating me for being an electronic Neanderthal. I bit back a sharp retort. These days I supposed Facebook was as unavoidable as death, taxes, and the Internet. I might as well get it over with. Closing my e-mail, I pushed my chair back and stood up. "Your fingers are just itching to get on these keys, aren't they, Cat? Okay, I can spare five minutes. Go ahead and set it up."

"Five minutes for my part of it, I mean. And then you'll fill out your profile information, choose who to friend—"

"Whom. *Whom* to friend. And is *friend* a verb now?" My grammatical training had been taking a thumping lately, what with all the neologisms brought about by the digital revolution.

"Sure is. Oh, yeah."

While Cat was pecking away at the keys, I strolled over to the window. The afternoon was cold and spitting rain. Behind the denuded trees on the Quad, Enfield's old buildings, foursquare and solid, seemed to have emerged directly from the blunt New England earth, a concrete expression of the foursquare morality of the Calvinist founders. A gardener was on his knees on the Common digging holes to plant what looked like daffodil bulbs.

"All done," Cat said. "All you've got to do now is fill in your profile, download your photo, and choose your friends and you're in business."

"Thanks." *And no thanks.*

"And, look, I'll be your first friend." She did something with the keyboard and her…page?…popped up on the screen. "See, it says you're now my friend. Goody. I can't wait to get back to the dorm and give you a poke. Bye."

She skipped out of the office, leaving her page up on the screen. I sat in the desk chair and stared at it, bemused. Okay. There was Cat's photo with green hair. And lots of vapid messages from friends. Marcy was eating Pop Tarts—Yum! Fred was cramming for a Poly Sci exam—Bummer. Wendy was dying to go home for some real food.

Did I need to know any of this? I closed Facebook down without waiting to be poked. I needed coffee and an hour or so away from campus.

If I had my little green house in town, I'd go home and take a bath.

Instead, I'd call Greg and ask him to meet me at Starbucks. He was on the President's Council this year; he'd know what was going on with the overall tenure situation.

◇◇◇

And how are you doing, Karen?" Greg asked. He gave my hand a friendly squeeze. "You any less strung out this week? Let's see—tenure materials are due…Friday. Right?"

"Everything's ready. I'm all set to submit them this afternoon. Just have to print out one more essay." It was odd, but I couldn't feel any sense of jubilation or relief—just a numb, passive anxiety, something like a latent, lurking toothache.

Cat Wharton bounced into the coffee shop. At that distance she could have been anyone, but I recognized the bedhead. When she spotted me, she turned in my direction with a big smile. Oh, no. Not Cat again. At the last minute, however, she stopped, made a sudden pivot on her heel and swerved away—maybe because Greg had become visible behind a pillar.

It was a funky Starbucks—olive-green walls, huge cast-iron Corinthian pillars, black-painted overhead metal air vents, and mismatched, distressed-wood tables—some corporate honcho's idea of what would make professors and students feel like they weren't being manipulated by some corporate honcho. Greg and I sat in an alcove by the bathroom door and spoke in low tones. The rain had turned into a cold deluge. My umbrella, hanging from a coat hook, accompanied us with a monotonous *drip, drip, drip.*

"So Irina and I will throw a party."

"Ha! Better wait to see what happens first." I took the top off the coffee cup and spooned out latte froth. "It ain't over 'til it's over."

Elbows on the table, he leaned toward me, dead earnest. "Karen, you're a shoo-in."

My friend was beginning to annoy me. "But what if Joe…"

Greg had captured both my hands now. "You're super-stressed, aren't you? Maybe Earlene is right; maybe you *should* see a therapist."

I pulled my hands away. "What could a therapist tell me that I don't already know? Academic life has been my escape route from ignorance and poverty, right? Becoming a tenured professor is the holy grail of that life, right? And I'm not going to get tenure because of that god-damned *Joe Lone Wolf*." I pounded out his name.

Greg sat up straight and put a finger to his lips. "Keep it quiet. People are listening. Now you don't have to believe me if you think it will jinx the process, Ms. Doom and Gloom, but you are a shoo-in. As for me, I'm ready to party."

"Party all you want to," I snapped. Yes, he was definitely annoying; the last thing I needed was a little Miss Sunshine in my life. I pushed back my chair, which screeched against the concrete floor. "I've got to get back to campus and print out my essay." I snatched my umbrella from the hook. Greg stepped aside to let me pass. The coffee shop had filled up, and I nodded at Garrett Reynolds and Stephanie Hart, who had taken seats near us and were speaking quietly together. Damn! Had they been in a position to overhear me fulminating about Joe? I sure as hell hoped not.

We made our way between the jammed-together tables and the damp, woolly-smelling students, and, once on the sidewalk, turned toward campus. For no good reason, I'd just snapped at my faithful friend. I felt as if I were headed directly to the funny farm.

Chapter Nine

Tuesday 10/13

When the phone rang an hour or so later, I had Hank on my mind. I wondered if maybe this call was from him. Had he changed his mind about asking for help?

But, no. The caller, a man with a cigarette voice, was on a cell phone; I could hear the connection crackling and cars whizzing past in the near distance. "This Karen Pelletier?"

"Yes. Who's calling?"

"Neil Boylan. Remember me?"

"*Lieutenant* Neil Boylan?" Charlie's colleague at the Massachusetts State Police B.C.I. What the heck?

"Yeah. Got something I need to talk to you about."

My first, icy, thought was that he was calling to deliver some horrible news about Charlie: *He'd been blown up by a female suicide bomber in a market square in Basra. He'd been shot in fighting between Shiite and Sunni militants. He'd been killed in a firefight with some obscure militia connected to the Taliban. He'd been...*I'd seen it in the movies: sober men in uniforms, stepping out of cars in some anonymous American suburb, proceeding gravely up a narrow cement walk between rows of scraggly marigolds, knocking resolutely at the door...But, surely, if this were about Charlie, it would be the National Guard at my door, not the state police on a telephone. I remembered to breathe.

I'd met Neil Boylan several times at cop parties. He seemed like a real hard-ass. His crisp ginger curls and pinkish skin were deceptively childlike, but his manner, while often ingratiating, could quickly turn crude. Charlie neither liked him nor trusted him—and Boylan knew it. "Okay, Lieutenant, I'm listening. What's up?"

A moment of crackling and whizzing and a man's shout in the background. The phone went silent, as if muffled by a hand over the speaker. Then he was back. "I want to talk to you about the death of your colleague, Professor Joseph Lone Wolf."

◇◇◇

I should have gone directly to college authorities with Boylan's news. Why didn't I? Instead, I snatched up a heavy sweater and sped off campus as fast as I could go without actually running. I was stunned. *The death of Joseph Lone Wolf. The death of Joseph Lone Wolf.*

Why did Lieutenant Neil Boylan want to talk to *me*? Shit! Someone had blabbed to him about…about *what*? Nothing! I was simply being paranoid. Wasn't I?

I should have gotten on the phone with President Avery Mitchell immediately. But I didn't. Maybe I'd forgotten who Boylan was. Yeah, he was a state police homicide investigator, and yeah, I owed him, as such, all the assistance I could provide. But I also knew he was a nasty piece of work. His news must have shocked me into unquestioning obedience; I should have been more wary. When I'd asked Boylan why he needed *me*, he said I'd find out when I got there. "Make it snappy. And I want to keep a low profile on this, so don't call anyone—and I mean *anyone*. I'll inform the proper parties when we know what we're dealing with here."

Joe's apartment was three or four blocks from campus, at the bottom of a long hill that sloped past the college gymnasium and playing fields, then past nineteenth-century frame houses with miniscule front yards, and then a row of small apartment buildings the college rented out to faculty and staff. The raucous shouts of girls playing soccer created a strange dissonance with the words echoing in my head: *The death of…*

From a block away I could see the pulsing emergency lights on a half-dozen state police cars. Night was beginning to fall, and the walls of the small dark-brown brick apartment building flashed in a psychedelic frenzy. So much for keeping a low profile. On the street, cars were slowing down to catch a glimpse of the excitement. A small group of onlookers huddled outside near the police cars, their faces likewise psychedelic: blinking white and blue. These must be Joe's neighbors, like him benefitting from the subsidized campus housing.

Neil Boylan was Homicide, like Charlie, but at this point, I assured myself, that didn't necessarily mean murder. In the case of any unattended death, an investigator would be present to assess the situation. So, as I put one foot in front of the other, I consoled myself: not another Enfield College murder. Joe was dead—a vigorous man in his thirties. But it could have been a stress-induced heart attack, couldn't it? A fall in the shower? Suicide? Maybe he'd choked on a chunk of buffalo jerky.

"But why call me?" I asked myself, again. *Me?* I hardly knew Joe. Or Boylan, either, for that matter.

When the lieutenant saw me coming he straightened up and trotted over. Lieutenant Neil Boylan, a man of medium height, was whippet-thin with a receding hairline and an expression often bordering on sardonic. A snappy dresser, he wore ironed jeans and a well-cut brown wool jacket over a black polo open at the neck.

"You know this guy, Lone Wolf?" No preamble. No thanks for coming. Just, "you know this guy?" Boylan's expression was neither hostile nor friendly, just the guarded neutrality these guys learn in cop school.

"Yes, of course I know him—we're in the same department. What happened to him?"

"English Department, huh? How well did you know him?" He had a cat's grin.

"Just about as well as I know anyone I've sat through ten thousand department meetings with—meaning, not well at all. What happened to Joe?"

Before Boylan could answer my question, a tall uniformed officer with a beak of a nose beckoned to him. "Don't go anywhere," the lieutenant cautioned me, with a pointed index finger. He strode over to talk to Trooper Lombardi, who gave me a discreet nod. I knew Lombardi. He was Sergeant Felicity Schultz's husband, and Felicity was Charlie's partner. Currently she was on maternity leave, caring for Buster Schultz-Lombardi, the biggest, most rambunctious six-month-old I'd ever known. I smiled at the trooper—at least I think it was a smile. It might have been more of a nauseous grimace.

Cold and shaky, I sat down on the cement steps that led to the apartment building's courtyard. I fastened the leather toggles of my hand-knitted sweater and turned the collar up against the chill breeze. It was beginning to hit me—Joe Lone Wolf dead, Lieutenant Hard Ass getting on my case. What would Charlie tell me to do? I knew—he'd tell me to shut up and watch my back.

Boylan stalked up again, running a hand over his short-clipped hair. "To answer your question, Professor, Joseph Lone Wolf was found dead in his apartment this afternoon. Cause undetermined."

"Jee-zus!" Joe Lone Wolf. I may have resented Joe's claim on what I saw as *my* tenured position, but I'd never wished him any ill. And now he was...no longer an obstacle. I felt terrible for ever badmouthing him.

I thought it would be prudent not to mention any of that to Boylan.

He pointed in the direction of a police car Lombardi seemed to be guarding, a statie blue-and-gray. Its rear window was rolled up again, the occupant invisible through the tinted glass. "There's someone over here I need to talk to you about." He took my arm to lead me the ten yards or so to the car, but I shook myself free. "He's the reason you're here."

"Who is it?"

"Someone who says he knows you." He grabbed the back-door handle of the police sedan but didn't open it immediately. "Fat chance of that."

I could see only a shadow through the glass. Who could it possibly be? Had they caught the killer already? Was it someone I knew?

With a flourish, Boylan whipped the door open. I half expected him to say, "Ta! Da!"

Then I did recognize the backseat occupant: shivering and miserable, hazel eyes looking up at me, pleading. Hank Brody.

"Hank? My God!" I pivoted around to the lieutenant. "What are you doing with this boy? He's one of my students!"

"He is, huh? Whaddya know—he was telling the truth after all. Well, sure doesn't look like a college boy to me. That ratty hair. Looks homeless or like some kinda Deadhead."

I began fiddling with the toggles on my sweater. "And you've arrested him?"

"Thing is, don't know if we've got us a witness here—or a suspect. He's the one found the body. Called 911. But the whole story sounds fishy to me."

I pulled out my cell phone, scrolled down to Earlene's number.

Boylan grabbed my hand before I could press the send button. "Hold your horses, Professor. We haven't arrested him—he's just being detained for questioning."

I snatched the phone back and pressed the button. I heard it ring in Earlene's office. She picked up right away. Secretary must be gone for the day. "Earlene—Karen. Listen, Joe Lone Wolf's dead, and the state police have Hank Brody in detention." I told her where we were.

I motioned Hank to move over on the hard plastic backseat, then I slid in next to him. The car smelled of cleanser with a faint overlay of cigarettes and vomit. "The dean's on her way, Hank. Don't you say another word to this man till we get you a lawyer."

He nodded, wide-eyed and speechless.

"The dean? Hey, now," the lieutenant said. "Don't go overboard. If he's really one of yours, that's a different story…"

I turned my back on him, closed the door firmly, and was alone in the car with my student.

Tears were beginning to fill Hank's eyes. "Professor Pelletier, you did say I could call you if I had a problem.…"

"I'm glad you did. What happened, Hank?"

"I c … c … came to see Professor Lone Wolf." Hank was shivering so hard he could barely speak. I pulled off my heavy sweater and draped it around his shoulders. "The door was unlocked. It always is. When he didn't answer I went in. He was in the living room, just lying there on the couch—like he was asleep. But the place didn't smell right. I didn't want to use his phone—you're not supposed to touch anything, right? And I don't have a cell. So, I started banging on doors. A guy let me call 911. I told that cop all this, but he wouldn't stop asking questions."

I had questions for him, too, not least of them how he knew the door to Joe's apartment was always unlocked. But now was not the time, and besides a campus police car came to a screeching halt at the curb, and Earlene jumped out. It was cold in the blue-and-gray; I was envious of her long wool coat.

I handed Hank over to Earlene with a sigh of relief. I'd intended to stay with them, but she told me to go back to my office and get warmed up before I came down with pneumonia.

The college cop, a black man of about sixty named Artie Crawford, offered to take me back to campus, but Boylan wasn't done with me. I'd barely gotten myself settled in the passenger seat, when he hustled over. He held the car door open and leaned in to speak to me. "Hey, wait a minute, Ka…ah…Professor.…" He didn't know what to call me. Good. I didn't want him getting all palsy. "I'm not done talking to you. You say you knew Lone Wolf. But you didn't really say how well you knew him." He ran his tongue over his front teeth.

At Boylan's smarmy tone, I heard Officer Crawford suck in his breath. His graying military brush-cut seemed to bristle. Immediately he turned the key in the ignition.

I tried to tamp down my rage, but Boylan must have seen it in my burning face, because he held up a hand to silence me. "I gotta ask these questions, ya know. Gotta look at all the angles. Good-lookin' lady like you, I wouldn't blame a guy—"

I snapped at him. "Cut it out, Boylan."

I hadn't noticed before, but his eyes were pale gray, almost like Nordic ice. "Answer the question."

"I already did—he was my colleague."

Officer Crawford slid the gear-shift lever into drive. The car lurched forward. Boylan slammed my door, but not before he got the last word in. "I'll be talking to you again," he said. The eyes were slits of glass.

I think I must have been in a state of shock, because as Crawford drove me back to campus, I was still struggling to frame the situation in terms of cold logic. People who've done nothing wrong will be okay. Hank hadn't done anything wrong; therefore Hank would be okay. *I* hadn't done anything wrong; therefore I would be okay. Faulty syllogism.

In a crisis, reliance on pure logic is a sign of denial. I went home and wrote an anguished e-mail to Charlie. And then I deleted it. There was nothing he could do about this anyhow. Why worry him?

Chapter Ten

Wednesday 10/14

From: nedhilton@enfield.edu
To: englishdepartmentfaculty@enfield.edu
Subject: Death of a Colleague

At ten a.m., the English faculty will meet in the department lounge to process the untimely death of Professor Joseph Lone Wolf and review the ramifications, procedural, pedagogical, and psychological, of that death for the department. This meeting is mandatory.

Please inform your students by e-mail of the cancellation of tomorrow's English Department classes.

As I walked toward the English Department lounge the next morning, I first smelled the burning incense, and then I heard the flute music and the birdsong. Good God, don't tell me the department was going to get all touchy-feely about Joe's death. Oh, no—not emotion! Could we survive the self-exposure? I gulped and walked through the door.

The long mahogany table that sits against the lounge's side wall had been pulled out a yard or so and held a projector, a laptop computer from which the Native music emanated, and a small clay smudge pot from which smoke emerged, smelling something like cedar or sage. Folding chairs were set up facing in the opposite direction. I turned. It was as if the pallid blue wall had vanished, and I was confronting the forest primeval, sunlight flickering through ancient trees, branches blown in a gentle breeze. *Trees. Breeze.* It rhymed. It scanned. I was thinking in poetry. *On the shores of Gitche Goomee, / Of the shining Big Sea water...* The room was nearly full of my colleagues, shifting in their chairs, shuffling their feet, clearing their throats. I glanced over at Sally Chenille, seated next to me. She rolled her eyes. It was the first time ever I'd felt like smiling at Professor Chenille. Then I recalled that the last time I'd ever seen Joe he'd been getting out of Sally's snazzy sports car. And he seemed to be in a bit of a snit.

An empty easel sat in the corner of the large room, and as Miles Jewell took the seat on my other side, sighing deeply, Chairman Ned Hilton came through the door lugging a photograph the size of a wall poster. Centering it on the easel, he stepped back to contemplate the effect. It was a black-and-white portrait of Joe Lone Wolf in full ceremonial garb: fringed leather shirt and pants, feathered war bonnet, menacing face paint.

The English Department faculty was too civilized to gasp out loud. Oblivious to the discomfort of his colleagues, Ned took the podium. He was dressed all in white, loose cotton pants and tunic, and around his neck he wore a black leather thong with a circular pendant in a Native style—a silver rim with dangling feathers. A dream-catcher, that's what it was. Ned was wearing a Native dream-catcher.

"Colleagues," our chairman intoned, "we are here to pay tribute to our Native friend, returned now to the Great Father and to Our Mother the Earth. *Ahwhooah. Ah woo ah ay.* Let us—"

My gaze was focused intently on my folded hands, for fear of catching someone's eye. Ned sounded a little...off-center...to me, but what did I know? Beyond mastery of the Native songs, speeches, and narratives I'd learned for my American literature survey courses, I was as clueless as most literary scholars about American Indian life and culture.

"What is this crap?" The voice that boomed from the doorway belonged to Clark McCutcheon. He stood there with each hand up high against the doorframe and his feet spread wide. He looked like Da Vinci's Vitruvian Man, only with fewer limbs—and wearing denim.

I recalled seeing Clark with Joe at Rudolphs' bar. I breathed a sigh of relief. They'd seemed friendly. Maybe this was the cavalry riding to the rescue.

"Hilton, don't tell me this is some bungling attempt at a Native ceremony! For God's sake, don't you understand the egregiousness of a politics of appropriation? This farce exploits sacred traditions, desacralizes shamanistic rituals, and perpetuates hegemonic misrepresentations of outsider culture. Cease at once!" I thought I heard the hoof-beats of the great horse, Silver.

"No, no." Ned appeared shaken. To the extent that a pale face could become paler, his did. "This isn't cultural appropriation—just a respectful effort to reenact the signifying practices of Native Indian bereavement ceremonials."

"Crap," McCutcheon repeated, striding to the front of the room.

Harriet Person interrupted him before he could go further. "Ned means no disrespect—"

McCutcheon sputtered, "Replication without authenticity equals appropriation—"

But Miles Jewell jumped up and cut him off at the pass. Moving spryly to the podium, Miles assumed the age-old stance of department chairman: shoulders squared, feet wide, confronting his fractious faculty head on—something like an aged bison. "This is an egregious waste of time. Hilton, sit down and shut up." Ned closed his mouth abruptly and plopped down into a front-row chair. "You, too, McCutcheon."

Clark stood his ground for a second or two, an alpha male studying Miles and then his colleagues. His eye caught mine and held. He took a deep breath, relaxed his stance and winked. Surprisingly, he sat down, too.

Miles continued, "We've got real work to do here. The death of Lone Wolf presents us with crucial administrative issues. Here we are, halfway through the semester, and we need an immediate replacement for one of our colleagues. Who's qualified to take over Ned's classes for two or three sessions until a replacement can be hired?"

Twenty or so colleagues stared at each other in hapless bewilderment: *Not me.*

Miles cleared his throat and continued. "Karen, as an Americanist, you meet the criteria." He paused. "But would it be fair to ask you to teach his classes while you have a tenure decision looming over your head?"

Nobody breathed—least of all me. As it had for me, realization dawned—I could see it on every face—that, with Joe's death, I suddenly had no opposition for the English Department's one tenured position. Everyone stared at me: *Professor Plum, in the faculty apartment, with...* what? We hadn't yet been told the cause of death.

"Okay, Hilton," Miles barked. "What are Joe's courses?"

"His course in the major is American literary Outsiders," Ned squeaked.

"Okay. Hmm, literary Outsiders." Miles seemed to have grown two or three inches in the moments since he'd wrested the reins of power from Ned. "Who'll take over this course? McCutcheon, sounds right up your alley."

McCutcheon, seated now, pushed both hands out in front of him, palms out. "Oh, no. Not me. I've got too many duties as it is—I'm on the editorial staff of *American Literature*, I hold an MLA office, I oversee a section of the *Heath* anthology—"

"I'll teach it," I said, with a sigh that came from somewhere beneath my insoles. How hard could it be? An extra class or two? "But you'll find someone else right away, won't you? Maybe someone from the university? A Ph.D. candidate..."

Ned looked at Miles. Miles looked at Ned, the chairman. Ned looked away, abdicating responsibility. Thus do dynasties fall in academe. "Yes, okay," Miles said. "I'll get right on it." I swear he grew another inch. "And what's his other—"

A brusque knock and the lounge door flew open. Lieutenant Neil Boylan strode into the room, snapping his badge case open in front of him. "Boylan. Massachusetts state police. Homicide." He was followed by Trooper Lombardi, tall, saturnine, and impassive. I nodded at Lombardi, but he remained expressionless.

"Professors," Boylan said, wearing his neutral face. "I'm sorry to interrupt, but we're going to have to interview each of you about the death of your colleague, Joseph Lone Wolf." He gestured around the room. "Is everyone in the English Department present at the moment?"

Miles, who had pushed forward toward Boylan when the investigator had entered, huffed at him. "We're holding a confidential meeting. You can't just barge in here!"

Boylan's fair Irish face was solicitous as he bent toward Miles, but his voice was flat. "I'm sorry about that, sir, but I'm afraid we can. Finding you all together like this makes it very convenient. Are you in charge, sir?"

Miles regarded the lieutenant as if the younger man was a truant freshman. "Yes, I am. And your unannounced arrival is highly inconvenient, not to mention rude."

"Well, sir, as I said, I am sorry. I understand that you are all important, busy people, and we'll do our best to keep the… inconvenience…to a minimum." Without actually achieving sarcasm, something ambiguous about the tone of his mellow baritone on "important, busy people" took all the ego salve out of the words. "Sergeant, get this…ah…senior gentleman's name and put him on the interview list."

Lombardi flipped open a notebook and began to write.

Miles lost his newfound inches. I don't know where they went—just got swallowed up by his old-man clothes.

The lieutenant slowly eyeballed the members of the department, one by one, with his cool, gray gaze. There was nothing unpleasant or confrontational about his expression; being scrutinized by him was an experience akin to going through an airport security scanner. While he may not have thrown the fear of God into my colleagues, he certainly had impressed them as being in earnest. Cell phones appeared in the hands of those department members most likely to have their attorney's number on speed dial.

Clark McCutcheon, one hand-tooled boot crossed casually over the opposite denim-clad knee, seemed the most unfazed. "Lieutenant, may I respectfully ask just, exactly, how Joe—ah, Professor Lone Wolf—died?" Although his voice was as smooth as soy milk, the boot remaining on the floor jiggled up and down.

Boylan checked out McCutcheon—the shoulder-length gray-blond hair, the faux working-man's denim, the expensive boots. "You may certainly ask, Professor, but that information is strictly on a need-to-know basis."

"Was it really…murder?" This came from Ned Hilton, slumped in an armchair in the corner. If he'd been pallid before, now, in his white cotton togs, he was bleached and hung out to dry.

"His death is being investigated by the homicide division," Boylan responded. "You're free to draw your own conclusions." Then, squinting his eyes at Ned, he asked, "You sick or something, fellow? You don't look very well. Should I be calling EMS?"

"No," Ned squawked.

I spoke up for the first time since the officers had entered. "He'll be okay, Lieutenant Boylan. He just…doesn't handle stress well."

"Is that so? Lombardi, get him on the list, too—along with the cowboy, there." Then Boylan turned to me, smiled his cat's smile, and waited a long beat before he spoke again. "Of course Professor Karen Pelletier and I have already spoken."

Every professorial head turned. Every professorial eye fixed itself upon me. Every professorial imagination went to work— on overtime.

◇◇◇

"Pssst, Karen!" Monica, red-eyed and blotchy faced, beckoned me into the department office, closed the door and locked it. She pulled a pink tissue from the box on her desk, raised a finger indicating that I should wait a minute, then blew her nose. With another tissue she mopped her eyes. It was the first time I'd ever seen the feisty department secretary reveal the slightest vulnerability. "I'm sorry, Karen, but it just got to me—that sweet man. I can't believe he's gone." She plucked another tissue from the box.

Sweet man? "Joe?"

"Yeah," she said. "But I didn't get you in here just so I could cry on your shoulder. I've got a message for you from Felicity Schultz. She wants you to call her."

"*Sergeant* Felicity Schultz?"

"Yeah, she's your boyfriend's partner, right? She says you're in deep doo-doo with the staties and need to talk to her, ASAP."

I narrowed my eyes at Monica. "Why would she tell *you* all this?"

"Felicity and I go way back. I sat for her."

"You mean—for her baby?"

"No, for her. When she was a little kid, a real brat, she lived downstairs from me. One of those triple-deckers in Springfield? You know—rickety porches and dripping radiators? Anyhow, Felicity knows I work here, of course, and she thought I'd be the most—what'd she say?—discreet—way of getting in touch with you. *Discreet*, whoops! Better keep my voice down.

"She said to tell you—and these are the exact words—she said to tell you not to tell that asshole, Boylan, anything and to call her at this number." Monica pulled a pink memo slip from inside her bra, glanced left and right before palming it over to me. "Good luck," she whispered and unlocked the door.

◇◇◇

At the Dunkin' Donuts in Greenfield, Sergeant Felicity Schultz was sitting in the back booth with Buster asleep in the stroller beside her. Motherhood didn't seem to have transformed her at all—still the same plain oval face and roundish cheeks. Her red-brown hair was longer, though, probably because she didn't have time now to get to the barber every two weeks like she used to. And she smelled of baby powder.

On the phone she'd told me she wanted to meet somewhere away from Enfield so Boylan wouldn't catch her fraternizing with a "suspect."

"A *suspect?*" I'd squeaked. "Me?" I'd thought *Hank* was a suspect, but Earlene had gotten him back on campus after only a couple of hours working the phone. But now Boylan's crude question about "how well" I'd known Joe began to take on a new and sinister significance.

I ordered coffee and a doughnut, carried them to the table, made the expected admiring noises over the bald, pudgy baby.

Despite her name, Felicity had never been lighthearted or spontaneous. Now she seemed even heavier in mood. "To tell you the truth, Karen," she said, "I love this kid to pieces, but I miss the action. I don't know what's the matter with me. I'm bored out of my gourd. Bad mother, I guess."

So that was it—Ms. Tough-Mama-Cop was bored. I took a good look at her: more than *bored*, I bet; she looked depressed. I remembered my own post-partum depression, the deep feeling of despair and helplessness, the stark knowledge that I'd gotten myself in far, far over my head. As in fact I had, having been only nineteen when Amanda was born. I put a sympathetic hand on Felicity's arm. She looked at it coldly, until I pulled it away.

So I got right to the point. "Monica says you told her I'm in deep doo-doo with the homicide squad."

"Yeah, well, maybe I overstated it, but Lombardi's worried about Boylan, says he's got a real hard-on for you."

I pushed away my chocolate-glazed doughnut. "Lady, watch your language, pul-eeze. The mere thought makes me nauseous."

"You know what I mean. It's all about Piotrowski, of course. Those two go way back, used to partner together, I heard. But something happened no one's talking about. Charlie wrote him up for a breach of procedure or something, and now it's nothing but cold, hard testosterone twenty-four/seven with those two. You could be in hot water here."

"Great! Just what I need." I was genuinely touched by her concern. I'd had nothing to do with the death of Joe Lone Wolf, but everyone knew I had a motive for wanting him out of the way. And Boylan, in his interviews with my colleagues, would hear that more than once. I was grateful for Felicity's support.

"I tried to call Piotrowski in Iraq last night," she continued, "but couldn't get though, so I thought I'd better let you know what's going on."

Suddenly I was suspended between one heartbeat and the next. "What do you mean, you couldn't get through?"

"They're way out in the provinces, and communications at the local base are down. Dust storm or something. Even National Guard headquarters in Baghdad can't get through."

The next heartbeat didn't come.

"Hey. Karen? You okay? Take a deep breath and let me finish before you freak out."

She handed me my glass of water. I took a sip.

"Headquarters told me this happens once in a while. One time a computer virus took things down for a couple of weeks. The guy I talked to was spouting all sorts of alphabet soup—"

"Acronyms?"

"Whatever." The baby stirred in the stroller. She glanced over and gave him a perfunctory pat, then turned back to me. "So, apparently it's nothing to worry about."

I'd worry if I wanted to.

"So," Felicity went on, "I've decided to keep an eye on what's happening in the Lone Wolf case. Lombardi says Boylan was hassling you at the scene. If he ends up giving you grief, Piotrowski'll have my ass. But I'm on leave, and it's strictly against regulations for me to get involved, so anything I do I'm gonna hafta do it on the sly.

"So, now tell me, about this Lone Wolf homicide, what does Boylan think he's got on you." She'd perked up at the thought of getting back in business.

"Nothing! He called me because the student who found Joe dead asked for me. After that, he was just being obnoxious."

"With him, that's par for the course. Is there anything between you and the victim I should know about that Boylan's likely to uncover?"

"Well, there's been some departmental friction lately, but it has nothing to do with the murder."

"I'll be the judge of that—tell me."

I told her about our rivalry for the same position, also about our little squabble over Ayesha Ahmed. "But there's no way Boylan could have known about either of those things until he interviewed my colleagues, which he only this morning began to do."

"Well, things like workplace friction don't stay hidden long. You can bet he knows by now." She wrote something on the Dunkin' Donuts napkin, and then looked up at me. "Anyone else besides you have it in for him?"

"What do you mean, 'besides me?' I didn't have it in for him."

"Hmm. Just answer the question."

I shrugged. "The students liked him, but he was a real loner with his colleagues. I don't know about anything specific—oh, wait a minute!" I remembered that scene in the college parking lot.

"What?"

"One night a few days ago, I saw a car without lights follow his van from the parking lot. It was strange—after midnight and no lights on."

"Really?" The word had at least four syllables. More writing on the napkin. The baby jerked awake in the stroller and started to whimper. Felicity unstrapped him, and then discreetly lifted her shirt. "Anything else?" Little Buster latched on to his mother's nipple and began to suck.

My coffee cup was empty and the donut was gone. *Anything else?* I thought hard. "The only other thing is that…You're going to laugh."

"Tell me."

"Well, he has absolutely no Internet presence. In this day and age—"

"Now, that is interesting. Sounds almost like he was working undercover."

◇◇◇

All the way back to campus I was thinking about what Felicity had said: Charlie's base was out of touch. I wasn't worried. Not really. I knew communication glitches happened now and then. It was just that being completely cut off from him made me feel sick to my stomach. But perhaps it was just as well: I really didn't need Charlie to know about all this trouble when he was too far away to help.

Chapter Eleven

Still Wednesday

With Joe's death, things had become so chaotic I'd almost forgotten that the deadline for submitting my tenure file was only two days away. From Greenfield I sped back to campus. Indian Summer had passed, and the brilliant blue skies had turned cold and gray.

Dodging colleagues and students, I made it to Dickinson Hall without being waylaid, a minor miracle. A uniformed officer was walking down the hall, knocking on doors. Miles Jewell peered out of his office at the far end of the hall, gave the officer a glare, but let him in, allowing the door to close behind them with a thunk.

Standing in the open door of my own office, I glanced around at my little realm. Everything was there that was supposed to be—desk, computer and printer on desk, conference table, chairs, overflowing bookcases, coat rack. And yet, as I closed the door behind me, I felt a vacancy in the room: something that was supposed to be there was gone. I'd been in a state of disorientation to begin with, and my sugar-and-caffeine lunch at Dunkin' Donuts hadn't helped. *You're imagining things*, I chided myself, but I couldn't shake the feeling that something was missing.

Okay, Pelletier: time to get this dog-and-pony-show on the road. I called up the essay on the computer, clicked the proper function buttons and sat in the green vinyl chair, watching the pages accumulate in the printer's tray. When it was done I could pack it in the tenure box, heft the whole thing into the chairman's office. Then my tenure petition would be official and final—all I'd have to do was to wait.

And remember to breathe.

But Felicity's comment about Joe was haunting me: *Sounds almost like he was working undercover.* My automatic internal grammarian automatically corrected her grammar: *almost as if he were working undercover.* While I was waiting for the document to finish printing, I typed Joe's name into the Internet search engine, as I had done the day Miles had informed me of the chairman's ardent support for my *professeur-sans-doctorat* colleague. Perhaps I'd missed something then. This time I did find a few more mentions, but they were all brand-new, journalistic reports of his death.

Then I called up the Enfield College website and clicked on English Department Faculty. Each of us had our own page on the department site, listing whatever we thought would be of interest to current and prospective students. My webpage, for instance, featured my scholarly credentials, a brief paragraph each for research and teaching interests, a list of courses taught, and a deer-in-the-headlights photo taken by the student photographer for the radical alternative campus paper, the *Hatchet*. You couldn't miss Sally Chenille's photo, which had somehow navigated to the department home page. It was a glamour shot, with cleavage, bronze hair, and multiple piercings. I couldn't help it—I clicked on her webpage. It was replete with her culture-maven TV appearances. But Professor Joe Lone Wolf's home page offered only a blank spot where the photo should be and a list of courses offered, past and present. Felicity was right—it *was* as if he were undercover. I closed the college website. Joe was distinguished by his absence; how can you read what isn't there?

The printer stopped. My essay was complete. I gathered the pages, evened up the edges, clipped the printout together with a heavy-duty paper clasp, and looked toward the box. It wasn't there.

Abruptly I sat up straight in my chair: Oh, God! My tenure box! *That's* what was missing from the office! The god-damned *tenure box*! It was gone!

I saw then, in the corner of the office, the box-shaped emptiness. That sturdy black-and-white speckled cardboard file box I'd packed so very carefully, a months-long preparation of the records of my entire academic career. The box that held everything I was submitting to the department except for the one final essay sitting snug in my printer tray. Gone. Vanished. Disappeared.

An emptiness in the shape of the rest of my life.

I don't remember collapsing into the green vinyl chair, but I must have. It wasn't that I passed out; it was just that my entire consciousness riveted itself on that vacant corner where I'd last placed the box of materials. My focused vision was cold, like my brain and my heart. My box of tenure materials was gone. As usual, Emily Dickinson gave me the words I needed: "As Freezing persons, recollect the Snow—/ First-Chill—then Stupor— then the letting go—"

I took a deep breath and let it out. The room was dim, and I shivered as the cold of shock released me. I was left to the wintery chill of late October and the small mean rain dripping down the windows.

◇◇◇

When I barged into the department office, Monica stopped typing and gazed at me with unconcealed curiosity. "So, you're not in the hoosegow, yet?"

"Not yet. Listen, I have a question for you."

"Shoot." Today I was in her good books; after all, Felicity Schultz, her former downstairs neighbor's kid, liked me.

My query was a long shot, but I had to ask. "Monica, by any chance," my voice was shaky, "did you collect that box of tenure materials that was in my office? Maybe you thought it was all ready for submission?"

The English Department secretary controls the cookie key, the passkey for all English department doors. It had gotten its name from a plastic key ring in the shape of an outsized chocolate-chip cookie, cumbersome so absent-minded professors wouldn't pocket it. Therefore Monica has access to everything in the department and can wander in and out of faculty offices at will.

She ran a stubby hand through her chopped-off hair and frowned at me. "So, your tenure file's missing, huh? Whoa! You sure you didn't take it home?"

"You think I'd forget something like that? Have you given the cookie key to anyone today?"

She shrugged. "Nobody's asked for it. That's not to say someone didn't come in when I was gone and take it from the desk drawer." She opened the drawer and, dangling the key before ne, said, "It's here, now."

I swallowed hard, and went to call Earlene. "Help! What am I going to do?"

"Maybe you took it home last night and forgot about it."

Not her, too. "You've got to be kidding—I've been working on this all semester. It hasn't left this office. I know it was here this morning—I...I *dusted* it."

She laughed, but it wasn't funny, and she realized it. "Are you okay?"

I had no answer for that. "Do you think someone has it in for me? Who would steal my tenure file? And why?"

There was a long pause on Earlene's end of the line. Then she asked, "Are you absolutely certain you saw it today—this very morning?"

"Ye-e-e-s." But my head was spinning. *Was* it this morning I'd dusted the box? Or was it yesterday? Or the day before? I was no longer absolutely certain. "Why does that matter?"

A huge sigh from the other end of the line. "Because... well, you know...if it was there, say, Monday, but not today...

well, maybe Joe Lone Wolf had motive to hamper your tenure process...I'm not making an accusation, you understand. I'm just saying...Are you still there, Karen?"

She'd stunned me into silence. *That. Son. Of. A. Bitch.* "I'm here," I breathed. A thought consumed me—a possibility so outrageous that I instantly convinced myself it was true. If I'd been suffering the hellish pangs of tenure agony, Joe Lone Wolf must have been, too. He had American history on his side, but still...I had quality and quantity. He must have known that. I hadn't even thought what it would be like to be in his position.

"Earlene, do you think...?"

"What?"

"Is it possible...?"

"Is *what* possible?"

I jumped up from the chair. "Do you think Joe Lone Wolf actually *did* steal my tenure box?"

When she spoke again, she was extremely somber. "That was irresponsible of me. Forget I implied it. I was just thinking off the top of my head. Don't repeat it—you hear me? Not to anyone. Especially not to the cops. You understand?"

I was slow in getting her point, but I finally did. "Oh, right," I said. If Boylan thought that I thought Joe had sabotaged my tenure case, he'd have good reason to consider me a suspect. "Right. Mum's the word. But, listen, Earlene, the tenure file's due on Friday. What am I going to do? I'll never get a new one ready in two days."

"Talk to Ned about it. Ask for an extension. There must be provisions—"

"Ne-e-e-ed?" I wailed.

"Well, okay. Not Ned. But talk to the academic dean. He'll tell you what to do about a delayed submission. Life is full of complications. Don't think you're the only one who's ever faced a last-minute problem. Tenure policy must make exceptions for extraordinary circumstances."

"I don't knooooow." I wasn't ready to let go of the trauma. Then I pulled myself together. "You think?"

"Now, that's a good girl," she said, Dean of students talking to some dimwit freshman.

I hung up knowing she was right about what I should do next. But…

But the box *had* been in my office this morning. I was certain. Well, almost certain. And Joe Lone Wolf had been dead at least since Monday. There was no way he could have taken it. Who else could have and would have? And why?

◇◇◇

Dean Sanjay Patel sat me down in the spacious office in Emerson Hall with its large Oriental carpets in rich tones of blue and crimson spread across an oak-parquet floor. He made me a cup of tea and talked me through my panic. Sanjay reminded me that most of the tenure materials—my letter, c.v., activity report—were on my computer and could be printed out again, that books and magazine articles could be replaced, that the college was not inflexible about deadlines. All I had to do, he summed up, was to begin to print everything out—one more time—submit it when it was ready, and then gather up copies of books, etc. He would see that the English Department knew to waive the Friday deadline. But, for right now, this was his advice: go home, put my feet up, relax, have a glass or two of wine, watch a Jane Austen video, get a good night's sleep, and come back to my office in the morning with renewed energy and an extra printer cartridge.

I resisted the impulse to kiss his feet and drove home through the late afternoon dusk. Tomorrow I would cancel all my obligations so I could begin the work of replacing my tenure portfolio. I don't have classes on Thursdays, so I could single-mindedly concentrate on printing everything out again and gathering copies of books and essays. For the first time I thanked whatever stars rule my life for leaving me so totally unencumbered with family this semester; I might be as lonely as hell, but at least I could focus on this one vital project without having to worry about anyone else's needs.

Well, Amanda. I knew I'd lie awake and worry about my daughter. Traveling in Nepal with a man she's only known for a handful of months! What if they were attacked by Maoist thugs? Or what if they came down with hepatitis? Or what if...

◇◇◇

It was rush hour, so it wasn't until I turned onto my country road that I noticed the car following me. It was fully dark now and raining harder. A few late leaves, red and brown, splattered onto my wet windshield, the wipers sweeping them back and forth. The air circulation system of my aging Subaru was shot, plus I needed new wipers, so between the fog and the smears, my visibility was not what it should have been. Anytime an oncoming car approached, I had to hunker over the wheel, wipe the windshield with a tissue and squint. The market for condos and McMansions hasn't reached this far into hicksville yet, so the road was isolated and dark, passing through played-out and abandoned onion farms. Having to pay so much attention to what was ahead, I ignored the rear-view mirror. Passing a darkened farm stand with heaps of Halloween pumpkins, I happened to look behind me: a car with odd cats-eye lights. A minute or two later I glanced in the mirror again. Cats-eye was still behind me—closer now.

I felt a sudden chill, and my hands began to shake. Was someone following me? Who? Oh, no, not Lieutenant Neil Boylan? Felicity's warning echoed in my mind: *Lombardi says Boylan's already hassling you.* As I signaled to turn right into my driveway, I kept my eyes on the mirror. If it was Boylan, he wasn't driving a squad car—the headlights were all wrong. I slowed down to begin the turn. Cat's-eye followed suit, turning on its right blinker. Oh, God, maybe I should have kept going straight ahead until I came to a more populated area. But it was too late; I was already into the turn. Cat's-eye began flashing its lights.

Damn, damn, damn. I pulled right up to the kitchen door. The other car followed me into the narrow driveway and stopped. There went my escape route. What was wrong with me?

Why hadn't I kept going—found a police station or something? Too late now. I yanked the keys from the ignition, snatched up the big magnesium flashlight that Charlie insists I carry in the car at all times, squared my shoulders, and stepped out of the car. My feet sank in the soft leaf-loam.

The other car was an old maroon Dodge. Familiar? Maybe, but I couldn't quite place it. The driver's door opened. I clutched the mag light. I would use its heft to brain the Dodge's driver. Yes. But what if it was Boylan? Assaulting a police officer was not a criminal charge the college administration would be happy about tenuring the perpetrator of. Or, whatever. Okay, whoever it was, I wouldn't hit him. I'd use the big flashlight's glare to blind him while I made a dash for the house, door key extended.

The passenger door opened. I turned the still-dark lens toward the emerging person and pushed the high-beam button. A bundled-up gnome stepped out, arms up to protect its eyes. "Hi, Karen." The gnome had my mother's voice.

I stood there, dumbfounded. My mother? Then another well-known woman's voice screeched, "For God's sake, Karen, get that damn light off of her." Out of the foggy darkness my sister Connie stepped forward, dressed in a dark-blue business suit and clunky dress shoes.

"Connie!" I shrilled. "What the hell?"

"I'm on my way to the airport," she said, her eyes wide and wary, as if she did indeed expect me to brain her with the mag light. "Mom's gonna stay with you."

"She's *what!*"

My mother answered meekly. "Karen, Connie said she simply didn't know what the hell else to do with me. I promise I won't be any trouble."

Connie dumped Mom's suitcase, told me about her medications, and then sped off. Very few words were exchanged. She was in a hurry to get to Bradley International in Hartford (and to get away from me). I was mute with shock and outrage. And, oh, yes, dammit, compassion, too, of course. And love. My poor little mother; how could I resent her, no matter how unexpected she was? But why did she have to show up *now*, when my career was hanging in the balance? She couldn't be left alone, and I had to prepare my damned tenure application—again. And I had to do it tomorrow. What would I do with Mom when I was on campus?

There she stood in my kitchen, still in her pinkish-gray down coat—my very own personal crisis. My mother. My love. "Here, let me take your coat, Mom. Have you had supper? Would you like a cup of tea?"

"That's very nice of you." Struggling out of the bulky coat, she spoke formally, as if I were a stranger. "But I don't want to be any bother."

I dropped her coat on a yellow-painted kitchen chair and threw my arms around her. "Mom, don't be silly. You're no bother. And we both have to eat." I gave a gentle squeeze and let go.

"That was a nice hug," she said, and my heart melted. I took her by the shoulders and held her away from me so I could get a good look at her. My Mom is short and puffy like a dumpling, and her gray-white hair had been recently set, then backcombed into a Queen Elizabeth coiffure. But it was her eyes that held me. I'd last seen her during the summer, when she was alert and smiling. Since then something had happened to her eyes. The light had gone out of them.

Connie had tried to tell me.

Chapter Twelve

Thursday 10/15

The following morning, Mom was ensconced in my green vinyl office chair turning pages in a copy of *People* magazine that Monica had given her. Unexpectedly Monica had taken quite a liking to her—and she to Monica. I didn't know what I would do with Mom on Friday, when I had two classes to teach, but for now she was safe and content with her gossip magazine.

I turned my computer on and scrolled through the list of Word files, intending to check for the ones I needed to rebuild my tenure file—resume, activities report, letter, etc. But first I checked my e-mail—eleven "friend" requests from students. I sighed, accessed my Facebook page and accepted them all. Then, curious, I scrolled down the page. There on the lower right-hand corner was something called a Friend Finder. I clicked on it, and sure enough half a dozen photos sprang up, mostly of people I hadn't seen in ages. How had Facebook found out I knew Stuart Horowitz? Or Shamega Gilfoyle? Or Mike Vitale? This was downright creepy!

I clicked on Stuart's icon. He was an old friend from the university I'd taught at in Manhattan, and we'd kept in touch, e-mailing once or twice a year, but it been six years since I'd actually seen him. Now here he was, resplendent in full color, still with his cyclist's fit physique and that general air of knowing more than it was politic for him to tell. *Cool*, I thought, and added him as a friend. Big mistake, I thought; first step on the long, long road to wasted time. So I added Shamega and Mike. Then, immediately, I got a message that Mike had accepted my friendship. A little thrill ran through me; I had two more friends. I looked up at my mom. She was still engrossed in *People*. So was I: I scrolled down the Friend Finder, clicking on familiar faces as I went. After all, it was all about *people*, wasn't it?

"Karen," my mother said, looking up from her magazine. "There's something I have to tell you." She sounded almost lucid. Almost like her old self again. "But you can't tell Connie or Denise."

"Really? What is it, Mom?"

"A secret," she said. "No one living knows it but me."

"What kind of a secret?"

There was a loud knock on the door, and we both jumped. My mother went still and silent. Who could it be? Students usually gave just a tentative tap.

Lieutenant Neil Boylan stood in the hall, dressed in his usual sharp civvies. Behind Boylan, the uniformed Lombardi towered over his lieutenant in full winter blues, his wide-brimmed hat in his hand.

My mother's small voice said, "Karen, there's a policeman here."

"Don't worry, Mom. You don't have to talk to him." I shut down my computer. "What can I do for you, Lieutenant Boylan?"

"Can we come in?" He stepped inside. "Just have a few questions for you."

"Looks to me like you're already in. Have a seat." I pointed him to the black-and-gold alumni captain's chair and turned to Lombardi. "Trooper, why don't you take the desk chair?"

"I'll just stand here, ma'am, if you don't mind." Lombardi was a stone-faced stranger as he pulled out a notebook and pen. I could see the trooper's Adam's apple move up, then down. It was a comfort to know he'd be keeping Felicity up to date on everything, but, oh, how, at that moment, I wanted Charlie.

"So, Professor, you have a cup of coffee handy?" Boylan leaned back and crossed one leg over the other, his ankle on his knee. "Sure could use it while we chat." He showed me some teeth. Were we going to be pals? That old ploy?

"What do you take?" I sat behind the desk, pressed the number for Monica's extension, and asked for coffee "for the police lieutenant." I wouldn't have dared ask her to bring coffee if it was just for me.

"Sure is a change in the weather," Boylan began.

I looked at him, expressionless. "It is, after all, mid-October."

"It is that," he replied, showing teeth again, more natural this time—a rueful grin.

The door opened and Monica hefted in two steaming mugs. Lombardi refused his, so she took it away with her. She took my mother, too, for which I was grateful.

The brew smelled fresh and terrific, and Boylan took a deep draught. Monica must have made it fresh, in the filter cone. Then he set the mug down. "So, what do you hear from Piotrowski?" His tone was friendly, but his attitude when I'd met him at the scene had left me wary. As had Felicity's warning, but he didn't know about that.

"Not much," I said. "He really just got there."

"Good man, Piotrowski."

I agreed.

He took another deep drink. "I'll bet his being over there has got you worried sick. Being left all on your own like that."

"Not really," I said. "Just what are you after, Lieutenant? You didn't come here to play Mr. Lonely Hearts."

His expression hardened, and he sat up straight, both shiny black oxfords flat on the floor. "Well, okay. If you want to play it like that. Word around campus has it that you and Lone Wolf were career rivals, Professor—both candidates for the same plush job."

I tried to keep a pleasant expression on my face, but my heart had turned to molten lead. "Well, we were both up for tenure in the same department, if that's what you mean by 'career rivals.'"

"Yeah, like I said, both up for the same plush job. And only one opening." He ran his tongue over his top teeth, then lifted the coffee mug.

I stared at him straight on. "Are you insinuating something, Lieutenant?"

"It's not my job to insinuate anything." There was the cat's grin again. "My job is simply to ask questions and pay attention to the answers. So, I'm just trying to verify the information gleaned from our interviews. I've seen it before—workplace conflict can lead to hard feelings and considerable strife." He took another drink, surveying my office while he did so—the floor-to-ceiling bookcases, the tall, multipaned windows. "Pretty nice set-up you've got here."

I held Boylan's flat gray eyes. "I've worked very hard to get where I am, Boylan. I've earned it. I don't have to think about killing colleagues."

The desk phone rang, and I blinked. I reached over and picked up the receiver.

"Hello?" My voice was expressionless.

"Babe. What's this crap Schultz is telling me?"

I signed so deeply I could hardly speak afterward; it was such a relief to hear his voice. "Charlie," I said, staring directly at Boylan. "Good timing. Your colleague, Lieutenant Boylan, is here asking me some questions." My voice was still flat. In the few second's long-distance lag before Charlie's response came, my eyes burned with tears.

"He is, huh? Put the son-of-a-bitch on the phone, willya, Babe?"

"Okay." I handed the receiver to Boylan, who rose and stood by the desk. His expression had turned to cast-iron.

"Yeah?" he said and listened for a long few minutes. His eyes narrowed as he turned from me to Lombardi, eyeing him assessingly, making the connection with Felicity. "Yeah," he said again. Then, "Right," and slammed the phone down.

Don't hang up on Charlie! I managed to keep my internal scream silent.

Lombardi loomed motionless by the door. Only his Adam's apple moved, up and down, as if he were trying to expel an acorn.

Boylan turned his gaze back to me, his expression now inscrutable. "Bringing in the heavies, are you, Professor?" The cat's smile was now the grin of a backyard predator.

I was beginning to wish Charlie had left well enough alone. Whatever he'd said to his colleague seemed to have antagonized him even further.

"I don't like to have to do this," Boylan said, his expression impossible to read. "But it does seem to me that 'reasonable suspicion' comes into play here. *Motive* and *opportunity*—you've got both. No matter what your…good friend might say."

He slid a legal-looking paper from his inside breast pocket and shook it open. "Search warrant," he said.

I jumped up.

"You creep," I said. "You had that all along. No matter what I said, you were going to toss my office!"

"Oh, no," he said. Without taking his gaze off me he ordered, "Lombardi, get the computer."

"No," I cried, totally losing any iota of composure I might have retained. "You can't do that!"

"Oh, yes, I can." Waving the document in my face.

"Just let me have a half hour to print out my tenure stuff. I need it for my tenure petition."

"Get that damn computer, Lombardi. Now. We're out of here."

"For God's sake," I whimpered, as they exited the room. "Not the computer. Don't take my computer!"

Neither Mom nor I said a word all the way home.

◇◇◇

I grabbed the phone the minute I got to the house. If Charlie could call me at my office, he must somehow be back in touch. I dialed the number for his Baghdad base, but got the same runaround Felicity had: comms were down at Piotrowski's temp base, and they were waiting for backup. Could be forty-eight hours, could be more. It all depended. It was just busted equipment. Not to worry, lady.

Chapter Thirteen

Friday 10/16

I usually pride myself on making the obscure topic of Native American political oratory come to vivid life. But Friday morning, with so much pressing on my mind—Mom, Joe's murder, my stolen tenure documents, the police seizure of my office computer—I was less engaged in the lecture than the students were. As I droned on, Garrett Reynolds typed away on his laptop—e-mail, no doubt—and Stephanie Hart nodded automatically, deep into her drawing. Cat Andrews was even more out of it than usual, and I wondered if perhaps she was in shock over Joe Lone Wolf's death. Was she one of the students who'd been particularly fond of Joe? I felt a miniscule pang of guilt: I hadn't returned her poke on Facebook.

Then Ayesha Ahmed walked into the classroom, and all heads turned. Not only was she late—unusual in itself—but, except for her face and her hands she was completely covered. Ayesha wore a floor-length robe in a fine, pale-green linen with long, wide sleeves and embroidered tucks across the bosom. The toes of a pair of scruffy sneakers peeked out from beneath the robe. Where were the sassy blue jeans that went with the sassy attitude?

Claiming her usual seat, she arranged her books and backpack, and lowered her eyes. She folded her hands, and they disappeared into her sleeves. The *hijab* was white today, pulled low over her forehead, showing not a tendril of her dark, shiny hair. In dress and demeanor Ayesha was suddenly light-years away from the girl she'd been all semester. A buzz went around the room, which I silenced with a prolonged icy stare. Only Hank Brody continued to gawk at the transformed young woman. Poor Hank; she didn't even seem to notice that he was in the room.

I continued to sleepwalk my way through the lecture, but now I was thinking about my (okay, I'll say it) my *pet* student. Something was going on with Ayesha—maybe something I couldn't hope to understand. All I could do as her English professor—all I had the right to do—was discuss with her the reason for not having handed in her mid-semester paper.

In spite of my distraction, I noticed Cat Andrews, wearing a wrinkled cotton dress over leggings, with her neon-tipped buzz cut a matted mess of hair and hair gel, focus for a long moment on Ayesha. Then Cat's gaze drifted to Stephanie and to Garrett. Suddenly, an expression that mimicked thought crossed her face, she snapped to attention and looked directly at me for a millisecond, as if she were about to interrupt the lecture. Then she seemed to think better of it. After class I again thought she was about to speak to me, but Garrett came up on one side of her and Stephanie on the other, and they all walked out together. Not wanting Ayesha to get away, I moved swiftly to the door. Between the holiday and the suspension of classes after Joe's death, there hadn't been a class in a week, so, of course, I hadn't had a chance to speak to her about her unsubmitted paper.

"Ms. Ahmed," I said, in a half-joking manner. She had tarried, packing up her backpack meticulously, and was the only student remaining in the room. She looked up at me, and I continued, serious now, "I was very surprised not to receive your essay last Friday."

"Oh," she replied. Her expression was inscrutable. "Didn't you get my e-mail?" It was impossible for me to read whether or not I was being played. She wouldn't meet my gaze, but averted her eyes in the way I'd seen with certain observant Muslim women.

"E-mail? No." For the ten-thousandth time I cursed the invention of the Internet, a professor's bane as well as blessing. "When would that have been?"

"Last Thursday. Before I went home. I attached my essay to it."

"Really? Hmm. No, I didn't receive anything from you. And you know my policy—no e-mail submissions for formal papers. Says so on the syllabus." Too tricky. Too prone to the-computer-ate-my-homework excuses.

"Oh." Then she did look straight at me. Her dark eyes seemed as free of guile as an angel's. "Well, then, I don't know what happened, but I do have a printout of the essay with me. Shall I just give you that?" She went shuffling through her backpack.

"Certainly," I said. The other students' papers were graded and returned. I could read this one tomorrow. As Ayesha held out the essay, her hand trembled briefly, causing the fabric to ripple on the wide embroidered sleeve. The slender hand was dark and beautiful against the pale green, but it was not quite steady.

I gave the girl a searching look. Was she, too, one of Joe Lone Wolf's student following? "Is everything all right, Ayesha?"

She started. Her eyes widened. "Yes, of course. What would be wrong?" Her body shifted, weight on one foot, as if she were ready to flee.

I took the paper, and she did—flee that is. The only question in my mind now was whether I should call the Dean of Students' office right away, or whether I should read Ayesha's paper first to see if it gave me any clue as to what was on her mind. I'd queried Earlene about Ayesha before the long weekend began, but at that time she'd heard nothing from her, and mine was the only professorial query she'd gotten.

"I'll wait until she's back on campus," Earlene had said. "Then I'll arrange a casual kind of chat. See if I can get a sense of what's going on."

I erased the blackboard, packed up my briefcase and headed toward the door. When I'd left my mother in the English office with Monica, they'd been talking about *Sex and the City*.

My *mother*? *Sex and the City*!

◇◇◇

The spacious hallway was oak-paneled to shoulder height and the dark wood floors worn into parallel paths by generations of student feet. Everything shone with polish and, this early in the morning, the smell of cleaning fluid from the overnight janitorial administrations still tinged the air. As I left the classroom a strong hand grabbed my upper arm. Startled, I let my book-bag slip. The heavy bag fell to the floor with a thud, landing on a well-polished brown oxford.

"Ouch!" Neil Boylan yelled, releasing me. He stood on one foot and flexed the other experimentally.

"You scared the hell out of me, Boylan!"

He stepped tentatively on the injured foot, then put his entire weight on it and took a step or two. Evidently I hadn't crippled him for life. "If you'd been watching where you were going—"

I could think of no reason for the lieutenant to be lurking outside my classroom that augured anything but trouble. He was alone this time, no sign of Trooper Lombardi—or any other officer, plain-clothes or uniformed. "What's with that girl?" he asked, nodding toward the robe-clad, head-covered Ayesha, who had just come out of the ladies room. "I saw you talking to her in the classroom. Looked pretty intense." His eyes slitted as he watched her begin to descend the stairs.

His cold scrutiny of my student gave me a little chill. "Nothing's wrong with her," I said. "She's Muslim. That's all." The response was louder than I'd intended—and sharper. A dark-haired student clutching a sweating Diet Coke gave us a wide berth. "What do you want?"

"I have to ask you about something."

"What?"

"Let's go to your office."

"No. I have someone waiting for me." I didn't want him anywhere near my mother. My mother! What was I going to do with her? I couldn't impose on Monica more than once.

"Let's talk here," I said.

"Well," he shrugged, "if you want to be seen in public being grilled by a homicide cop."

Boylan was right: I didn't want to be seen on campus with him. We descended the eroded stone steps to the first floor, and then I led him out of the building through a side door. Once we were outside, he gave me a sideways glance. "I've been talking to your colleagues."

"Yeah?" Wanting to get at least a couple of blocks away, I turned toward a street that headed out of town. I walked fast through this old light-industrial area with its remaining red-brick factories and mid-twentieth-century car showrooms with grimy plate-glass windows. Boylan kept step with me. A cold, damp wind cut through my wool coat. I tucked the knitted scarf tighter around my neck. The smell of Mexican food wafted from a small restaurant, and I realized I'd had no breakfast.

"Yeah. And I heard about your altercation." He was going to make me work. I'd seen Charlie use the same technique, edging toward the question, putting the interviewee off balance. I could play the game, too.

"What altercation?" But of course it could only be the one, and my breath grew shallow.

"Oh, a little squabble in Dickinson Hall. About ten days ago?" He wore a sleek yellow cold-weather hiking jacket. Now he stopped and zipped it up. "You know that stuff I said out by Lone Wolf's apartment the other day?" Then he stood still, not quite meeting my eyes. "Well, then I was just jerking your chain. Just for fun."

"Ha, ha." *Jerk* was the right word. But could this possibly be an apology?

"Even yesterday, hearing about how you both wanted that job, I thought, jeez, give the girl a break. But now, what people are telling me—I've gotta take it seriously." He snapped his jacket shut at the collar. "No matter what Piotrowski says." He pulled on a pair of fur-lined gloves. He hadn't been looking at me, but now he turned his head and gave me a long stare. "Or does."

I could feel my face freeze into a mask. "Is that so?" What was it between Charlie and Boylan? I wished I could ask Charlie, but, since that brief moment in my office, he hadn't called, and he hadn't answered my e-mail, either. I was beginning to worry about him even more than usual. What was it he'd said last time we'd spoken at length? That he'd be out of touch for a while? That they were going "out into the provinces"? I sure as hell didn't like the sound of that.

Boylan and I walked past a long-abandoned gas station, its pumps forever frozen at $1.19 a gallon. I tripped over a sidewalk crack raised a couple of inches by an errant tree root and caught myself before I fell.

"Yes, that's so," he blurted. "As you damn well know. Competition for the same big-time job? A nasty public argument with the victim? Workplace conflict—it's a motive as old as the hills." He tipped his head toward me. "That fight between you and Lone Wolf? What was that all about?"

I sighed, huffing out like a race horse. "It wasn't a fight. It was simply a disagreement."

"Over what?" His expression would have frozen steam.

Oh, God—I didn't want to bring Ayesha into this, but I was certain that Ned Hilton would have already told the investigator about her. "I didn't like the way he was treating one of my students—the one you just saw on the stairs." I stopped walking and lowered my heavy book bag down on a low cement wall outside an auto-parts store; he might as well hear *my* version of that ugly scene.

◇◇◇

"Sorry, Monica, I got delayed." My mother was sitting in a corner of the English office with a large bone crochet hook and a ball of bulky cerise yarn. "Hi, Mom. Looks like you've been busy."

She looked up and frowned. "I'm not ready to go yet." A nearly completed winter scarf was spiraling from her ball of yarn.

"Adele told me she likes to crochet," Monica said. *Adele?* So she and Mom were on first-name terms already. "We took an early coffee break and went over to the Hook Nook. And, see, she's only been on this for—what?—an hour? and she's got a whole scarf almost done." She smiled at my mother, who tucked her head modestly.

I took the soft rosy scarf in my hand. It was beautiful, crocheted in an intricate openwork pattern. "Mom, that's lovely—"

"What's going on here?" Ned's voice came from behind me. Had he been lurking there, waiting for me?

"Shit," Monica hissed.

"We're just—"

"Never mind, Karen. I have to talk to you." Why was Ned assuming such a tone of authority? Hadn't Miles resumed the English Chair?

"Okay. I'm listening."

"In my office. Monica, no calls."

As I followed Ned into the chairman's inner office, I glanced back with a puzzled look. Monica rolled her eyes.

Ned sat well back into the window alcove behind his desk as I took the facing chair. "I'll make it brief," he said. "You must know that it was my duty to inform that police detective about your...your *contretemps*...with Joe Lone Wolf."

"I do know that."

"You do?" He gazed at me assessingly. "Oh, yes. You have connections within the state police, don't you? But do you know that, here on campus, there are rumors that you killed Joe?" Light coming through the mullioned windows behind Ned momentarily bestowed upon him an aura of sanctity.

"What?" Gripping the arms of the leather chair, I tried to conceal my astonishment. My colleagues thought I was a killer? Boylan hadn't said anything about that. "That's nonsense!" I bit off the words. The image of Earlene pleading prudence steadied me; I would not lose my cool.

"Is it?" Ned's expression approximated one of sage authority. "In any case, you should know that I felt it necessary just now, when I saw that police detective—what's s his name? Boyle? Well, when I saw him entering the Administration Building, I thought I should pass that campus speculation on to him."

Sudden sheer hatred for my colleague shot through me. My first year at Enfield had been Ned's tenure year. I thought back to those months when his tenure had been under consideration—the way he'd skulked around campus toadying up to senior faculty. I'd vowed then, that if Ned's slavish servility was what academic life required of its denizens, I'd join my sister at WalMart. And since his tenure, Ned's secure position in the academy had not liberated his spirit; rather it seemed to have narrowed both his mind and his character. A life lived exclusively in the intellect can do that to you; I'd seen it before.

Ned pursed his thin lips. "I thought it was my obligation to let you know."

So that's why, when we were walking, Boylan hadn't brought up any campus gossip about my possible guilt; he'd only heard it after we'd parted in front of Emerson Hall. Yet another nail in my coffin.

But Ned was continuing, "And certainly because such… er…suspicion…will factor into any…hmm…any personnel deliberations."

Such as my tenure decision.

"Forewarned is forearmed," Ned continued.

I stood up and left his office without the words of humble gratitude he obviously expected.

"Prick," I muttered under my breath, once I'd gotten into the secretary's office.

"Watch your mouth!" my mother admonished.

"Mom," I said, "and Monica, how'd you like to go out for an early lunch? My treat. We'll go to Rocco's and get some of those great meatball wedges. Or maybe we'll have a late breakfast at the Dolphin. Waffles and whipped cream. If I don't get off this campus, I'm going to…to…well, let's just say, I've got to get off this campus for an hour or two."

"No shit!" Monica said. The door to the inner office had been open the whole time Ned was "forewarning" me. She turned to my mom. "Adele, how about it. Want some lunch?"

◇◇◇

The ginger-haired American hulking over the petite African girl by the main campus gate could not be mistaken for anything other than a cop. When I saw them, I gasped, and Mom said, "What's wrong, Karen?"

In her delicate traditional garb, my student looked extremely fragile next to Boylan's overbearing presence. I was too far away to hear what he was saying, but she almost seemed to be cowering under the onslaught of his words.

"What the hell, Boylan," I yelled, and took off at a run, leaving Mom and Monica behind.

Boylan glanced around and saw me, said something curt to Ayesha, spun on his heel and stalked away through the crowds of between-classes students.

"Ayesha," I called. She hesitated, then she too turned her back on me. Even in her long green robe, she took off at a pace I couldn't hope to follow.

Chapter Fourteen

Friday afternoon

Mom was with Earlene, until I finished teaching Joe Lone Wolf's American literary Outsiders seminar. My only preparation was to stop by Monica's desk and ask for copies of Joe's syllabus and class roster, and the cookie key so I could get into his office. The syllabus and roster were for classroom use, the key for a look through the office, where I hoped to find something pedagogically useful—detailed class notes would be nice.

Although Joe and I had been hired the same year, I'd never been invited into his office. I don't think any of his colleagues had. He'd been a real loner. Now, standing in the hallway in front of his door with the cookie key in my hand, I felt as if I were committing a violation—trespassing on the dead.

Nonsense. The man might be dead, but his classes still had to be taught. I was here legitimately, looking for a course plan and a grade book.

I inserted the key in the lock and turned it. The slatted window blinds were closed, letting in mere slits of light. Already the air was filled with motes of dust. With some dim notion of Native beliefs gleaned from reading Tony Hillerman's mystery novels, I wondered whether Joe's death spirit was hovering here. Whether those dust motes were…I shuddered. And what was that smell?

Very faint…It smelled like…like *the past*. Like my wilder days, tame as they had been. Like weed. Like Mary Jane. Like pot.

Surely Joe hadn't smoked marijuana right here on campus?

But I was here for a purpose, not for lurid speculation. I focused on Joe's desk. It was heaped from edge to edge with papers stacked to various heights. I groaned. No way was I about to find class notes, or even a grade book—not in that landfill. Taking a quick survey of the dim room, I saw that teetering piles of books and even more stacks of papers cluttered the floor, which was navigable only by paths leading to the desk, to a student chair, to the bookcases, to a little table by the window. Whew!

By contrast, the bookshelves that covered three walls were as carefully arranged as if in a museum, filled with Native Indian crafts, artifacts, and weapons. A bright woven rug hung on one side of the window, with a large hunting bow mounted vertically on the other side. A notched tomahawk with silver bands on the handle hung over the window-seat, and another, smaller war axe stood close at hand on a shelf by the door. But in that first glance I truly paid attention to only one thing, the fierce eagle-feather war bonnet, ermine skins dangling down each side, which crowned the coat rack. I stood in the doorway, staring at it: surely this was the headdress Joe had been wearing in that huge portrait on the easel that Ned had now positioned in the hallway by the department office.

It looked like a hopeless mission to find anything that would help with teaching. In the few minutes I had before class began at four, I'd be better off getting a cup of coffee than burrowing through the mess of books and papers. Sighing, I closed the door, turned the knob to check that it was locked, and headed to Emerson Hall to meet Joe's seminar. I'd have to wing it.

As I approached the seminar room, I could hear a hubbub of nervous chatter that died as I walked in. From a dozen matching green-leather upholstered chairs set around the square cherrywood table, the students eyed me warily. Their real professor had been murdered; who was this imposter? And what fresh hell was she about to unleash on them?

I wished I knew the proper protocol for taking over a murdered colleague's class, but I must have missed that session in graduate school. So I just sat there for a moment, looking around the table from face to face, attempting to get some sense of the classroom atmosphere. *Wary*, as I'd noted from the start. Quite wary. But why?

Ethnically it was a more diverse class than any I'd taught at Enfield: young people of Asian, Caucasian, African, and Native descent, two or three of them gloriously multiracial, looking to me like the American future. Of the dozen students on the roster, three had the surname Lee. I took attendance; one Lee was a Caucasian with a Southern accent, who looked as if she'd descended from a Virginia plantation family, the other two were Chinese. Hank Brody was in this class, along with Cat Andrews and Ayesha Ahmed, the latter still dressed in her long pale-green robes. At least I had a friendly student base I could call on to help me out—if I needed to.

"So here we are," I said, "after the tragedy of Professor Lone Wolf's death, you with a new professor and me serving as a stopgap teacher until the department can find someone permanent to continue the course. I'd like to make the best use of our time today. Tell me—how far have you gotten in the syllabus?"

"Oh," said a girl with a ski-slope nose and a waterspout of chestnut hair jutting from the top of her head, "we haven't been using the syllabus. Joe said he just put that together to satisfy departmental requirements." She looked smug, as if she were operating on a higher plane of sophistication than I was. "Anyhow," she summed up, "literature is *passé*."

"It is?" I glanced at the syllabus Monica had given me. It looked like literature to me, beginning with native oral literature, moving through slave narratives, ending with current Latino fiction and Asian-American poetry. Pretty standard multicultural American lit course: I'd taught all of these texts myself at one time or another. I raised my eyes to the class again, and then it hit me: yes, I had taught all of these texts, and had taught them all at the same time, in the same exact order and from the identical anthology, two or three years ago in a course called multicultural american literature.

This was *my* syllabus, and Joe Lone Wolf had copied it word for word, substituting only his name and a new course title! My hands tightened on the stabled-together paper sheets and I took a moment to steady myself. Which was more appalling? That Joe had stolen my syllabus? Or that *literature*, to which I had devoted my entire adult life, and in which I had a hard-won Ph.D., was now…what had the girl with the hair said?…*passé?*

"So," I continued, sitting back in the comfortable chair, my tented fingers at my lips, "literature is…obsolete, is it?"

"Yeah, so over." She looked a bit like a Dr. Suess character. "Along with print and with writing itself—so twentieth-century. Joe said that this syllabus represented the ossified concept of the Outsider mandated by the Western literary tradition from which we would depart." She sounded for all the world like a well-schooled parrot. I waited for the concluding squawk, and it came. "That, of course, is a concept ordered by outmoded terms such as 'truth,' beauty,' 'content,' 'quality'."

Oh, no, don't tell me—Truth and Beauty are also passé.

Hank Brody broke in. He was very earnest. "You see, Professor, we've been attempting to transcend the constraints of established categories." Hank looked better today. He'd traded in his baggy shorts and his battered sandals for more seasonable attire: a gray Enfield sweatshirt, new jeans, and sturdy low-cut brown boots. A navy winter jacket hung on the back of his chair. I felt warmer just looking at him.

And I knew that he only had these comfortable clothes because Earlene, having found him freezing in the police car, had bought them for him. That was how destitute the poor kid was.

He continued, "We were moving beyond even the more recent but nonetheless irrelevant categories of class, sexual orientation, and ethnicity.

"Really? Beyond class? Beyond sexual orientation? Beyond ethnicity?" The Enfield College Comparative American Studies

Department, which considered itself daringly liberal, hadn't advanced *that* far yet. "And beyond *literature*?"

"Beyond even the category of 'category' itself," Hank said. "Professor Lone Wolf thought 'literature,' for instance, was outmoded as a critical tool, as, of course are those worn-out terms, 'meaning' and 'relevance.'"

"*Meaning* and *relevance* gone, too?" I mused aloud. I found myself shredding the "ossified" syllabus with unconscious fingers. "So, tell me—what criteria do you use, then, in defining Outsider literature? Which is," I added with some acerbity, "after all, the subject of this course."

"Oh, you know," chimed up Waterspout Hair, "*Rawness.*"

"*Rawness?*"

There was some shifting in the seats, and the black student with the shaved head and little goatee stopped her with a hand on her arm.

"Yes—raw literature," the young man said, his dark eyes hooded. This was Elmore O'Hara, and I'd seen him talking to Joe earlier in the semester. "Lit *brut*—narrative liberated by the Internet and other cutting-edge advancements, and…well, er, media…" To a student, faces went blank. What the *heck*? "Narrative liberated," he continued, "from cultural monitoring, thus allowing *authentic* expression, expression that escapes entirely the dead hand of literary and academic establishments. Blogs, e-mail, websites, listservs, chapbooks, underground lit, self-published stuff and, er, *experiential narrative.*"

A tall young woman with black-rimmed narrow glasses and brown hair in a conservative bun chimed in. "The Internet, among other…um, media, has liberated us even from the concept of 'writing' itself. 'Writing,' like 'print' is passé. Our texts include Facebook and YouTube."

"Is that so?" What the *hell* had been going on in this course? I pushed myself up from the chair and walked over to the ancient leaded window. Trying to keep my face expressionless, I gazed out the wavy glass at a campus in dusk. Student migration had turned in the direction of the dining hall. Garrett Reynolds walked past our window, a Burberry scarf tied loosely around the collar of his navy-blue wool pea jacket. He held his Blackberry in an ungloved hand and was punching buttons furiously.

Facebook? YouTube? The kids clearly had been captivated by the adventure of investigating outside even the most recent canon, and I didn't want to alienate them. But there was a difference between cutting-edge literary investigation and absolute twaddle. *Facebook!* How to approach this nonsense?

We were in one of the oldest and more elegant classrooms on campus, cherry-paneled, with tall, narrow recessed windows and, decorating the walls, portraits of bewhiskered gentleman from two previous centuries. There was nothing either *raw* or *brut* about it. Nor should there be about the education these young people were paying through the nose to receive on this distinguished campus. *Cutting-edge* was one thing; sheer literary anarchy was another.

"So," I said, turning my attention back from the window. "Raw lit, huh? Lit *brut?* I assume Professor Lone Wolf adopted those categories from contemporary visual art fads, er, trends. But, if you think about it, even Americans educated in the Western literary tradition have cast themselves as Outsiders." I opened the anthology I had brought with me to its nineteenth-century pages and gave an impromptu lecture on "Outsiders" such as Walt Whitman, who wrote in what he called a "barbaric yawp" and set the type for his own poems, which were so "raw" no conventional publisher would touch them. And I reminded them of Emily Dickinson, who celebrated herself as "Nobody" and refused to participate in print culture at all, by making little sewn-together "fascicle" books of her verses for herself alone. "How dreary—to be—Somebody! / How public—like a Frog— / To tell one's name—the livelong June— / To an admiring Bog!"

"The instinct to write 'outside' the literary establishment, you see, can indeed be radical and liberating, but it wasn't pioneered by the Internet and, er, other media—whatever they might be."

The students glanced at each other, and then looked back at me. Something wasn't being said, and they were still wary. Hank and Ayesha exchanged enigmatic glances. Well, whatever was going on here, it was none of my business. By next week's meeting, I hoped, the seminar would have a new teacher.

I assigned a selection of Whitman and Dickinson and dismissed the class.

It wasn't until I was halfway down the hall that I realized Ayesha Ahmed hadn't spoken a word during the entire discussion.

◇◇◇

The Dean of Students office was close by in Emerson Hall, on the second floor. My mother had spent most of the afternoon there, crocheting, I assumed. On this unseasonably chilly October day, Earlene had built a small, well behaved fire in the old fireplace. My mother sat in an armchair, hands quiet in her lap now, and the flickering firelight dancing across her face. When had she gotten so old?

"Hi, Mom," I said. Oh, what was I going to do with her tomorrow?

"I'm hungry," she replied.

I smiled at her, gently. "We'll take care of that right away." Then I turned to Earlene. "I'm sorry, pal. I didn't intend for the class to run so long. But, man, that Joe Lone Wolf was into some weird shit."

"You're telling me." my friend responded, twisting her lips.

Any other time I would have caught the enigmatic tone in her voice. But right now I was so outraged by what I'd just been hearing that I spilled it all out. Then I finished up: "Can you imagine! When you have Walt Whitman and Emily Dickinson available in a literature course, choosing to study YouTube and Facebook! Outrageous!" But, in spite of the outrage, I was curious and wondered if there was some way I could find out just exactly what Joe and the students were up to with Facebook. If I ever had a free moment again in my life—which was doubtful.

"I'm not surprised…considering what else he was into."

"What?"

She waved off my question with a beringed hand. "Never mind. You'll know soon enough." Then she sat down behind her desk and began to toy with an elongated African head carved in ebony.

"Whaaaat?"

Earlene laughed. It was a musical sound. "Sorry—can't tell you. But it sounds to me like Professor Lone Wolf thought Outsider literature didn't have anything to do with outsiders, but that it meant 'literature *outside* of literature.'"

I was struck by the astuteness of her analysis. I'll have to remember that," I said, "literature outside of literature."

"I'm hungry, Karen," Mom repeated.

I turned to my mother, distracted from Earlene's comments about "what else" Joe had been "into."

"Do you like chili, Mom?" I asked. "We'll go home and you can watch Nick at Nite while we eat." I'd take some of Charlie's fiery chili from the freezer, heat it up, and try desperately to forget that this day had been the deadline for submitting my tenure petition.

And that I'd missed it.

Chapter Fifteen

Saturday a.m., 10/17

The knock on my front door at two a.m. didn't wake me, but it woke my mother. She was bedded down in Amanda's room, and when I'd peeked in before I'd gone to bed myself, she was tossing and mumbling. I'd stood in the door and watched her for a moment: what was going on in her dreams? Did she still have dreams? I knew she still had secrets, anyhow. What was it she'd been about to tell me yesterday when Neil Boylan had interrupted us?

Then *I* was dreaming—a special handcrafted nightmare designed especially for a handcrafted tenure dilemma.

Oh, stop it, Karen, said the Schoolmistress, stout, corseted and certain, index finger raised in scolding mode. *You've done good work, you've been an asset to the department, your students love you. It's only logical that you'll be tenured. What is all this juvenile whimpering? Do I need to take you into therapy again?*

No. No. Not therapy. Not again, I said. I was back in Lowell bouncing a rubber ball on a cracked sidewalk. **K** *my name is Karen and my husband's name is…*

Don't listen to her, Karen, my love, whispered the Waif, her tattered skirts whipping in the psychic storm. *Only I know how accustomed you are to hardship and loss, how your dreams evade you, how inconceivable it would be for a Girl from the Wrong Side of a Factory Town to succeed at Enfield College. You'll never make it, and you'll be inconsolable. Quit now. Just walk away. Don't set yourself up for a fall.*

"Karen? Karen?" Why was my mother in my dream?

"Karen?" Someone wouldn't shut up. "Karen?"

I opened one eye, then the other.

My mother stood in the lighted rectangle of my bedroom door in white flannel pajamas with little red birds on them. "Karen, get up. Men are at the door. Get up." Her hairdo was flattened on one side.

I could hear the pounding now and threw back the blue thermal blanket. "Who on earth…?"

"Policemen. Out the window. Policemen with hats."

"Cops!" I went cold all over; what had happened now? Grabbing up a crimson wool robe from the bottom of the bed, I headed for the door, my mother behind me clutching a handful of my robe.

"Who's there?" I called, turning on the standing lamp by the door, still shivering.

"It's Boylan, Ms. Pelletier. Open up." The lieutenant's tone brooked no refusal.

"Boylan? Again?" What was going on? But he was a legitimate officer of the peace; I had no legal right to refuse him entry. I slid the chain from the bolt and unlocked the door. There were two of them, backlit by the motion-sensor light, the dark woods stretching behind them. Lieutenant Neil Boylan and a uniformed female trooper I didn't recognize. She'd taken off her stiff-brimmed blue hat and stood behind him, slightly to one side, turning the hat in awkward hands. Where was Trooper Lombardi, Boylan's usual partner?

The lieutenant took an uninvited step into the living room, the trooper right behind him. Cold air swarmed in with them; it smelled like night. "Ms. Pelletier, this is Trooper Dunbar." The tall black woman nodded at me expressionlessly. "Dunbar and I, we're here to ask you some questions." His mouth had gone lopsided, as if he were feeling a sore tooth with his tongue.

"What's so urgent it couldn't wait until morning?" I began. Then the kitchen phone rang, and I startled. It was an old phone, and it shrilled in the darkness like the portent of doom from a 1930s black-and-white film—something, maybe, starring Claudette Colbert.

"Don't answer that." Boylan moved to block me, but I side-stepped him and grabbed the receiver. "Hello?"

"I just heard." It was Felicity Schultz. "Don't say a thing. I'll be there in twenty minutes. Maybe less." The line went dead.

"Who's calling you this time of night?" Boylan barked. "Piotrowski?"

If only…

I recalled that, after *hello*, I hadn't said a word on the phone. "No one," I replied. "Wrong number. What are you here for?" I moved into the living room, turning on lights as I passed them. Mom sat in Charlie's big armchair. Boylan plopped onto the couch without asking permission, and the uniformed oficer stood by the door—as if, I thought, to prevent any attempt at an escape. I eyed her: she was big, but using my old Lowell street moves I could probably take her.

Not that I would, of course, being a respectable professional now and having different and far more effective defensive moves, but it was comforting to know I could.

"Why am I here, Professor?" Boylan replied. "I guess the answer to that would be…" big dramatic sigh…"it's your *third strike*."

"Third strike?" All I could think of was a baseball game.

"Yeah. *Strike one*—rivalry with Lone Wolf for that cushy job."

"Uh huh. We already talked about that."

"Yeah, we did. *Strike two*—that fight you had—"

"It wasn't a fight!"

"Altercation, then. Your *altercation* with the victim."

"And we talked about that." A suspicion began to flood my mind. "I know! You're here because of what that damn Ned Hilton told you!"

Boylan looked surprised. "Hilton? Hell, no. I didn't pay any attention to his bullshit. What is wrong with that guy, anyhow? I've talked to everyone on campus—there are no rumors out there about you. Which surprises me, actually—Hilton's the only one who seems to suspect you. Otherwise, you've got a lot of friends on that campus."

"I do? I mean, of course I do." It was ridiculous; in spite of the dire implications of having a homicide investigator in my house at two a.m., I felt a flush of gratification: *I had a lot of friends on campus.* "Well, then…?"

"We're here because of *strike three.*"

"What the hell is strike three?"

"On Friday, October 2—ten days before he died—you conducted a comprehensive cybersearch on Joe Lone Wolf. That's *strike three.*"

Goddammit! My computer. "Yeah, I Googled him. I'd forgotten all about that."

He stared at the banked coals of the wood fire that was burning in the old fieldstone fireplace. "You had, huh? Well, Professor, now's the time to remember."

"It was nothing. I Google people all the time. We all do. Don't you?"

He turned back to me, his eyes cold and hard. "Yeah. But it's my job to investigate—not yours. I want to know why you were suddenly so interested in Lone Wolf."

I told him about Miles' tenure bombshell. "I guess I panicked a little. I wanted to find out just who it was I was up against. Funny thing, though—there was nothing there."

He nodded. "Lone Wolf kept a pretty low Internet profile. Unlike you, of course." He stopped. And waited.

"What are you implying?"

He didn't answer me. "And he had very little e-mail correspondence."

"Is that so?" Why was he telling me this?

"Also unlike you, Professor," he continued, giving me a sly sideways glance.

I stared at him, stunned. "You read my e-mail!"

"*Oh, Charlie,*" he said, expressionless, "*I miss you so....*"

"You...you bastard!" I felt as if I'd been slimed.

"Perfectly within my rights," he replied, stony-faced, "in the course of an investigation."

Then, out of the darkness, headlights suddenly flooded the living-room windows. "What the hell?" Boylan snapped. "Dunbar, see who's out there."

Trooper Dunbar had barely gotten the front door open before Felicity Schultz, dressed in jeans and a red plaid hunter's jacket, came storming in.

"The hell you doing here, Schultz?" Boylan towered over her.

"I'm asking you the same, Lieutenant." She stood facing him, leather-gloved hands on her hips. A pit bull facing down a fight-trained Rottweiler.

"I'm here officially, and it's not your business. You're not even on active duty."

"I'm making it my business. Unless you have reasonable suspicion, disturbing a citizen at home in the middle of the night looks like harassment to me."

For a moment Boylan kept silence. Then, "You're just sore about Lombardi."

"Damn right I'm sore. You slapping a suspension on his record! But that's not why I'm here. Just because you and Piotrowski have a beef going on is no reason to persecute his lady."

His *lady?* Jee-zus! "Felicity—for God's sake. I can take care of myself." But I might as well not have spoken.

"Wha-a-a-t? That's an actionable accusation! I'm not persecuting anyone." He turned his back on her and walked over to the fireplace with its glowing, half-consumed coals. Grabbing the iron poker, he hefted it. She stiffened into a defensive stance, but he used the poker only to push back the iron-mesh fire screen and then to stir the coals. He stood there, his back turned to us, for a long, uneasy moment. Suddenly the poker landed on the stone hearth with a clang, and he spun on his heel back toward Schultz. "That Polack bastard put you up to this."

Schultz strode over and replaced the poker on its hook. "'That Polack bastard,' as you call our colleague, is in Iraq—he doesn't know nothing about it, Boylan. Give me one good reason not to report you for harassment." They went into fighting-breed stance again, eye-to-eye. I had a brief nonvisual flash of jaws and teeth.

Sergeant Dunbar had been watching the spat with unbelieving eyes. I saw her take a deep breath, let it out in a sigh, set her stiff-brimmed hat carefully on the narrow oak table behind the couch, and stiff-leg it toward the combatants. She didn't say a word, just stood there, stone-faced, looking from Boylan to Felicity, from Felicity to Boylan.

Lieutenant Boylan's fair complexion was suffused with an angry red. He bit his lip so hard drops of blood oozed through the skin. For another long moment he stood motionless. Then he spun around again and headed for the door. "Dunbar, we're out of here." With his hand on the knob, he turned back and growled, "Schultz—don't think I'm gonna forget about this."

Before following her furious superior out the door, Dunbar turned back. The long look she and Schultz shared was heavy with meaning, but it was meaning in a cop dialect, and I was an outsider. I couldn't read it.

When Dunbar eased the door shut behind her, I slid the bolt into place. In a suddenly quiet room, the chain rattled against the paneled door. I looked over to see how my mother had weathered the scene. She was no longer in her chair. I found her in Amanda's room, crouched in a small space tucked between the dresser and the bed.

◇◇◇

While I was getting Mom calmed down and back to sleep, I could hear Felicity in the kitchen making coffee: water ran from the faucet, then was poured into the coffee machine; the beans rattled into the built-in grinder, then came the screech of coffee beans being pulverized into grounds. Then I smelled the aroma of the brew itself.

Charlie had given me this expensive machine for my birthday, along with a gift card for a near-endless supply of Colombian beans. The sound and smell of the coffee-making bought a sensory illusion of his presence so strong it almost made me cry to know he wouldn't come striding out of the kitchen to announce that breakfast was ready.

Felicity poured herself a cup and sat down across from me at the kitchen table. "I think you know that I'm not here officially."

"I do know that. I also know that you've just bought yourself a world of trouble with Boylan." I blew on the black coffee, which was still too hot to drink.

"Ha!" She slammed her mug down. "Trouble! That son of a bitch put Lombardi down for suspension—conflict of interest; divulging information on an active investigation. Lombardi roared into the house a couple of hours ago—furious. Then a pal of his called from the barracks and said Boylan was on his way over here. I thought you shouldn't be alone with him."

I huffed out my breath. "Thanks!"

She regarded me with curiosity. "What the hell does he think he has on you?"

I told her about the three strikes.

"Bullshit! That stuff's all circumstantial. He can't make an arrest unless he's got material evidence. Unless he can place you at the scene of the crime."

"Arrest? Me!" In my innocence, I'd been seeing only harassment in Boylan's behavior. The word *arrest* shocked me into a new understanding of my vulnerability. This was not some abstract academic quarrel; it seemed I was in serious trouble in a homicide investigation. Would I ever get tenure after that?

Felicity ran her fingers through her mop of short hair. "Why else go to a citizen's home at this insane hour? We're trained not to take such steps lightly."

"You really think he was here to arrest me?" One dominant consequence came to my horrified mind, and it had nothing to do with my innocence or my career. "But what," I asked, "would happen to my mother?"

"They would call elder services, probably." She gazed at me solemnly. "But on second thought, I don't think he would actually have arrested you. It would never hold up in court, and, whatever else Boylan is, he's not stupid. But it sure as hell looks like he was trying to make you think you were in danger of that. It's personal with him—it's gotta be. You know, Karen, you really should report the fucker for harassment."

Abruptly she jumped up from the table and went into the living room. Standing at the fireplace, she selected a chunk of birch and settled it skillfully atop the glowing coals.

I followed her in and, with a sigh, settled on the saggy couch. "Just what happened between him and Charlie, anyhow?"

She stared at the coals, stirring them with the poker. "I don't know for sure—there are rumors…" Her face went suddenly blank, cop-face, as if she'd just remembered something. "I think it had something to do with a prostitute." She cleared her throat. "In any case, I wouldn't be authorized to tell you."

"Okay, Felicity," I said. "I get it. Something that would not reflect well upon the force. So, this guy's a real problem, but he's your senior colleague, and Lombardi's already in trouble with him. What I want to know—doesn't your coming here exacerbate the problem. You've just further antagonized him."

"Too late to think about that," she retorted. "He was already antagonized to the max." She'd removed her jacket and I could see black-and-white-and-red Scottie dog pajama tops sticking out at the neck and waist from beneath her oversized UMass sweatshirt. "You know, Boylan's between a rock and a hard place here. He's been simmering for months, and he's too blinded by your connection to Piotrowski to be able to think straight. He's ready to go after you on motive and opportunity alone, without hard evidence, all of which is against standard procedure. But Piotrowski's a formidable enemy, and Boylan knows it. That's one reason why I showed up here—to remind him of the consequences." She finished her coffee and sat with her chin resting on her hand, elbow planted on the scrubbed pine table.

We were unlikely allies. I'd first met Felicity five years earlier when she'd been assigned to shadow me undercover. I'd loathed her instantly, and she'd returned the emotion in full measure. But she was Charlie's partner, and over the years we'd come first to a tepidly cordial détente and then to a grudging admiration of each other. Now I said to her, "I know you're doing this for Charlie's sake, not mine, but I want you to know how much I appreciate it."

She was looking exhausted, the silly Scottie pajama collar sticking up around her face, but she raised her head from her hand. "I know we didn't always get along, Karen. But since you and Piotrowski have been together, I've gotten to know you better." She fiddled with her coffee spoon, probably so she wouldn't have to look me in the eye. "You're okay…I think."

"Well, yeah. And you know what? I like you, too."

But she was frowning again, and cleared her throat. "That's not to say you shouldn't find yourself a good lawyer—and quick."

My heart jumped so far up my throat so fast that I almost choked on it.

"Here's what you tell the attorney. You think Boylan's operating only on motive and opportunity. He's forgetting about *means*. "How the hell would you, of all people, get hold of *any* peyote buttons—let alone enough for an overdose?"

"Peyote? Is that what killed Joe?" Speculation had been rife on campus as to the means of death, but no one had come anywhere near guessing *peyote*. My god!

"It's assumed. Tox report isn't in yet, but peyote buttons were found on the scene. And from what I hear, it takes a hell of a lot to o.d. on that stuff. Where would someone like you find that kind of drug?" She made a sweeping gesture toward the window that indicated my little barren plot of land and, by extension, the entire stony New England countryside. "Sure as hell don't grow them cactuses nowhere around here."

"Those cacti," I corrected her, automatically. I had a vague memory of seeing cactus plants.

"I know that," she said and grinned.

A recent memory. Where had I seen them? I'd thought of something else, however, that I ought to tell her. "I know Joe did drugs—at least I know he smoked pot. That peyote might have been his. He never said what his tribe was, but out in the Southwest among the Navajo and Zuni, peyote is used in some religious ceremonials."

"So I understand," Charlie's young partner said. "So I understand."

Chapter Sixteen

Saturday, early a.m.

Around 3:30 a.m., when her breast milk began to leak, Felicity went home. Wired, I knew I wouldn't be able to sleep, so I called up e-mail on my laptop. Wow! I already had twenty-seven more friend requests on Facebook. My former colleague, Stuart Horowitz, had written on my wall: *Why don't you ever come to Manhattan anymore? Out there in the wilds of Enfield you might as well be on the moon. I MISS you.*

Stu was the consummate New Yorker. Aside from having done his graduate work at some state university out in the West that I couldn't remember the name of, he hardly ever set foot outside Manhattan. I poked him, and went to bed. Then I lay awake until dawn began to lighten the room, my brain spinning.

I'd done nothing more about my overdue tenure application, because I'd been focusing on trying to juggle classes, the care and feeding of my mother, and all the complications that had arisen from Joe's death—including the extra course. My eyes refused to close: who would take Mom during my Monday classes? Was Ned—or would it be Miles—working on finding a new teacher for the Outsiders course? Why hadn't I heard from Connie? When was she coming back? Was she ever coming back? It was days since I'd heard from Amanda. Was she now so spiritually enlightened that she'd cut all her earthly ties? Or was her battered and broken body lying at the bottom of some Himalayan crevasse? And…Charlie? Where was he? Why hadn't he called again? I reached over to the bedside table and took up the framed photograph of him at the beach in Wellfleet. He was wearing his bathing suit and a soaked Springsteen tee. His blowing hair was lightened by the sun, and the ocean water dripping from his arms and legs highlighted well-developed muscles.

How could I bear not seeing this man again for almost a year?

And, then, just as the rising sun had me thinking about getting up to make coffee, the true dilemma hit me—the real McCoy—the one I'd been blocking out by obsessing over everyday details and far-fetched fears: I was a suspect in a murder case, a case being investigated by a seemingly vengeful rival of my beloved Charlie. Was it really possible I might be arrested for homicide? Oh. My. God.

Like a beacon in a pea-souper fog, a steely resolve began to emerge from my nighttime dithering: there was more at stake here than my tenure application or elder care or the pedagogical oversight of an orphaned American literature course. It was beginning to look like, if Lieutenant Neil Boylan had his way, I might well be charged with killing Joe Lone Wolf.

Goddammit, I told myself, as I felt rage heat my veins, if I'm ever going to get my life back, I'm going to have to get serious and investigate this murder myself. Felicity's support by itself won't be sufficient. What could I do?

First thing would be to talk to as many of my colleagues as possible, interview them, really, but make the interviews seem like casual gossip sessions. Next, get myself back into Joe's office and look for evidence that might not have seemed significant to the police investigators. Third…Third? Well, third probably depended on the results of *one* and *two*.

I took a deep breath. Then I fell sound asleep until nine, when my mother came into the room saying, in a voice very like her old-time self, "Karen, I simply don't understand your coffee machine."

◇◇◇

I parked downtown so I could leave Mom at the drop-in Eldercare program I'd found on the Internet: it was at the Enfield Congregational Church, and they called it a respite program. Respite, indeed. I hadn't heard from Connie, didn't have her cell-phone number, and couldn't continue to impose on my friends. But respite was expensive; how on earth was I going to pay for it in the future?

Mom's short flash of clarity this morning just about broke my heart—because it *was* so short. We'd gotten through the coffee-making together and sat down at the table laughing like girls at the silly, overly complicated coffee machine. And, then, in a minute, between one sip and the next, she was gone, lost in the brain miasma that was obliterating her soul.

Because the air was brisk and dancing with late October light, I left the Subaru at the church and walked through town to campus. Bread & Roses smelled of fresh bread and doughnuts as I powered by. Townsfolk and students mingled on the sidewalks, brushing elbows and nibbling the bakery's special Saturday cinnamon rolls. I waded right through a clump of five or six freshmen girls. The one who was wearing a child's silver birthday crown and carrying at least eighteen motley balloons scowled at me.

My first stop on campus was Java Zone, the old coffee house on the far side of the academic buildings. It was modeled after a traditional rathskeller and had been there forever. Here I had the advantage over the police. They wouldn't know that Saturday morning at Java Zone was schmooze time. Stress was high on campus during the week, and time was short; professors didn't have the leisure for casual chats. But on Saturday a.m., faculty working in their offices or in the library gathered here mid-morning, for conversation more than for caffeine.

I strolled in the back door, keeping an eye out for likely gossip sources. Immediately, however, I had to jump behind a wide distressed-wood pillar covered with a motley assortment of flyers: requests for rides, advertisements for mountain bikes, and posters for campus events. Lieutenant Neil Boylan, grim-faced, was standing in line at the cash register with Trooper Dunbar, the latter now also in street clothes, her short hair moussed into spikes. Behind the pillar I was face-to-face with a poster advertising a student poetry slam to be held in memory of Joe Lone Wolf that evening here at Java Zone. Okay, that would be phase three of my investigation—the poetry slam. Attending it would allow me to get a better fix on how the students felt about Joe.

I stood there, behind the pillar, engrossed in "reading" the poster, hoping no one would come along and blow my cover. Fortunately I was close enough to the check-out counter to be within earshot of what the police were saying.

"That Muslim kid, Alice something," Boylan said. Today he wore ironed jeans and a blue blazer.

"Ayesha," Dunbar corrected him. Sporting gray sweats with ENFIELD plastered across her butt, she was evidently trying to pass as a student. "Ayesha Ahmed." She was holding two cups of take-out coffee while he wielded a cash card.

"Whatever. We gotta take a closer look at her. Those Arabs—"

"She's African, not Arab." The trooper, an African-American who clearly did not like Boylan confusing the two ethnicities, was brusque.

He frowned at her. "Whatever. There's a good chance she's some kind of extremist, you know, wearing that head towel—" He took the coffee she handed him.

"*Hijab.*" She pronounced the two syllables carefully—*heh-jaab*—as if she were speaking to a developmentally impaired child.

Boylan's frown turned into a full-blown, focused scowl. "You're pushing it, Dunbar."

"Sir," she barked, military-style.

As they left the coffee shop, I emerged from behind the pillar—just a moment too soon. Trooper Dunbar, who was following Boylan out, turned around in the doorway and looked straight at me. Her gaze was long, assessing, and grave. Then, raising both hands, she made a smoothing motion, as if covering her short, dark hair. It was some kind of a coded warning.

As she turned back to depart the building, I felt my spine go cold—could Ayesha Ahmed be in even more trouble with Lieutenant Boylan than I was? I turned on my heel and headed for the dorm.

◇◇◇

"Professor?" Ayesha queried, frowning, as she opened to my knock. "What can I do for you?" She was alone in her dorm room, wearing jeans and a Barak Obama tee. Her feet were bare, as was her head, and her black hair was plaited in soft, thin braids. In short she looked like an American kid.

I entered and closed the door behind me before I responded. Like most dorm rooms it was minimalist—two beds, two desks, two desk chairs, two dressers, one heaped with unfolded laundry, the other holding only a red-lacquered jewelry case, a bottle of Tea Rose Jasmine perfume, and a professionally photographed family portrait: mother, father, two young men and Ayesha. All were fashionably dressed and smiling—a handsome, prosperous, modern family.

"Did you just get a call from the police?" I asked, out of breath. I had rushed over from Java Zone. After Boylan's "extremist" remark, I had a sick feeling about how he might approach my student.

"No," she responded, looking puzzled. "I mean, a detective talked to me the other day about Professor Lone Wolf. That was all." She motioned me to the desk chair, but I shook my head and remained standing. "There was nothing I could tell him. And no one's called me since then."

"Good," I said. "I think we should get out of here." I stared over her shoulder at the family portrait in its wide gold frame; something about it seemed a little...unexpected.

"Get out?" Her brow furrowed. "But I'm working on a poem for the slam tonight. I have to—" The phone rang, and she turned toward it; I grabbed her arm.

"Don't answer that—unless you want to be grilled by...by an ethnophobic detective."

"Grilled?" The phone kept ringing. "Because I'm Muslim?"

A Yankees' cap topped a pile of books on her roommate's bed. I snatched it up and jammed it on her head. "Get your coat and shoes. We're out of here."

She was still frowning, but she obeyed. The phone rang again as the door closed behind us. I could picture Boylan, cell phone slapped to his ear, striding across the noontime campus against a flow of lunchward-bound students and toward Ayesha's dorm. "Hurry," I said.

Noon Saturday

I took Ayesha home with me and made grilled-cheese sandwiches for lunch. In the car I'd explained to her what I'd heard Boylan say, that he thought she was likely to be an "extremist."

"Ha!" she replied. "Where have I heard that before? It's the *hijab*, isn't it? What is it about Americans? Terrified of a piece of fabric not much bigger than a hand towel. What does he think? I have a warhead under there?"

I let her have her say before I continued. "Then he said he was going to question you again. What do you want to do?"

"Do?" She was so calm it astonished me.

"I may have overreacted in coming to warn you," I replied. "But I know from personal experience that this guy is a...," then I decided it might behoove me not to go around using words like "jerk" about members of Massachusetts law enforcement "... that the lieutenant can make things uncomfortable for anyone he suspects." I shrugged. "I wanted to give you a chance to go home and speak to your parents—or, if you stay here at the college, to talk to Dean Johnson. Or you could simply take the time to prepare your story, which you'll probably need as soon as you get back on campus."

"My *story*?" She sat across from me at the kitchen table with her perky braids sticking out from beneath the oversized Yankees cap. She wasn't reacting at all as I'd expected she would. No fear.

No hysteria. As a matter of fact, a small lopsided smile seemed to indicate that she was...what?...amused.

"Professor Pelletier," she said, "you are very sweet to worry about me, but I assure you that I'm in no danger from your police lieutenant."

"But..."

Ayesha smiled widely, teeth regular and creamy in her dark face. She evidenced a level of poise and maturity unusual in a woman of twenty. "I had nothing to do with Professor Lone Wolf's death. I'm perfectly innocent. I do not think your state policeman will give me any trouble. But if he does, well..." Her dark eyes were inward-looking, her expression unreadable. "...if he causes me problems, I have family resources to fall back on."

"Family resources?" What could she mean? That sounded like Mafia to me. Was there a Moroccan Mafia? A Muslim Mafia? I found myself, inexplicably, shivering. And Ayesha's profound self-assurance made me feel as if I had over-reached in trying to protect her.

Ayesha set her sandwich down on its plate and pulled off a small piece, the gooey yellow cheese dangling droopy strands, like Silly Putty. She popped it in her mouth and chewed. Then she looked up at me, and now her eyes really were troubled. "Something *has* happened, however," she said, "that I would like to talk to you about, but it has nothing to do with Professor Lone Wolf." She hesitated. "It's very difficult, and I don't know if I'm doing the right thing."

I understood in a flash. I'd had this conversation with women students before: *she's pregnant!*

Pregnant? But wasn't she supposed to be...

She continued, "The first time it was—"

"Blue," I interjected.

"Blue?" She looked at me askance. "No, it was an e-mail. I use white paper."

"An e-mail?" My brain was trying to make sense of this: some new electronic pregnancy-testing technology?

"Yes. Then a note on my pillow. That really scared me—someone had been in my room. Then there were more e-mails and a letter in campus mail."

"Oh?" *Not pregnant, then.* "Hate mail," I breathed in sudden comprehension.

"Yes. And they were vicious from the start. The first one told me to go back to Africa where I belonged. It said I should go to college with the Taliban and not threaten American college students with my *jihad*." Her brown eyes were large, the iris almost as dark as the pupil. Did they hold tears?

I handed her a paper napkin. "Unsigned, I take it."

She nodded, and mopped her eyes.

"Any idea who it is?"

She didn't answer my question. "Until this happened, I felt really comfortable at Enfield, as if people appreciated me for who I am. As if they liked me. But this has shaken my confidence. For a few days, I didn't know what to do." She twisted the bangles on her slim wrist, one finely wrought gold and three woven in various strands of colorful thread.

This old yellow kitchen had seen crises of many kinds over the years, but never before had any of them involved suspicions of *jihad*. "Is that why you went home for the long weekend?"

"Yes."

"Why didn't you tell Dean Johnson?"

"I was so stupid! My first reaction was to feel ashamed… demeaned. I didn't want to tell anyone. Then I read Zitkala Sa's memoir about her school years, and it sounded so much like what I was going through that I got really angry."

"Yes, I remember." I gave her a wry smile. "You scolded the class. I wish you'd come to me first."

"I really am sorry about that, but I just had a sudden impulse to…educate these complacent American kids. Afterwards I realized that this isn't really about me. Just like at Zitkala Sa's school and college, it's about ignorance. I looked in the student directory to see whose e-mail address the hate mail had been sent from. But, of course, it wasn't there—how could I expect a

coward to use his own address? So I wrote back to iamurjihad@
yahoo.com."

The threat implied in the address made my expression freeze.
"Weren't you afraid of reprisal?"

"I didn't confront him at all—I just wrote in a spirit of inquiry.
I asked him if my presence on campus caused him discomfort
and why? Then I said that if he told me what the problem was,
I'd be happy to discuss it with him, either by e-mail or in person."

I gaped at her in astonishment. So smart. So mature. She'd
framed the attack as *his* problem, not hers, and offered to help
him with it! "Then what did he say?"

"That was yesterday. Last time I checked my e-mail there
was no response." She removed the baseball cap and ran a hand
through her braids.

I filled up her milk glass from the container. She'd referred
to the hate-mail sender three times as "he."

"You know who it is, don't you?"

She gave me a wide-eyed gaze of pure innocence, and her
shoulders went up, then down. She picked up the sandwich
again and bit into it.

My heart contracted in fear. I narrowed my eyes at her. "Don't
do anything foolish," I said. "Ignorant people are frightened
people. They can be truly dangerous."

◇◇◇

As soon as I returned Ayesha to the dorm and went back to my
office, I read her essay. It was terrific. She wrote about Zitkala
Sa's school experience and the concerted attempt of white educa-
tors to eradicate unique attributes of Native culture. She then
made the connection between her own situation as a Muslim
at Enfield College, insistent on "maintaining and practicing my
heritage and culture." The true genius of her essay came in her
acknowledgement of similarities between the Native woman's
situation and her own, but also in the awareness that identity
is not fixed but mutable. "All cultures evolve," she concluded,
"and to freeze an evolving culture in time, enshrining the static

version of that culture as its sole authentic manifestation, while perhaps making things easier for scholars, is less than truthful or useful."

"A-plus," I scrawled at the top of the first page. "Terrific work!"

◇◇◇

From: APelletier@sbcglobal.net
To: KPelletier@enfield.edu
Subject: Moving On

Mom, we traveled on from Nepal through India. Now in Sri Lanka. If I ever get married, which I don't intend to, I want the wedding to be in an ancient Buddhist temple. Such serenity.

Speaking of serenity, stop sending so many e-mails. Cybercafés are few and far between. And stop worrying—I'm fine. I'll call when we're back in Kathmandu.

Chapter Seventeen

Saturday afternoon

It was too late now to find any of my colleagues in Java Zone. I'd have to delay talking to them about Joe until at least Monday. In particular I wanted casual chats with Clark McCutcheon and Sally Chenille. Two images were beginning to resonate insistently in my memory: McCutcheon clapping his big hand on Joe's shoulder that night at Rudolph's bar, and Joe at midnight exiting Sally's yellow sports car in the college parking lot with an angry slam of the door.

When I went back to Dickinson Hall to retrieve my briefcase before picking up my mother at eldercare and going home, the door to the chairman's office was open. That surprised me; Ned never came in on the weekends. I poked my head inside. The young college custodian turned from the terra cotta planter of cacti on the wide windowsill (ah! That's where I'd seen them!) with a green plastic watering pot in his hand. He smiled his lovely Incan smile.

"*Hola*," I said. I don't speak Incan, but I do know enough rudimentary Spanish to be polite.

"*Hola, senora. Buenos dias.*"

Here was an unexpected opportunity. I could get the key to Joe's office, and no one in the department would ever know. Of course I had every legitimate reason to be in the office—to find his grade book and class notes (although I was beginning to doubt that he would ever have stooped to use class notes). But right now I needed to exonerate myself and Ayesha by finding evidence that might suggest who else wanted Joe Lone Wolf dead.

I smiled my lovely French-Canadian-American-God-knows-what-else smile at the janitor and strolled over to Monica's desk. The drawer glided open without a squeak, and the cookie key was sequestered safe in my hot little hand. I slid it into the pocket of my jeans. Mission accomplished.

Seeing no one around as I walked down the hall, I slid the passkey into Joe Lone Wolf's door lock, and I was in. Nothing in the cluttered office had changed since I'd peeked in here yesterday, except for the rain suddenly pelting the windows. I closed the door quietly behind me, turned on the light, and headed for the desk—which still resembled a landfill. If his computer was still here, I'd try it first; its files should be far more orderly than the piles of paper I could see on the desktop. The dusty monitor was on a small computer table. I sat on the rolling desk chair and peered down to the lower shelf, hoping against hope the investigators hadn't taken it. No computer. Damn!

I sat up again and sighed. Okay, I'd have to do my research the old-fashioned way, on paper. The desk was Mount Papyrus, in some places papers piled as high as my chin. No labels identified the manila folders, but most of the material looked like Internet printouts. I reached out to take a sheet, immediately causing a calamitous landslide, spilling printouts all over the floor. Double damn! I'd pick it all up later. Now I simply grabbed a random sheet of paper.

This printout detailed a Native story about a pre-Columbian voyager, Prince Madoc of Wales, who had sailed to America three hundred years before the Italian explorer. According to tradition, Prince Madoc and his crew reached the Gulf Coast and eventually founded a colony of Welsh settlers on the Missouri River. Reports from the earliest European explorers document a tribe of blue-eyed "White Indians" in the region.

Could this story possibly be true? I mused. "White Indians?" Well, why not? And what of it? In Western epistemological classifications, law, government, society—not to mention literature departments—institutional identity categories have too often been treated as absolute and immutable, while history and experience show us that race and culture have always been in flux. That's academicspeak: what it means for English professors is that career advancement depends on whatever literary fiefdom the individual scholar has carved out for him or herself, and therefore lines are drawn in the theoretical sand as if they were etched into concrete. What does "pre-Columbian" mean anyhow? The same thing as "pre-Madocian"?

But, wait, I was looking for clues, not for yet another intriguing intellectual conundrum. I tossed the printout back where I'd found it and opened the top desk drawer.

There it was—Joe's grade book.

Right next to the bong.

There was a tap on the door. I slid the desk drawer shut and held my breath. Whoever it was, maybe he or she would go away. Another knock, more imperative. Then Clark McCutcheon's voice said, "Karen, I know you're in there."

I did have a few questions I wanted to ask Clark about his relationship with Joe Lone Wolf, but now was not the time. I rose from the desk chair and opened the door. Clark loomed in the doorway, beaming at me. I almost expected him to drawl, "Now what do we have here, little lady."

"Well, I'll be damned—so this is the Lone Wolf lair? Guy was sure no neatnik." In his large hand-tooled boots Clark strode into the room; no qualms about trespassing for Professor McCutcheon. "Can I help you find something?"

"Just looking for class notes," I said, attempting an innocent expression.

He gestured expansively around the chaotic space. "Any luck?"

"I haven't had time yet to make sense out of this mess."

But Clark wasn't paying any attention to the clutter. His eyes had suddenly fixed themselves on the wall hangings and on the shelves that lined the three unwindowed walls, their contents the only organized part of the room. "Well, I'll be…" he said, and strolled over to the displays: a shelf of hand-woven baskets lined up according to size, another of hand-thrown pots arranged according to color of the clay, kachina dolls, etc. A finger to his lips, as if deep in thought, Clark hefted a pot, studying its glaze, lifted the corner of a hanging rug to check the weave. The eagle-feather war bonnet hanging on the wall claimed intense scrutiny. "Interesting," he said, *sotto voce*, "interesting." But he didn't say why.

Finally he picked up a small, colorful pottery figure of a Native woman with several children clustered around her and held it toward me. "You know what this is, don't you?" he asked, turning it in his hands.

"A mother and her children?" I ventured. *Mother*, I thought, and recalled that mine was waiting for me at the eldercare center.

"No," he said, caressing its smooth surface with his thumb. "It's a story-teller doll from one of the Southwestern tribes. See, the large figure, the story-teller, has her mouth open, speaking, and the small figures, the listeners, are clustered around her, rapt with attention." He gazed at it with what could be seen as an expert's concentration.

"How do you know so much about this material?"

He shrugged. "I come from Indian country. You pick it up."

"Well, then, what do you make of all this?" I asked, with a sweeping gesture of my arm around the room.

He shook his gold-and-silver head. "It's a real surprise, that's for sure. I don't quite know what to think. There doesn't seem to be any organizing principle. It looks like a mish-mosh of stuff from a number of widely scattered tribes. Nonetheless Lone Wolf's got really nice things here. Some of them might even be of museum quality, historical artifacts—like that pipe-tomahawk over the window."

He climbed up on the window seat for a close look at the notched tomahawk. "See, this is a very fine item, obviously a ceremonial object. You can tell by the solid brass blade and the inlaid silver on the haft." He laughed. "It's ironic. This weapon must have been fashioned for important ceremonial and diplomatic purposes, and now it's hanging in an academic office, nothing more than fashionable wall décor."

"I disagree with you, Clark. It looks to me like these things were more than simple décor to Joe—it's as if they really meant something to him." I scanned the shelves. "But, one thing—on an English professor's pay, how did he afford all these expensive objects?"

He ran his tongue over his top lip, looking at me intently. "I wouldn't have a clue," he replied. Then he stared me right in the eye, as if there were some unspoken meaning in his gaze. "And I'll bet you and I are the only ones who know about this collection." I stared right back at him, a little chill running down my backbone. I didn't know quite what to make of this man, but if he intended to suggest, or even *imply*, the possibility of any collusion over Joe's collection, he needed to know that I wasn't about to bite.

"He brought his students here," I said. "They know."

He shrugged, gave me a semicomplicitous wink and left. I locked the door behind him, abandoned the printouts and gave my attention to the shelves of Native arts; after Clark's close perusal of Joe's collection, I wanted to make certain that he hadn't walked off with anything, specifically the storyteller figure that had so attracted him. But, no, there she was, lovingly formed by hand, her beautiful colors smoothly glazed, the small brown woman telling her stories to an enraptured group of listeners, her mouth open forever. Joe had chosen this. Joe had treasured it. Now he had left it behind. For the first time I felt a pang of genuine grief for my murdered colleague.

As I was leaving the room, I recalled my original errand. Searching for class notes seemed to be a hopeless endeavor, but I had found Joe's grade book. I opened the drawer again, and, without touching the bong, I slid the grade book out, tucked it under my arm, and took it back to my office. Then my cell phone rang: Enfield Eldercare. Yikes!

I hid Joe's grade book in my own top desk drawer, and took off like lightning.

Mom was hungry when I showed up at the eldercare center, and we went for General Tso's Chicken at Amazing Chinese. Before we entered the restaurant, however, I wiggled the department pass key from its chocolate-chip cookie ring and dropped it off at Enfield Lock and Key to have a copy made. After all, no sense in bothering Monica every time I had to enter Joe Lone Wolf's office.

Saturday evening

The memorial poetry slam for Joe Lone Wolf was open mic, and Java Zone was packed. A panel of five student judges sat at a table by the fireplace in front of which the poets performed. At night, with the lights lowered for dramatic effect, it was easy to see the coffee house's origins as a rathskeller. The low, beamed ceilings, leaded windows, the long, narrow tables, massive stone fireplace, all spoke of a long-ago time when the college was all male and all white, the drinking age was eighteen, and one could smoke in any public building. I could almost smell the cigarette smoke and beer fumes embedded in the off-white walls and the dark chiseled pillars. I could almost hear the smoke-husky voices of inebriated ghosts singing *eins, zwei, drie, vier, lift your steins and drink some beer*. And what would those old ghosts of young people think of today's student incarnations, men and women, black, white, Asian, and New-World natives, no one smoking (at least not here), no one drinking (at least not openly), all engaged not in singing drinking songs but in partaking of a new kind of student pastime: the poetry slam.

Mom was at Felicity and Lombardi's place for the evening so I could attend this student memorial service for the dead professor. I wasn't here so much for the sake of commemoration as for purposes of investigation. Poetry conveys and elicits powerful feelings, and I hoped an image or a reaction might help me get some insight into the hold my colleague had had on these students.

I arrived in the middle of a…a *what?* Was it a poem? Was it a rant? Was it a dance? Well, anyhow, I arrived in the middle of what I imagined would be called a spoken-word performance. Hank Brody danced and chanted, his feet moving in what could possibly be called native ceremonial footwork:

> Eagle is dead. Eagle is dead.
> Eagle is dead. Watch out for your head.
> They won't scalp your skin,
> They won't scalp your hair,
> But your brains and your hearts
> Until you despair
> Of the sky, of the wind, of the blue, blue, blue air
> Of FREEDOM.
> Eagle is dead. Eagle is dead.
> Eagle is dead. Watch out for your head.
> FREEDOM
> (*shouted*)
> Freedom
> (*spoken*)
> freedom
> (*whispered*)

The reaction was unexpected—to me at least—a standing ovation with tears and sobs. And there were more poems and testimonials in which I heard about a Joe Wolf I never knew, an engaging teacher who spoke without notes and stimulated students' interest in all kinds of texts and contexts and who used his own identity as a Native Indian as a springboard for discussion of "Outsider" peoples of the world.

Except for me, the sole audience member remaining dry-eyed and seated was Ayesha Ahmed, in a blue robe and white *hijab*. She gazed at me, her expression sober. And she didn't read a poem.

Chapter Eighteen

Monday 10/19

As the plump Latina server at the Blue Dolphin diner slapped our platters of eggs, sausage, and home fries on the table early Monday morning, I decided I liked eating with Felicity Schultz. In a town of no-carb, no-fat, no-sugar, no-caffeine dieters, she was a down-to-earth, no-nonsense eater. If I'd been with Earlene, we'd have had oatmeal. Both of us.

"Who gets the pancakes?" the waitress asked.

"That's me," Felicity said, hefting her fork. Then she gave me a sideways look. "Hey, I'm breastfeeding the baby Hulk. Okay?"

"Did I say anything?" Overeating in company is always more fun than overeating alone. "Pass the ketchup."

The next few minutes were spent in near-silence, with only the sounds of forks clicking on plates and cups clicking on saucers. This early on a Monday morning the diner was frequented by UPS drivers, mailmen, local police officers, and medical personnel from Enfield Regional Hospital a mile down the road. It was too early for students, and professors would have their French Roast fix at Starbucks.

◇◇◇

After the poetry slam Saturday night, when I'd gone to pick Mom up from the Schultz-Lombardi apartment, Felicity, bless her heart, had suggested a temporary solution to my eldercare dilemma. "Lombardi and me, we've been talking. Your mom's so good with Buster—we think it would be real helpful if she stayed at our place daytimes this week to play with the kid. Lombardi's gotta be here anyhow. That'd give you a break, keep Adele safe, give Lombardi some relief from all the ga-ga goo-goo, and make the baby happy. And maybe you and I can do something to get Neil Boylan off our backs."

"But taking my mother, that's too much to ask—" I'd been calling Connie's house once a day, in case she'd gotten home without letting me know. I had no idea how long Mom would be with me, so Felicity's offer was a godsend. But I still had no idea whether or not I should be planning a long-term solution.

"Hey, you're not asking—I'm offering. And listen, it'll get me outta the house and save my sanity. This kid is something else. I had no idea what I was getting myself into—fourteen hours a day of servitude." She jerked her head toward her tall, panther-like husband, who was on his knees by the playpen spinning a musical top for the baby. "Might as well make use of Daddycakes while I can." She grinned at me.

Daddycakes?

So I told her what I'd decided that morning, that the most effective way to get Boylan off *my* back would be to investigate the murder myself, and she declared herself my unofficial partner "strictly on the q.t., of course." Thus was greatness born—the new investigative team of Schultz and Pelletier—an investigative collaboration that might actually work.

◇◇◇

"So," Felicity said, having downed the last triangle of pancake, "What have we got to go on?"

I told her that on Saturday I'd overheard Boylan talking about going after Ayesha; that Ayesha wasn't worried because she had "family resources."

"What the hell does that mean?"

I could just see all sorts of racist stereotypes bombarding her imagination: tall young men in skull caps and flowing robes, brandishing hand grenades or scimitars. I knew exactly what she was imagining, because the media had done a similar job on my own unconscious.

"Come off it, Schultz! She just means…" I didn't know what she meant, so I told my new partner about the hate mail Ayesha had been receiving. "I'm worried about her—I think she knows who's sending it and is trying to deal with him herself."

Then I told Felicity about the clutter I'd found in Joe Lone Wolf's office and about Clark McCutcheon's interest in the collection of Native arts and artifacts.

"Hmm," Felicity said.

The final thing I told her was about the affection students had revealed for Joe at the poetry slam. "For a man who was so distant and unpleasant with his colleagues, he certainly seems to have been adored by his students. Listening to them, I began to see new depths in the man."

Felicity was writing down bits and pieces of what I said in a little notebook. I'd regretted immediately having told her about Ayesha's "family resources," so I didn't say anything at all about the girl's dry-eyed demeanor at the poetry slam. Enough was enough.

Felicity slipped the notebook into her jacket pocket. "Okay, you've got your connections, and I've got my connections. Together we should be able to fill out the big picture on this guy, Lone Wolf," she said. "Now, here's something for you. I got a call last night from a confidential source."

"Yeah?" I motioned for more coffee.

"Boylan's been trying to locate Lone Wolf's next-of-kin."

"Yeah?" Someone had put quarters in one of the miniature juke boxes, and Willie Nelson was on the road again.

"In the college personnel records he listed a Margaret Lone Wolf in Erewhon, Montana as his mother."

"Yeah?" I contemplated the remaining home fries on my plate, and then pushed it away.

She gave me a straight look. "Not only is there no Margaret Lone Wolf in Erewhon, but there's also no Erewhon in Montana. What do you make of that?"

"It's strange—that's for sure. Are you saying 'Arrow-won'?"

"No. It's *Erewhon*. Not sure I'm pronouncing it right."

"Spell it." I had the glimmer of a clue.

"E.R.E.W.H.O.N."

As she said each letter I wrote it out on my paper placemat, but, before I was halfway through, I knew what we were dealing with. "Nowhere!" I said. "Why that mendacious little twerp."

"No! It's Erewhon," Felicity protested. The waitress poured coffee and removed our empty grease-slicked platters.

"Write it backwards." I sipped fresh coffee.

She did. "For Christ's sake. It is 'Nowhere,' but it's not spelled right."

"Just an English major having a little fun," I said, "and deceiving the college about his origins in the process." I told her about *Erewhon*, the nineteenth-century novel by Samuel Butler, which featured the fictional country of Erewhon—or Nowhere, slightly misspelled.

"Well, hell." She slapped both stubby hands on the tabletop. "And how am I gonna get this info to Boylan without compromising my source?"

"Why not just have your Deep Throat 'suddenly recall' an old college class. She (I was thinking Trooper Dunbar)—or he—could look it up in his or her college English lit textbook"

"If she—or he—ever took a course in English lit." She grimaced. "Which is unlikely. You'd have to supply the textbook."

"No problem. We get free textbooks from academic publishers all the time." It's one of the perks of the profession. Medical doctors get free drugs and holiday junkets—we get a truckload of almost identical textbooks.

"Great—that's an excellent idea, Karen. You know, you could have been a good criminal investigator. You're wasted in higher ed."

"I coulda been a contender!" I sighed melodramatically, secretly pleased by her praise. "But right now I've got to go teach a class in American literature."

We descended the diner's concrete steps into a cold misty rain. Felicity fished for car keys in the pocket of her hooded jacket.

"I told you about that strange car, didn't I?" I suddenly asked, remembering.

"Which one?"

"The one that followed Joe from the college lot at midnight, not this past Saturday, but a week ago Saturday."

"A week ago Saturday?" Felicity became very still. "That's two days before...Maybe you did, but tell me again."

"Well..." I began.

She put a hand on my arm. "Wait a sec." She scanned the lot again and the busy street that ran past it. "We'll talk in my car. You never know who'll be driving by here and see us together. We can't let this get back to Boylan."

Felicity's car was an old Toyota Camry with a child safety seat in the back. The front passenger seat was littered with take-out coffee cups, fast-food wrappers, and at least a half-dozen pacifiers. She brushed the garbage to the floor, but the pacifiers she dropped into an empty McDonalds' coffee cup. She set it carefully in the cup-holder, close to hand for when Buster demanded one.

I told her the whole thing: Joe arriving in Sally's car, getting in his VW bus, the dark sedan following him with no lights.

"I'll be damned. Chenille? And then an unknown driver? But you say that was Saturday night? So that means the driver of that car isn't necessarily the perp. The ME says Lone Wolf died early on Monday. And he was definitely around on Sunday night. He had some kind of party—"

"He did?"

"Yeah. Didn't I tell you? We heard about it from the neighbors—a lot of noise. Drumming and chanting."

"Really?" *Huh? Drumming and chanting?*

It was cold and damp in the car. Felicity turned the key in the ignition and the heat dial to MAX. The CD player came blasting on, Michael Bolton singing about heartbreak.

I held my hands over the heater vent. "Should I call Boylan and tell him about that car?"

She thought about it. "I don't think so, Karen. He's just gonna say, 'very convenient timing, Ms. Pelletier, very convenient timing.'"

◇◇◇

All the way through teaching my morning class, I'd been thinking about what Felicity had said: "You've got your connections and I've got mine." She'd been referring to my Enfield College connections, of course, but I had a much wider network than that: the entire academic brain trust of American literature scholars. This whole social networking phenomenon of Facebook had made me recall my professional online network, the various e-groups I belonged to for professional discussion and information. I was beginning to think about ways in which I could use my e-groups to learn more about Joe Lone Wolf and his past.

Monica had somehow requisitioned a computer for my office, and I accessed its search engine. I seemed to recall that Joe had done his graduate work at Montana University, so I called up the Montana U alumni website. Joe Lone Wolf's name didn't come up. Bummer! Then I slapped my forehead: of course it didn't! Joe had never completed the Ph.D. He'd never graduated, so he wasn't listed as an alum. Duh!

I checked the time readout on my desk phone: 11:11. I was brain-dead. Time for emergency rations. At Java Zone, I purchased black coffee and a Snickers bar. If I could have, I would have ingested them intravenously. Then I went directly back to my office and posted a query on the largest American literature discussion group: "Anyone know anything about an Amlit scholar named Joseph Lone Wolf?" Okay, that would go out to thousands of people. It was the best I could do at the moment. Time to prep my afternoon freshmen class. We were reading *Invisible Man*.

◇◇◇

Before I left campus later that afternoon, I checked e-mail. No responses to my query re: Joe Lone Wolf, but I now had sixty-seven Facebook friend requests. Hmm—that gave me an idea. I'd just picked up *actual* mail from my department box and had found a memorial card with Joe's portrait, the one in full tribal regalia. Ned was saturating campus with these little cards. What if I scanned Joe's picture into my computer and sent it out to scholar-friends on Facebook? An electronic "wanted" poster. *Anyone know this man?* So I worked my privacy settings and sent the portrait out to thirty-eight people in the academic field of American Literature. *Somebody* had to know this man.

Then I went home to cook for company. In this chilly weather, beef stew sounded like manna from heaven.

Monday evening

Outside the kitchen window, slender black branches crisscrossed the cloud-mottled gray of the darkening sky. I stood at the sink peeling potatoes, looking out the window, and wishing Charlie were here with me, drinking this rough Spanish *roja* while we shared the happenings of our day. Without him, dusk was an empty hour, and my solitary glass of wine a worrisome indulgence. What was it they said about people who drank alone?

I didn't want to think about it.

The beef, onions, and garlic had been stewing all day in the crockpot. Now I cut potatoes, carrots, turnip and parsnip into chunks and lifted the lid of the pot. Fragrant steam wafted into the air, clouding the eyeglasses I wasn't too vain to wear at home.

I was expecting Felicity and Lombardi for a brainstorming session on the murder investigation. Felicity's husband did have a first name. I knew what it was but never used it, and Felicity referred to him only by his surname. I simply couldn't imagine that no-nonsense tomboy cop whispering sweet nothings in the ear of a hunk named *Egidio*.

They'd bring my mom home with them, of course. This morning she'd been anxious when I took her to that "strange place" again, but she'd perked up when she saw the baby. And the baby—they'd bring that pudgy little Goliath. It had been so long since I'd spent time around an infant, I hardly knew how to behave with this serious small person who looked me directly in the eye, frowning, as if I failed to meet his exacting standards for an acceptable human being.

The vegetables plopped into the stewpot, turnips first, then the carrots, potatoes, parsnips. Each made a little splash in the beefy broth. The peas I would put in at the end, so they wouldn't mush up into soggy, flavorless nothings.

I replaced the top on the pot, sat down at the scrubbed-pine table, and pulled my wine glass toward me. It was empty. Damn. I got up, retrieved the bottle from the counter, refilled the glass and took a sip.

Had it only been two weeks earlier that my primary concern was the compilation and submission of my tenure file? That seemed as far in the past as the Garden of Eden. Since then murder had intervened—and not only murder, but police suspicion of me and of my two best students, Ayesha and Hank. I'd tried again to call Charlie, the only person in the world who could help me make sense of all this, but the base operator said his unit was still out of contact. Worry about him ate away at my gut like an unmentionable disease.

And then, on top of all that, came the care of my mother and her increasing senility. And, of course, the theft of my box of tenure materials.

But right now tenure was the least of my worries. I was a damn good English professor, fuck it! If Enfield College wanted to consider me for tenure, they could just wait until I'd finished dealing with other matters, matters of life and death. I took another slug of the red stuff.

By the time the headlights of Felicity's Toyota swept the dark kitchen window, the wineglass was empty again. Two car doors opened and then clunked shut. Only *two*? I had the house door open before they knocked. Felicity stood there bareheaded, her shaggy hair askew and her jaw pugnacious. Mom was right behind her, puffy coat buttoned to the chin. I peered around them at the car. The delayed-action interior light revealed no further passengers.

Felicity noted my curiosity. "Don't ask," she snapped. "I'm hungry. Let's eat."

◇◇◇

Mom had finished her meal and was watching Nick at Nite in the living room when Felicity and I settled ourselves on the shabby kitchen couch with our coffee. I'd had another glass of wine with my stew and she'd had two. Now I watched as she splashed scotch into her coffee—things did not seem to be good with Felicity Schultz tonight. When she handed the whiskey bottle back to me, I screwed the top back on tight and set it to one side. No more for either of us. The way it looked, I might end up having to serve as this Massachusetts state trooper's designated driver.

She took a sip of the coffee. "He said to make his apologies to you." She blurted it out. "Otherwise he's not talking to me. I had the kid in his snowsuit and the diaper bag packed, then Lombardi announces he's not coming. 'Oh, yeah,' I says. 'Then have a happy boy's night in with the little squirt.' I snatched up the car keys and got out of there. If I'd stayed, Lombardi would have gone out drinking somewhere—that was the mood he was in. And I just couldn't take being alone again with that demanding little twerp."

I winced, and she noticed. "Oh, I love the termite to pieces, but, God, being cooped up with him at all hours, night and day, for weeks on end, months and months—sometimes I think I'm half-dead." She covered her face with her hands. "Oh, God, I'm such a terrible mother. I can't wait to get back to work. What's the matter with me?" Her shoulders heaved. Sergeant Felicity Schultz was crying?

Yes, stalwart Sergeant Felicity Schultz was crying, great gasping, unladylike sobs and sloppy, nose-running tears. Poor thing. I wasn't the only one, it seemed, in a state of family crisis. I put my arm around her shoulder and grabbed up a box of tissues with the other hand. "There, there," I said, soothingly, like a kindergarten teacher, "it'll be all right. Just wait. You'll see."

I wasn't certain which one of us I was trying to comfort.

Until now, I hadn't stopped to think about the stress placed on the Schultz/Lombardi marriage by Lombardi's suspension. And, really, wasn't that my fault, since Felicity had been acting in my interests by allowing her husband to keep her up-to-date on developments in the Lone-Wolf homicide investigation? He must resent the hell out of that. And, of course, on top of everything, she was suffering post-partum depression. I remembered again—in both body and soul—how merciless the baby blues could be.

While I comforted my friend, I indulged in my latest "grounding" exercise, picturing myself and Charlie in that little green house currently for sale on Elm Street. If I got tenured I would put a down payment on it immediately. I grabbed another tissue and wiped my own eyes. In that little green house, no one would ever cry.

◇◇◇

I sobered Felicity up and sent her home for the midnight feeding. Mom was long asleep. I sat at the laptop computer in my cramped study and wrote:

From: kpelletier@enfield.edu
To: Charles.piotrowski@army.mil.gov

Charlie, my love, I don't know if you'll get this or not, but I'm frantic about you. I can't get you by phone, and you don't answer my e-mails. Please, please call me. Please, please be safe. All my love, Karen.

P.S. Things are insane here. I'm drinking too much wine, and I'll probably be arrested for murder.

I stared at the e-mail for a long time, and then I pressed the delete button. At least I thought I pressed the delete button, but I'd had yet another glass of wine, and I couldn't be sure.

Chapter Nineteen

Tuesday 10/20

The next morning I found Sally Chenille right where I hoped to—in Java Zone—and sat down at her table. She looked up from a sheet of scrawled-over class notes and blinked. Her mascaraed lashes flickered like the legs of dying centipedes. I needed to find out what the deal was between her and Joe. I'd managed to talk to a number of colleagues about him, but hadn't been able to find Sally on campus.

"I just wondered," I began, "if perhaps you might be able to…ah…tell me anything about Joe Lone Wolf. I feel bad that I didn't really know the man, and now he's dead." As an interview ploy it was pretty weak, but I hadn't had my coffee yet.

Sally denied that she had any particular knowledge of Joe Lone Wolf.

"Really?" I widened my eyes. "But I saw him get out of your car in the college parking lot a week ago Saturday night—and it was past midnight."

Sally laughed. "Oh, that! It was just that we got to talking about casinos, and he volunteered to show me the ropes at Mohegan Sky over in Connecticut. We had a few good hours, but on the way home he definitely had something else on his mind."

"Sex?" I ventured.

"Right. And I wasn't up for it. He got pissed and slammed out of the car. That's all there was to it." She cocked her head at me. "So—why do you ask?"

"Oh," I said, "just curious. That's all." I picked up my coffee and headed for the office. An entire free day lay ahead of me in which to try to reconstruct my tenure file.

◇◇◇

"This is a voice from your past," said a deep voice from the telephone receiver.

"Stuart Horowitz! My God! It *has* been a long time. What's new? You got my Facebook invitation."

"Well, yes, and I'm calling because I have kind of a strange question to ask you."

"Ask away."

"You know that photograph you sent out? The American Indian. Why the hell is Frankie Vitagliano wearing feathers?"

"That photo? That's Joe Lone Wolf, my colleague." I added, ridiculously, "He died."

"Joe—*Who*? It's Frankie Vee. I swear it. We were in grad school together. I'd know him anywhere."

"Frankie? Frankie *Who*? That portrait is of Joe Lone Wolf. Yes, he was an Indian."

There was a gap of silence, and then I could hear Stuart's incredulous chortle. I could almost see him throwing back his head as he laughed and laughed. When he finally caught his breath, he said, "Holy shit! Don't tell me Frankie actually did it?"

It turned out, at least according to Stuart, that not only was Joe Wolf not Native, he wasn't even Joe Lone Wolf. He was Frank Vitagliano of Brooklyn, a former grad-school classmate of Stu's at the University of Montana, a guy nicknamed "Snake-Eyes" because of his gambling habit. "You know," he said, "I think I remember the very night Snake-Eyes 'became' Native American. A bunch of us doctoral students were sitting around, smoking weed. You remember how it was in grad school? We'd have this once-a-week dissertation support-group meeting in someone's room—it always smelled like beer and ganja and cigarettes and dirty socks. So one night we were bitching about how hard it was to get anything published. I said we needed an affirmative-action program for white men—I was pretty wasted at the time—and Snake-Eyes said, *hmmm*, maybe he'd become Joe Snake Eyes, because he sure as hell wasn't getting anywhere as Frank Vitagliano. We all laughed, took another hit, and I thought that was the end of it." He paused, then laughed again. It was more like a cough than a laugh, a wheezy *har-har-har*. "I haven't thought about old Frankie in years! Jeezus, so the little S.O.B. went through with it! Who would've thought?"

Now that I did think of it, Joe had looked more Italian than Native. His skin was dark olive rather than brown. His cheekbones were pronounced, but in a less sculpted manner than many Indians. And his eyes were not quite black. I'd assumed all that was because Joe had European ancestry as well as Native, but maybe we'd all been misled. "So Joe wasn't really American Indian?" I said, slowly, as the implications began to dawn on me. No wonder the police hadn't found his home town or his mother—both were fictions.

"Not even remotely Indian. Frankie was a Brooklyn paisano. As I recall, he said his family ran a hole-in-the-wall pizzeria somewhere—maybe Bay Ridge. We got sick of him bitching about how you couldn't get a decent slice in all of Montana."

I grabbed a pen and a scrap of paper and wrote down *Vitagliano, pizzeria,* and *Bay Ridge*. "If you're right, Stu," I said slowly, "Joe was nothing but a slick opportunist—passing himself off as Native American so he could snag a prime teaching job."

"I'm right. Believe me."

I shook my head. "I'm stunned. I can't get my mind around it. Well, that answers some questions, for sure. Like why he kept such a low profile in the profession—he never, ever, went to conferences."

"Of course not. Someone would have recognized him as Frankie Vee and blown the whistle. And, really, in the long run, he wouldn't have a chance in hell of getting away with it forever, would he? The academic world is like a gossipy small town. Sooner or later your sins will find you out."

Joe Lone Wolf's years in the cushy Enfield College job had been based on a lie. Had his petition for tenure pushed the envelope of that fabrication just a little too far? Was his death related to his deception?

Stuart said, "so, Frankie Vitagliano became an affirmative action con man, huh? You gotta at least admire the *chutzpah!* But how the hell did he pull it off?"

◇◇◇

How the hell *did* he pull it off? And what should I do about it? I took a brisk walk around campus, my brain in turmoil: what should I do with this knowledge? Should I go to the police first and tell Boylan that his Native victim was really a guy from Bay Ridge? Or should I go to the English Department? Or the Dean? Or maybe even President Avery Mitchell? And tell them…what?…that for six years a con man had pulled the wool over their clueless eyes. I was stunned, in a quandary I could never have imagined. I was the sole denizen of Enfield College who knew that we'd been bamboozled by an academic fraud, a shape-shifter of the first water. A Trickster.

When I walked past Miles Jewell's office on my way back to my own, the door was open. I took that as a sign—Miles, the history and institutional memory of the department, sitting in his winged armchair, stalwart and ancient as an old oak tree. He was reading the *Globe* and eating a tuna-fish sandwich on whole-wheat bread. A cup of tea steamed on the side table, next to a flattened square of waxed paper spread with a dozen regimentally aligned carrot and celery sticks. I tapped on the open door and entered, pushing it shut behind me with a click. He looked up, startled. Junior colleagues were not in the habit of visiting Miles Jewell unsummoned.

When I told him Stuart's story, Miles went parchment white. "Oh, God," he moaned, "and I was department chair when he was hired." He mopped his face with a white handkerchief. "That damned search committee. I knew something was dubious about the hiring, but the more questions I asked, the more they stone walled me. I never should have trusted them."

"Who was on the committee that year?"

"Oh, let me see…hmm, it was Sally Chenille, Harriet Person, and Ned Hilton."

I groaned.

"I should have known that triad would be nothing but trouble. It's never about literature with any of them—and *hiring* is always about politics. They were so ecstatic about an application from a minority candidate they just rammed him right through the process. It was the perfect opportunity to expand the ethnic diversity of the department."

"That's a good thing, of course, but didn't anyone do a background check?"

He shrugged.

"What about letters of recommendation?"

"The letters were glowing." He dropped his sage old head into his hands. "Must have been faked."

"No one double-checked?"

"No. I asked about that. Hilton said the committee didn't want to. He said it would be patronizing and offensive to do a background check on a Native candidate. Only by a policy of absolute trust could we erase from our literary praxis the psychic vocabulary of genocide."

"Oh," I said.

"That's just what I said, 'oh.' But how can you counter that kind of smug self-righteousness?

"That was, what, six, seven years ago? How could Joe have gotten away with the deception so long?"

"Oh, God!" Miles groaned and ran his fingers through his tousled white hair. "How could I let him take me in like that?" Now his pallor was greenish gray. "I bent over backward for him. I'm such a patsy!"

"Wh-a-a-a-t?"

"You know how he refused to go to scholarly conferences? Well, that damned impostor had the effrontery to come into the chairman's office one day and plead debilitating illness." Now Miles' face was in his hands. "I should have known! I'm such a dupe!"

"What kind of illness?"

Miles looked me straight in the eye. "Severe social anxiety related to a psychosocial disorder compounded of dyslexia, racial trauma, and a disadvantaged childhood. All of which manifested themselves in a crippling and incurable agoraphobia triggered by large scholarly gatherings, where his symptoms could become exacerbated to the point of aphasia. If I wished, he told me, he could bring me a note from his psychiatrist."

"Slick," I mused. "At any academic conference he ran the risk of running into someone who knew him as Frankie Vitagliano." So that's how he'd gotten away with it for so long. My colleague and I stared at each other, equally aghast. Ironically, after years of acrimony the elder statesman of my department had suddenly become my ally.

"But, you know," Miles concluded, "I'm not responsible for handling this, thank God. That goddamn pantywaist Hilton insists he's still department chair, so you can throw this hot potato right in his lap."

◇◇◇

Ned Hilton seemed even more horrified by Joe's fraudulent identity than he'd been about the man's death. "Don't you dare," he said, "tell the police about this. Or anyone at the college." He stared into my eyes with a intense single-minded determination to subjugate any independent action on my part. "I've got to call a meeting of the senior faculty right away—before this appalling news becomes public." He'd been losing weight all semester, and his pasty skin now pulled tight over his eye sockets, bony nose and jaw. His thin hand trembled. "The Enfield English Department," he said, "will be the laughing stock of the profession. Allowing ourselves to be duped into hiring a false minority." The shaky hand was already straying toward the phone. "Let me see, yes, tenured professors for a crisis-management meeting...."

A pow-wow, I thought. *Big chief medicine men.*

"It's imperative that we gear up immediately for damage control." Ned gave me a warrior's fierce glare, and I felt like laughing in his face. If I'd wanted to, I could have knocked the puny dude flat on his back with his hot-pink stress ball. "After all," he continued, "our first loyalty is to the department."

Lottsa luck, Department, I thought.

"And, I repeat, Karen, not a word to anyone until I tell you. Especially not to the police."

◇◇◇

As soon as my office door clicked shut behind me, I called the police.

Of course the police officer I called was Felicity Schultz, who was not currently on active duty. "This information changes everything, you know," she said. "It's a whole new ball game—widens the investigation way beyond Enfield, Massachusetts. Now we gotta take Brooklyn into account and the entire friggin' state of Montana. Well, we don't gotta—Boylan does. That onionhead probably hasn't even thought to look at anyone outside Enfield."

"I'll call Boylan, then," I said pensively, "and tell him I need to see him. Not that I want to have anything more to do with that S.O.B., but, you're right, this does change everything. No wonder the investigators couldn't find anyone from Joe Lone Wolf's past—he didn't have a past. Only Frankie Vitagliano had a past. You know," I continued, "the knowledge of Joe's true identity could really take the focus off of Enfield College."

"And off of you," Charlie's loyal partner said.

"And off of Ayesha Ahmed." Which lightened my heart; I hadn't realized how worried I was about my Muslim student. Well, I worried about all my students—I was an equal-opportunity worrier—they were so much more vulnerable than they knew, so lacking in experience of the inequities that the world could hurl at them. Well, most of them, anyhow, I thought; life had not been kind to Hank Brody, the coal-miner's kid from Pensylvania—at least so far. Enfield College was his chance to turn it around.

"Be careful, though," Felicity said. "Boylan's likely to think you've concocted the entire story in an attempt to derail his investigation." Young Buster began to cry in the background, and Felicity sighed. But it wasn't the bawling I might have expected from such a bruiser; something more like an informational cry: *Poop! Poop! Hey, lady, poop here!* Nonetheless I could hear Felicity give another deep, resigned sigh. "Adele, no, you don't have to do that—I'll change him." Then she addressed me again. "Listen, see if this Horowitz guy can tell you a little more precisely where Vitagliano came from."

"I'll sic Boylan on him," I said. "Stu will be thrilled. A little homicidal drama will take his mind off the horror of grading midterms."

◇◇◇

I left a message on Neil Boylan's voice-mail, and headed immediately for Earlene's office. "Earlene, I've got a serious problem."

"Hmm?" She pressed the Save icon and turned from her computer, eyes still unfocused from concentrating on her work.

I crossed the office and sat in the chair by her desk. "I know this isn't your bailiwick, but Miles said he doesn't want anything to do with it, there's no one else in my department I feel comfortable talking to, and I don't know the college protocol for dealing with such a…an urgent issue."

"You've got my interest now, girlfriend." She pushed her chair back and stood up. "Want coffee?" She gestured toward her intricate little black machine. "I was just about to make some."

"Sure." But my head was already constricted by a band of caffeine pain. "No, wait—I've had too much already." But I'd had a fearsome responsibility placed upon my untenured shoulders; maybe more caffeine would jolt me into action. "Oh, all right. You talked me into it."

My friend laughed. "You're easy." Then she took a second look. "Man, you sure look a wreck today."

"Yeah," I swiped a lank strand of hair out of my eyes. "Thanks for reminding me."

"What's up?"

I told her about Joe having deceived the department about being Native American and about Ned's decree that I not tell a soul. "So, I'm truly in a quandary. Ned doesn't seem quite... quite stable at the moment, and I feel that it's my obligation to go over his head with this. After all, for six years the college has employed a professor with fraudulent credentials. Who do I tell?"

An entire panoply of expressions from amused to appalled to aghast had played across Earlene's face. "Well, yeah, no question—you've got to inform someone, and right away. But whom? I'd say go to the dean of faculty. He'll probably call the president right in on it. Oh, God!" She slapped her forehead with the palm of her hand. "Think of the headlines in the *Chronicle of Higher Education*!"

◇◇◇

I went to Sanjay's office immediately, only to learn that both President Avery Mitchell and Dean Sanjay Patel were off at a higher education administration conference in Detroit. Neither would be back until Thursday. I didn't want to call them and give the bad news long distance, nor did I feel right about leaving it with their assistants. Oh, well, the college had survived six years without knowing the truth: another day or two wouldn't hurt.

When I got back to Dickinson Hall, Sally Chenille pushed past me in the heavy doorway, seemingly without seeing me, and hustled into the English Department office. The air in the department hallway was rank with crisis. Sally was followed by Miles Jewell, who rolled his eyes at me. Clark McCutcheon strolled past, favoring me with his slow, appreciative smile, and vanished into Ned's office, closing the door behind him.

Okay, let the games begin. Responsible department members were about to be informed of Joe's deception. Surely one of them would inform the proper college authorities.

◇◇◇

When I got to my office, Lieutenant Neil Boylan was stationed outside the door, tapping the ferrule of his sleek, black umbrella impatiently against the wood floor.

"You wanted to see me, right? Ready to turn yourself in?" With anyone else the quip would have been a joke.

"Come in, Lieutenant," I said, "and close the door behind you. I've learned something you need to know."

Grateful for the desk's oaken mass, I barricaded myself behind it. Joe's grade book was still in the top drawer, but unless the lieutenant had X-ray vision he wasn't going to find it. And what if he did? I needed the grade book; I was teaching Joe's course—at least for now. No one had to know that I planned to scrutinize the book for clues to his death.

Boylan stood ramrod straight, as if he had never heard of bendable joints, but when I gestured to the green armchair, he sat—stiffly. It was a discomfiting situation for both of us; he sure didn't want to be here at my bidding, and I couldn't wait to get rid of the man.

I told the lieutenant what Stuart had told me about the dead man's true identity. "And so he was never really Joseph Lone Wolf. He was Frank Vitagliano the entire time." I made my story simple, honest, and short, but Boylan sat there, silent, for a full minute before he spoke. "Convenient timing, Professor," he said, finally. Skepticism and suspicion played across his angular features. Running his fingers through his damp ginger curls, he said, "You sure you didn't brief this, er, old friend, Professor Horowitz, on what might make a good diversion from any… er…speculations about your possible culpability?"

I lost my hard-won cool. "Any 'speculations' you might have about me, Lieutenant Boylan, I fear are baseless. One thing I learned in graduate school was that speculation is merely a preliminary part of the process of reasoning and investigation. One begins with speculation, but one must have irrefutable evidence in order to come to a valid conclusion." Anger always brings out the Latinate in my language. I rose as if I assumed I had the right to dismiss him and handed him a sheet of yellow lined paper. "You'll find Stuart Horowitz's full name here, Lieutenant, along with his academic affiliation, phone numbers, e-mail address. He says he'd be more than happy to talk to you and to provide the names of several of his former fellow graduate students who would also be able to identify Joe Lone Wolf as Frank Vitagliano."

"I'll bet he would." Boylan was the master of the bad-cop evil eye—not even a cat's grin today. "I'll just bet he will. You sure do have a lot of male friends, Professor Pelletier, now don't you?"

Chapter Twenty

After Neil Boylan left, dragging his malice behind him, I went to the door and twisted the knob to make sure it was locked. Then I threw the bolt. In the cold, rain-blurred light of the departing afternoon, I shivered and pulled my thick sweater tighter around me. Then I opened the top desk drawer. Finally, I had a moment to look through Joe's grade book.

It was the usual thick-cardboard-covered class record and roll book, the kind I bought every few years at OfficeMax. This one had dark green covers, its light green pages featuring wide vertical columns for student names, narrow columns to mark attendance, and boxy columns at the end of each row to record mid-term and final grades. Oddly enough, throughout the book, the only columns filled in by Joe were the wide ones on the left for names and the boxy ones on the right side for final grades. In between, there was a huge swath of emptiness; Joe hadn't recorded attendance, quiz grades, essay grades, class participation, or any of the multitude of small cues that allow a teacher to remember whether or not her students are conscious in the classroom. Also, over the years of teaching at Enfield, he hadn't given actual letter grades; he'd chosen Pass/Fail grading, a not uncontroversial option. I leafed through the book. From Joe Lone Wolf's first Enfield course to his most recent completed course in the Spring semester, grades were marked in a bold black script. And without exception they read P—a solid column all the way down of P, P, P, P, P.

Then I reached his current class, and in an otherwise blank final-grades column, Hank Brody's semester grade was already listed—a bold black, indelible-ink F.

I gasped. An F for a scholarship student? That meant death. Well, not literally, of course, but it meant a severe blow to his financial aid. And Hank was an exceptional student; his essay for me had picked up on the discussion about magic in the Native tales. It had been both insightful and eloquent. This grade had to be a mistake. And why had Hank praised Joe so highly at the poetry competition? You would have thought he'd want to kill the man who had threatened his academic future.

Wait—bad choice of words, but I did have to talk to this kid as soon as possible. I checked my cellphone for the time: 5:35. Too late to see him today.

Then a worrisome thought plagued me; a failing grade could be seen as a motive. Someone who didn't know Hank might suspect him of the murder. I had to keep Lieutenant Neil Boylan from getting his hands on this grade book. Especially since Hank, as the student who'd found Joe's body, had been under suspicion at the start. This time Boylan would think he had his perp for sure.

I stood in the middle of the office and looked around. Should I keep the grade book in my desk? Should I hide it among my own books?

In the end, I decided to take it home with me. I'd call Hank first thing tomorrow morning and set up a talk with him.

Wednesday 10/21

"Do you believe in magic, Professor?"

"Me?" Hank's question took me aback. "Hell, no. I'm much too rational a thinker for that—maybe too rational for my own good. Why do you ask?"

"Because you gave me an A on that essay I wrote about magical transformation in the Trickster tales." The sun through the window next to our table in the Java Zone fell on his shaggy dreadlocks, and their straw turned to gold.

"I didn't *give* you anything. You *earned* it. You made a passionate and intelligent argument for the cultural importance of magic in the tales."

He sipped from his extra-large mocha latte with whipped cream. This early in the morning—not yet eight o'clock—the mere sight of the super-size concoction nauseated me. "It was just that Garrett Reynolds was so damn contemptuous about the magical elements in the American Indian stories that he pissed me off."

"Better lower your voice, Hank." Classes were about to begin, and Java Zone was more of a grab-it-and-go zone than a sit-and-eavesdrop zone, so we hadn't been particularly quiet. "Garrett's at that table, over by the doors."

Hank turned his head and stared. "That jerk! He—" He abruptly clamped his teeth over his words. "Never mind. I promised…Well, anyhow, I don't really believe in magic, either, but don't you think it's truly arrogant to say that something's impossible just because we don't understand how it works?"

I laughed. "Imagine someone turning on a light bulb in Puritan New England. She would have been burned as a witch."

"Yeah, and the light bulb, too."

I peeled the top off my cardboard cup of black coffee and took a cautious sip. "So…" I said, "that's why I asked to meet you here. After reading that terrific paper of yours, I was surprised to see the "F" Joe Lone Wolf was planning to give you in *his* course."

"Oh." His shoulders sagged. He pushed the latte away, half-finished, and slid me a glance I could only think of as cagey. "How do you know about that?"

I told him.

"Shit! I was hoping you wouldn't find out. Sorry for the language, but if I fail that course, I'll lose my scholarship. If I lose my scholarship, I'll have to leave Enfield." He dropped his head to his hands. "Oh, God—I'll end up just like my father."

A sigh expelled itself from somewhere deep in my torso. Life is in constant conspiracy to turn English professors into therapists. "Like your father?"

"Yeah, I come from coal mining country. Last summer Pop had a heart attack and died." Hank's head was still hanging and his hands were clenched into fists somewhere in the center of his chest. "He was only forty-three. I don't know whether it was the coal that killed him—or the alcohol."

I regarded him sadly. "And, really…" I sighed again. "Really, the coal and the alcohol were the same thing, weren't they? Hopelessness."

His head jerked up. "You understand?"

"Oh, yes. I understand. More than you can imagine." Garret Reynolds was directly in my line of vision, so I couldn't help but notice how agitated he seemed, tapping his fingers on the table, swiveling his head toward the door whenever anyone entered.

"This is what happened with Lone Wolf—I mean Professor Lone Wolf—I just couldn't write what he wanted me to. He assigned us offensive…creepy…topics, like 'In Defense of Killing Indians,' for example, or 'In Defense of Auschwitz.' We were supposed to write an essay endorsing that position. He said if we could develop the skills to argue the inarguable, then we could use those skills to persuade readers of anything."

"'In Defense of Auchwitz,'" I mused. What a hell of a topic to inflict on students.

"Yeah. Professor Lone Wolf said we should become provocateurs, intellectual firebrands. Whatever the common wisdom was, we were to argue against it, and do it well enough to outrage and infuriate readers. It seemed perverse to me, but…what do I know? I got the topic 'In Defense of Poverty,' and in the end I simply couldn't write it. What is there to endorse about poverty? Hunger? Ignorance? Fear? Disease? Listen, I've been living in poverty all my life—there *is* no defense. So I ended up writing a satiric essay, you know, like Jonathan Swift's 'A Modest Proposal.' But when he read it Professor Lone Wolf said we weren't allowed to be satirical. We had to present a straightforward persuasive argument. So that's why I got a failing grade."

"In essence you got a failing grade because you were sincerely satiric—or should that be satirically sincere."

"That's what he said—I was too earnest. Then I tried to drop the course, but he wouldn't sign off on it. He told me that if I rewrote the assignment to his specifications, he'd grade it again." Hank sat with his fingers twined together, twisting them over his stress-whitened knuckles. "I'm hoping you'll let me write about something different, something I can believe in." This unsophisticated kid had little practice in appearing blasé; his eyes pleaded like those of a Bassett hound.

"Oh." I really didn't have to think too hard about this. I understood that Hank's scholarship meant everything to him; what would his life become if he had to drop out of school? "You know what, Hank? No sense in you writing another essay. Just give me the satiric one. If I think it's worthy, I'll grade you on the effectiveness of the satire. If not, you can write about something else. Okay?"

He jumped up from his chair, and for a moment I was afraid he would throw his arms around me, right there in the Java Zone.

My coffee was cold now. And I still needed ten minutes or so to review my notes for class. But I simply couldn't run off without asking him: "Um, Hank? There's something I don't understand."

"What's that?" Hank folded his gangly limbs into the chair again

"I was at that poetry slam the other night—where you read the eagle poem. After such a bad experience with Professor Lone Wolf, what upsets you so much about his death? It just doesn't seem to compute."

Hank looked me right in the eye. "Damn right, I'm upset. He...he was terrific."

"Really? Even though he threatened to fail you?"

He sighed. "Did you know Joe Lone Wolf well?"

"No. Not at all, to tell the truth."

"Were you ever in his office?"

"Yes," I said. "That's where I found the grade book. He's got...interesting things."

"Yeah, he does. First day of class he let us handle those beautiful baskets, those kachina dolls—do you know some of them are sacred? Then he told us that Western culture had it all

wrong about the arts, separating them from ordinary life the way
we do—confining them to books and museums and academic
study. That drains the spirit from them, he said—stories and
pictures and exquisite objects should be part of daily life in order
to be alive. They should be beautiful and also be of use, like those
pots and baskets. They should always be *at hand* and *in hand.*
Then he picked up a plain little stone-headed tomahawk from a
shelf by the door—an authentic throwing axe, he called it. The
only truly ancient thing he'd been able to collect, he said. That
old tomahawk, he told us, was just as infused with spirit as any
Shakespeare sonnet."

"Really? A tomahawk?"

"Yes. And he showed us how to use it. Like this…" He raised
his arm high and back , then whipped his wrist forward. The
motion appeared so effective I half expected the window on
the far side of the room to splinter into shards. "Throwing the
tomahawk, Professor Lone Wolf said, was as beautiful a motion
as any ballet step in 'Swan Lake.'"

"Really?" I repeated. I raised my own arm high and replicated
his motion. Then I looked around sheepishly. Garrett Reynolds
was gaping at me. Damn. But the motion of my arm and wrist
had felt good, almost like a move in a dance.

"That turned my world around. I'll never be the same again.
Somehow," Hank said, "I just can't find it in my heart to hate
him."

Behind him, out of his range of vision, Ayesha Amhed entered
the coffee shop in a cool yellow flowing robe and green head
cloth. I couldn't find it in my heart to tell Hank that at a signal
from Garrett Reynolds, she'd sat right down with him and begun
an earnest conversation.

"Oh, by the way, Hank," I said, hoping I could distract his
attention as I led him past their table. "The day you found Joe
dead, you told me Joe's apartment door was always open. How
did you know that?"

"What? Oh, he told the whole class. Just drop by any time
you want to, he said. The door's always open."

Chapter Twenty-one

A breathless message from Stuart on my voice mail after my p.m. class requested that I call him at home. A woman answered the phone. "Yes, hang on, he just got back. *Stu, honey,*" she called.

He was still breathless when he got to the phone. "Boy, Karen, do I need to talk to you."

"That's nice," I said, "but can I first ask you about—"

"Clark McCutcheon?"

"What? McCutcheon? No, I want to know if you can tell me where exactly in Brooklyn Joe…er…Frankie came from." If I found out about Frankie's early life in Brooklyn—Brooklyn!—Felicity could work her cop connections for murder motives stemming from…from what?…childhood stoopball games?

But Stuart wasn't listening to me. "No. No! Clark McCutcheon—he's the one we have to talk about."

"What's Clark got to do with it?"

"So, you do know him?"

"Well, yeah. Of course I do. He's in my department."

"Whew!" I could hear the air whistling through Stuart's teeth. "Then I simply don't understand."

I was mystified myself, but more by Stuart's interest in McCutcheon than by McCutcheon himself. "Understand what?"

"How Frankie could get away with it. Here's the story. You got me really curious, so I went on the Enfield College website, just to see what I could find out about his Joe Lone Wolf persona. What courses he taught, and so on. Then I saw that McCutcheon was on your faculty, too. That was a huge shock. How long's he been there?"

"Just this semester, so far. Why?"

"It's really weird. McCutcheon and Frankie go way back, all the way to Montana University. McCutcheon was Frankie's dissertation director."

"He was?" I couldn't get my mind around it. "Then why—"

"Yeah, right. Then why wouldn't McCutcheon have recognized his former student when he got to Enfield, and why didn't he expose him as a fraud?"

"Exactly! Stuart, I'm going to look into this right now."

"Be careful, Karen. I remember McCutcheon as a guy who always has hidden agendas."

◇◇◇

"Karen, I knew you'd show up here one of these days." Clark McCutcheon leapt up from the desk chair in his meticulously neat office and clapped his hand on my shoulder. It was a large, tanned hand, warm and gentle, and, as always, it smelled of high skies and the wide open plains.

I couldn't smell any agendas—other than the usual, that is.

Smiling broadly, he guided me to a comfortable armchair upholstered in faded blue chintz, took a wooden side chair from his conference table, swung it around backwards and straddled it, arms resting on the tall slatted back, grinning the whole time. "You know that…drink I promised you? You ready for it now?"

Today Clark wore a Western suit with broad, top-stitched lapels. It was a light cord fabric, the color of desert sand, and with it he sported a black bolo tie with a turquoise-and-silver slide in the shape of a Navajo thunderbird. His blond-white hair was pulled back and tied at the nape of his neck with a leather thong. His shoulders were broad, his movements cheetah-like. He radiated physical strength and prowess. The man was masculinity distilled down to its pheromonal essence.

I sat as far back in the chair as I could. "A little early for a drink, Clark," I said, "at least for me. I'm here because I have a question for you. I know Ned met with the senior faculty yesterday to—"

His blue eyes widened, incredulous. "—To tell us about Lone Wolf's false identity. Isn't that *something*? What a fraud!" He upped the wattage on his smile and did the finger/gun thing. Behind him on the desk, piles of index cards were stacked as meticulously as if they were hundred-dollar bills. "And I understand that *you're* the girl detective who unmasked him."

I smiled. "I'm hardly a detective, but I just wanted to know... what you thought about the situation." I'd come directly from Stu's phone call meaning to ask Clark right up front why, when he must have known of Joe's deception, he hadn't turned him in to the college authorities. But, sitting here, face to face with Clark, I decided a more oblique approach might be prudent. It was something about his eyes. What had he said to me once? *Nothing escapes me*: that's what it was. When he looked at me, it was as if nothing escaped his gaze. "Especially since I remembered that you used to teach at Montana—where Joe, well, really Frankie Vitagliano, had come from. Did you know him at MU?"

Clark regarded me for a long moment. I thought those eyes were going to swallow me up; I'd end up drowning in a sea of blue. "Well, yes, I did," he drawled. Then he grinned at me as if we shared delicious secret knowledge. "Karen, you are one smart lady. No one else made the connection." He jumped up and grabbed my arm. "Let's get out of here. I've got a story to tell you, and there are better places to tell it, preferably someplace where we can get a drink."

◇◇◇

That early in the evening, Rudolph's bar was not particularly busy. The bartender was a former student of mine, dark-haired and skinny, an aspiring poet with a housefly tattooed on his right cheekbone. Not wanting to leave the sheer, untested promise of college life behind, some graduates hang around Enfield for years.

Clark overrode my abstemious request for a glass of ice tea, ordering a bottle of cabernet and two glasses. "Hey, I've got you to myself for once. I'm not letting you go so easy. So—you want to know about Frank Vitagliano and me, do you? Well, here goes."

Clark admitted that he'd recognized Frankie the moment he saw him in September at the first Enfield all-college faculty meeting of the year. "Then at the reception afterwards I walked over to him." He shrugged; his broad shoulders were shifting sand dunes. "I thought, of course, that he was at Enfield College as Professor Frank Vitagliano. I was surprised, because he hadn't been a great student, and I sure didn't remember him finishing his dissertation.

"But when he saw me, Frank went bone white and he staggered. I thought he was about to pass out, and I grabbed his arm to steady him. The way he tensed up you would have thought I was a cop with handcuffs and a warrant." Clark indulged in a crooked smile, shaking his head in amiable disbelief. Telling this story, he seemed to be enjoying himself hugely. "I might as well have been saying, 'Okay, buddy, the jig is up.' It's a wonder he didn't have a heart attack on the spot." He laughed his big, booming laugh. "But the funny thing is I still didn't have any idea he wasn't here as Frank V. himself.

"Have more wine." He filled my glass almost to the brim.

The wine was good, the story fascinating. Against my better instincts, I began to relax. "Did he tell you then that he was posing as Joe Lone Wolf?"

"Ha. He took me down to Moccios', got sloppy drunk, and begged me to keep silence—at least for the rest of the school year. Said he'd known for a long time that there was no way he was going to survive an Enfield tenure review, and he'd planned for it. He was working on yet a third identity into which he could vanish when the Enfield job disappeared. He planned on leaving Joe Lone Wolf behind."

"Really," I breathed. This was better than a novel. "Did he say what his new identity would be? Who…whom he would become?"

"He wouldn't tell me—only that, oddly enough, it 'still sort of had something to do with Indians.' Then he pleaded with me to give him some time, just until the end of the school year, before I made his deception known." He leaned toward me, his elbows planted firmly on the table, and frowned fleetingly. "I don't want you to think I was being frivolous by not reporting him to the college authorities. Truth is, I had the college's best interests in mind. Since Frankie-Joe…," McCutcheon flashed his sunny grin again, "…was planning to disappear anyhow, I kept quiet in order to spare Enfield the embarrassment of being known to have hired a fraud." It was amazing how well the expression of sheer disinterested benevolence sat on Clark's well-tanned face, but I didn't believe him for a minute.

I took a long sip of wine. "That was…thoughtful…of you."

My skepticism must have showed, because he sat back and winked at me. "We-e-e-ll, to tell you the truth, Karen, I was so amused by the whole thing, I didn't have the heart to turn the pathetic little phony in." He laughed heartily again. "And, besides, it was wicked fun to watch all these pretentious stuffed-shirt Eastern academics being bamboozled. It's not often you get such a good laugh, and I wanted to let it play out for a while." He shrugged. "And, besides, he seemed to be a good teacher—who was being harmed? Bartender, another bottle of the same."

"Clark, no. I've got to drive home."

"So do I. What's the problem?"

◇◇◇

At supper that night Mom said, "There's something I have to tell you, Karen, but you can't ever let anyone else know. Not anyone, not ever," she insisted, "not even your sisters."

"Maaa," I sputtered. "What could be so terrible that I can't tell Connie?" Denise, I could understand. We all tiptoed around

Denise. Given the slightest excuse, Denise drank. But Connie, she was as tough as chewed leather.

"Not Connie." Sitting at the table, eating her chopped-up spaghetti, she couldn't keep her hands steady. "It's too… shameful."

"Shameful?" Must have something to do with sex. I shook grated Parmesan on my pasta. Hmm, was it possible I had been born seven months after my parents' wedding at St. Brigid's, instead of the righteous nine?

She covered her plate with the paper napkin. Her fingers were white at the knuckles. "No. I can't tell you. Forget I said anything about it."

Across the table I took her trembling hands in mine. "You've got to tell me, now, Mom. What is it? Am I…Was I, maybe, born illegitimate?"

She muttered something almost inaudible. I heard it as, "Of course not."

"What is it then? What could be so unspeakable?"

Her head hung low and she muttered into our conjoined hands. "My grandmother's mother…oh, I can't tell you."

"My great-great-grandmother was illegitimate?"

"No, don't be ridiculous." She raised her head and looked straight at me with suddenly lucid brown eyes. "I heard you taking about Indians on the phone, you know. I never heard anyone talk about Indians before. So, I think it's time I told you—your great-great-grandmother, you know—when the family was still in Canada?—well, your great-great-grandmother was a full-blooded Mi'kmaq Indian."

With a whoop, I abandoned my own meal. "You. Are. Kidding. Me!"

Mom lowered her head and her eyes. If she were a turtle, she'd have been totally inside her shell. "I'm sorry, Karen."

Jumping up, I rounded the table and hugged her. "Don't be sorry. It's wonderful news."

She pushed her head up and forward. "It *is*?"

"Of course! I'm proud to be Native—well, I'm only a little bit Native, but I'm delighted. You should be proud, too. And, Amanda, she'll be thrilled!"

"But...Grandmère...she told me never to tell. She said it was a family *scandale*."

"That was then—this is now. We live in a different world. Things have changed." I could save the scholarly lecture on racial politics for another day. Little could my mother understand how much things had changed, how her "dirty little family secret" had created false shame, twisting—warping, really—her understanding of our family's heritage.

And, really, I wanted to laugh. Only yesterday I'd found out Joe wasn't an Indian. Today I was finding out that I was! And really, wasn't it ironic that departmental politics should give the tenure edge to the non-Indian and overlook the actual (if unconscious of it) part-Indian?

I decided on the spot that I would mention this to no one at the college until after my tenure petition was decided. I wasn't raised as a Native. I hadn't known until now that I had Native blood. I was who I was, and they could take me or leave me.

But, secretly, I hugged the news to myself. I did the math: what did that make me? One-sixteenth Native? I couldn't wait to look in the mirror, check myself out. So, maybe my high cheekbones and straight dark hair didn't come from French ancestors after all.

I couldn't wait to tell Amanda.

Chapter Twenty-two

Thursday, late afternoon

Ned Hilton looked like death, and there was nothing warmed-over about him. He was standing halfway up the granite steps that lead to Emerson Hall, the administration building, his lugubrious features frozen in an expression somewhere between indecision and horror. I was on my way to see if either the president or the dean had returned yet from Detroit. Just as I approached Ned, he turned, as if he'd decided to descend rather than ascend the stairs. He didn't seem to see me. He took a step down, one dusty brown loafer touching the lower step, then the other. Immediately he pivoted back and climbed up two steps. Then he stopped and began muttering to himself.

"Ned?" I queried, but it was as if his name went through some kind of force field before he heard it. Then he started, as if I'd set off a firecracker next to his ear, and stood staring at me. It was quitting time for the office workers, and people were streaming down the steps, clutching car keys and griping about the unseasonable cold. They eddied around us on both sides, buttoning fall jackets to the neck, turning up collars. Ned was shivering in his well-worn beige corduroy sports jacket over a rumpled white dress shirt with the tie askew. He still didn't seem to realize I was there.

"Ned, you're freezing. Let's go inside and get you something hot to drink."

"Hmm? Oh, yes. Something hot to drink." It was the voice of an automaton. He allowed me to take his arm and lead him up the steps into the Emerson Hall faculty lounge, where he then allowed me to sit him down and put my coat around his shoulders. I made him a steaming cup of coffee from the coffee-pod machine that sat on an ancient carved-oak sideboard next to an elaborate arrangement of sunflowers in a square dark-green vase. I was becoming increasingly concerned about Ned—he seemed disoriented. What should I do? Whom I should call? His wife? But she had never seemed much more stable than he was. Security? But that would be a bit overdramatic, wouldn't it?

After a few sips of the milky, sugary coffee, Ned looked around. "What am I doing in the faculty lounge?"

Good. At least he knew where he was. "Don't you remember?"

He peered, frowning, into the distance. After a minute he spoke. "I wanted to see the president."

"The president? He's been away at a conference, but he might be back by now." That's why *I* was at Emerson Hall; I wanted to make certain Avery had been informed about Joe Wolf's false identity. Was that why Ned was here? Had he also planned to divulge Joe's deception?

"You seem a little...distressed." Understatement of the year. "Could I help you with something?" What a statement of hubris; who was I to offer myself as a substitute for the college president?

"A woman came into the office." A long pause. "It was about Joe Lone Wolf."

A grey-uniformed security guard ducked his head into the room on his rounds. He stopped and stared at Ned, who was thin-lipped, grim, and shaky.

"The professor has had a shock," I said, and asked the guard to get someone over here from Health Services.

I could hear him on the phone out in the wide, marble-floored entrance hallway, but I didn't attempt to make out the words.

"You had a visitor?" I prompted, turning back to Ned. "It was about Joe Lone Wolf?" Another opportunity to follow through on my queries into the Lone Wolf murder.

"Yes. She was an Indian. She had a funny name. Tallchief or something." Suddenly he was talking at full speed. "What *was* her name? She knew Joe from Mohegan Sky Casino—she's a blackjack dealer there. She said he wasn't Joe at all—he was a professional gambler named Carlo Mangeri. I said, no, no, he was Joe Lone Wolf, a professor."

"Don't you remember?" I corrected Ned. "Joe was really Frankie Vitagliano from Brooklyn. I told you that on Monday. He was only posing as a—"

"That's what I said, *Joe Lone Wolf*. A professor. I tried to help him, to make the world right for him—the representative of an oppressed people. I tried…but I failed. And then he…Oh, what was her *name*?"

The wail of a siren, at first an inconsequential distant whining, grew louder and louder, until I realized, with a jolt of panic, that the ambulance was headed our way. Oh, no. Not an ambulance! I'd had in mind maybe a nurse with a couple of Xanax. But with a screech of brakes and one last flourish of the siren, the Enfield Health Services ambulance pulled up in front of Emerson Hall; student EMTs love dramatics. Two of them in their shiny green EMT jackets came rushing into the lounge pushing a collapsible gurney on wheels; what on earth had the security guard told Health Services? Hearing all the excitement, administrators and a handful of students began to gather, peering in the door of the spacious and formal faculty lounge. In his high-backed chair, Ned cringed, gripping tighter to the carved wooden arms; I could tell I wasn't going to get another word out of him about his mysterious visitor. And then, as if the situation could get any worse, the front door into the massive entrance hall just outside the faculty lounge opened. Sanjay Patel and Avery Mitchell, carrying briefcases, pushed their way through the crowd of onlookers and into the lounge. Avery, in a dark topcoat and a white wool scarf, said, "What's going on here?" Our president looked exhausted; he and Sanjay must just now be returning from Detroit.

One of the EMTs, my student, Cat Andrews, turned from checking Ned's blood pressure and answered him. "Professor seems to be losing it. Gotta take him to Enfield Regional for assessment."

"Oh, good God," Avery said. He set his briefcase on a chair and began to unbutton his coat. "Patel, why don't you go with Hilton? I'll call his wife—let her know where he is." He tossed the coat on top of the briefcase. Then he noticed me next to the gurney. "Karen?" he queried. His lips constricted. "I should have known you'd be in the middle of this. What's wrong with Hilton?"

Ned began to mumble again. "What was her…"

I raised a finger to Avery. "Give me a minute, and I'll tell you."

"What *was* her name?" Ned muttered, as the EMTs lifted him onto the stretcher. Cat Andrews handed me back my coat, then covered Ned with a blanket. "*What* was her name?" he repeated.

I took Ned's hand and held it as the EMTs bumped him through the massive outer door and down the steep granite stairs. "What *was*…" He seemed to have no idea he was being taken to a hospital.

The back doors of the ambulance were open.

"What…?"

I squeezed his hand and, as the EMTs began to raise the stretcher, I let go; I'd learn no more about Ned's visitor today.

"I've got it!" He tried to sit up, pulling against the wide restraining straps as the EMTs rolled him into the back of the ambulance. "I've got it! Her name was…Graciella! Graciella Talltrees!" The double doors slammed, cutting off any further disclosure. The ambulance took off with an earsplitting blast of the siren.

Graciella? Where had I heard that name? Graciella? Graciella? Oh, *Graciella!* Wasn't that was the name of the woman who'd slugged Joe Lone Wolf and floored him the night Earlene and I had seen him with Clark in Rudolph's Café? The beautiful Native woman Earlene had called Pocahontas? What on earth could Graciella Talltrees possibly have said to Ned Hilton that had sent him over the edge?

I knew, then, that I would have to go to the casino as soon as I could and find out.

◇◇◇

Flames crackled in the president's office fireplace; judging from the frequent loud pops, the wood must be pine or cedar, softwood laid to get a new fire up to quick heat. I edged one of Avery's maroon leather wing chairs closer to the fireplace and held out my hands to warm them.

Avery put the phone down and stood thrumming his fingers on the desk. Then he turned toward the neat little mahogany bar concealed behind sliding doors in the alcove next to the desk. "I've been doing bourbon lately," he said, handing me the amber liquor in a squat Waterford glass. "Do you want water in it?"

"No." I sipped decorously and let the heat of the bourbon challenge my mouth.

"Good choice." He moved the other wing chair closer to the heat, and raised his glass. "To Kentucky, where they know how to distill the elixir of the gods." He drank, sighed deeply, then sat back in the deep maroon chair and gave me an inquiring look. "So, what the hell was that all about?"

"Well—"

"And Loni told me you dropped by the office the other day but didn't leave a message. Did that have anything to do with this Hilton fiasco?"

Reaching out, I centered a crystal bud vase on the side table next to me. It held a single elegant miniature white lily, the blossom a tiny furled cup at the top of a thick green stem. I picked up the vase to sniff the flower—absolutely no odor. "I suppose so," I said, "in that Ned was mumbling something just now about Joe Lone Wolf."

Avery groaned and took another drink. He appeared to be bone-weary, the patrician features drawn, the thin lips turning down at the corners, where they ended in short, deep grooves. "Some obsequious homicide detective dropped by last week, and I'm afraid I wasn't at all convinced of his abilities. Whatever happened to...that friend of yours? Lieutenant Piotrowski, isn't it?"

This last was more than an idle question; like many of my colleagues, Avery seemed to be intrigued and puzzled by my relationship with a cop.

"Right now Charlie's with the National Guard. In Iraq."

"Really?" Avery straightened up in his chair. He was interested now. "For how long?"

"A year." It sounded endless to me. "Well, ten months, now. He'll be back next summer."

Avery wasn't the type of man who would know anything about the military—or have ever had anything to do with it. His family line went back to the Puritan dissenters who had colonized New England and who had learned quickly how to profit therein. Preachers had given way to planters, who had begotten merchants, who had spawned industrialists, who had bred statesmen and poets, who had given breath and being to Avery Claibourne Cabot Mitchell, prince of privilege and long-time president of Enfield College.

Why was I, daughter of the deep working class—and, as it turned out, of partial Native blood—so goddamn attracted to this aristocratic son-of-a-bitch?

Avery raised the glass to his lips again and tilted his head at me in silent inquiry.

I told him what I'd wanted to tell him on Monday, that Joe Lone Wolf was really Frankie Vitagliano. I told him how Ned had forbidden me to tell anyone about Joe but had imparted the knowledge of Joe's deception to the senior English faculty.

Avery's frown deepened. "Evidently none of your senior colleagues saw fit to inform me."

I told him about Ned's mysterious Native visitor and the effect she seemed to have had on him and how I had seen that very same woman slug, er, assault the putative Joe Lone Wolf in Rudolph's bar almost three weeks earlier. "I think Ned had developed some kind of a fixation on Joe," I concluded.

"Is that so?" He mused on the idea. "I wonder why?"

"My sense is that it may have been the *idea* of Joe even more than the man himself that fascinated Ned." I shrugged. "Because he was Native."

"You mean you think Ned had something like an *idée fixe?*" He let his voice rise in a parody of noble political discourse. "Joe Lone Wolf as a member of an exotic and endangered people whom it was Ned Hilton's higher duty as an enlightened white man to nurture and protect?"

I laughed, but really it wasn't funny. "I'm afraid Ned's failure to 'save' Joe may be what's now sending him around the bend. Something is."

The fire was dying down. Avery took the iron poker and shifted the coals around. He seemed lost in thought.

With his back still toward me, he spoke. "I really shouldn't say this, Karen." This sigh was the deepest yet. "But I will. What if it's the other way around? What if Ned somehow found out Joe was an ethnic fraud—before anyone else did—and he felt so betrayed that he killed him?"

I frowned. "But how would Ned have found out?" *Clark McCutcheon?* I bit my lip in silence. "But I'd swear on a stack of *Leaves of Grass* that when I took the news to Ned he knew nothing about it. He turned ghost pale and his eyes—well, I've never seen anything quite like his eyes at that moment—huge and defeated, like tar pits."

"Tar pits, huh?"

"And now Ned has this…what?…this *breakdown*. I don't know what to think."

"Well, I do. Let me put on my administrator's hat for a moment. Given certain…reports that have come to my attention over the past week or two, it seems clear to me that the English department has been seriously lacking adequate leadership since the beginning of the semester."

"Yesssss!" I breathed it out in a sibilant rush. *Adequate leadership*: Who would have thought those two words combined could have aroused such passion in my breast?

"And then you tell me Hilton actually forbade you to inform college authorities of an egregious academic deception perpetuated upon the college—and upon its students—and just now I come across this troubling scene with Hilton, this, as you say, breakdown…It looks as if I'm going to have to take some immediate steps…" The sigh came from the depths of an administrator's weary heart. Avery arose, empty glass in hand, and picked mine up from the side table. He poured bourbon, handed me my glass, and placed another log on the fire before he sat down again, crossed a long, well-tailored leg, ankle to knee, and sipped from his drink.

There followed a quiet few moments in which I basked in warmth, bourbon, silence, and the presence of Avery Mitchell.

"Tell me, Karen," Avery said, abruptly, "how's your tenure petition proceeding?"

"Tenure?" I'd almost finished the second drink. "Oh, yes, tenure. In all the chaos surrounding Joe Lone Wolf's death, I'd almost forgotten."

Avery snorted. I looked up at him, muzzy and startled. Avery *snorted*?

"Sorry, Karen. I don't mean to be crude. But, for God's sake, woman, you'd almost forgotten? You're up for tenure, and you'd forgotten?" He titled his head again, with a quizzical expression on his handsome, worn face. He was expert in encouraging people to confide in him.

I rubbed my hand across my eyes. "This is what happened." And I told him the whole story: the disappearance of my tenure file; the police confiscation of my office computer; my mother's untimely visit; Boylan's harassment. I even told him about working unofficially with Sergeant Felicity Schultz to try to solve the homicide case and clear my name. I didn't mention the two students who were also under suspicion; I wasn't that looped. And there was something else I hadn't told him, but I couldn't remember what it was.

When I'd finished my woeful saga, Avery sat up in his chair, both shiny wingtip shoes flat on the floor, and said "Whew!

And you've been trying to deal with all that by yourself?" He shook his head. Then he rose from the leather chair and said, "Let's get out of here, Karen. How about some dinner? I think we both deserve a good meal."

◇◇◇

I made a call to Felicity, and she offered to keep Mom overnight. This couldn't go on, I knew. I'd soon have to make professional arrangements for my mother. But, oh, I couldn't, simply couldn't, pass up a chance for an evening with Avery Mitchell.

We went out of town, to a French restaurant in an old farmhouse, a place I'd never heard of, but where he seemed to be a regular, and he ordered *coq au vin* for both of us. We ate and drank, talked and laughed. It was all so easy—the best time I'd had since Charlie left for training camp.

Charlie.

After dinner, in the restaurant parking lot, Avery opened the BMW's passenger door for me. Before I could enter, he took me gently by the shoulders and turned me toward him. His slender hand stroked my hair once. I felt as if I were melting into a dark, sweet puddle. Then I put both hands on his shoulders and eased him away, too breathless to speak.

Avery gazed down at me, thoughtfully, his eyes soft, and after a beat or two in time, he said, "We can't do this, can we?"

My brain was spinning. *Charlie. Oh, Charlie.* "No, we can't," I said, my throat ragged.

"After all," he continued, "you're up for tenure."

Tenure? Oh, yes, *tenure.*

"And it would be seen as an abuse of power." Ever the administrator. Already he was doing risk management assessment.

"And then there's Charlie," I said.

I got in the car and he went around to the driver's side. He turned the key in the ignition, and the BMW's tires whooshed in near silence over the leaf-strewn roads.

Chapter Twenty-three

Saturday 10/24

Even through the haze of strobe-lighted cigarette smoke, I knew her the moment I saw her: bronzed skin, high cheekbones, dark eyes, silky black hair in two braids falling past her shoulders.

"That's her," I whispered to Felicity, who accompanied me. My cop friend was almost unrecognizable in undercover mode, lipsticked and mascaraed, her hair gelled and spiked, wearing what she called her "lucky outfit," black velvet pants and a red satin shirt unbuttoned to display her considerable cleavage. "That's Graciella Talltrees—at that table." I nodded toward the felt-covered semi-circular blackjack table presided over by the beautiful Native woman.

When we had pulled up to the Mohegan Sky casino just a short while ago, it had been an ordinary late-fall midafternoon. Then we'd walked into the giant domed wigwam supported by tree trunks of mythic strength, tall enough to hold up the sky, and, suddenly, it was mystical night lit by flaming braziers, neon sunset glowing around the edges of the painted ceiling. Was this how my Mi'kmaq ancestors had lived? I didn't think so.

"Blackjack, huh? You play?" Her gaze darted here and there. She was casing the joint.

"God, no." It was hard to make myself heard over the pounding beat of "Born in the USA." I raised my voice. "All I know about gambling is how to slip quarters into slots. I just want to talk to the woman."

"Sure thing. I'll set it up. Let me sit in on a hand or two with her, and I'll…you know…establish a rapport. Find out when she's taking a break. I know how to do this stuff." She edged over to Graciella's table, sat down, leaned forward confidently, slapped her money down, stacked her chips, and she was a player—no different from the others.

◇◇◇

I'd considered passing Ned's information about Graciella Talltrees on to Lieutenant Boylan, as I probably should have. But he'd been so nasty when I'd told him about Joe's Frankie V. identity, I didn't want to muddy the waters any further—at least until I could find out more about this Carlo Mangeri persona from Ms. Talltrees. So I recruited Felicity, and we set out together to learn what we could from—and about—Joe's Native friend.

Driving east on the Massachusetts Turnpike toward Connecticut, Felicity and I had summed up what we knew about Graciella Talltrees. It wasn't much. One: I had seen Graciella slug Joe Lone Wolf in Rudolph's bar; she had a good, solid right. Two: She worked as a blackjack dealer at Mohegan Sky. Three: She had come to the chairman's office to talk to Ned about Lone Wolf, whom she knew as Carlo Mangeri, a professional gambler. The second two facts I had pieced together from Ned's mutterings. That, and whatever else Graciella had told him, was clearly enough to freak my chairman out.

Ned was not a natural risk-taker, but by supporting Joe for tenure against me he'd gambled big-time. I assumed that with all good intentions he'd made a commitment to himself to see that the first Native American ever was installed in a tenured position at Enfield College. If he couldn't do anything about the long sorry past of American history, at least he could redeem his own sorry whiteness by giving an Indian a job. Then Joe's duplicity had knocked the foundations right out from under him; the man he'd gone out of his way to promote turned out

not to be a dedicated Native scholar of American Indian literature, but an imposter and an opportunist. No wonder Ned had
lost it; all his good intentions toward Joe had been based on an
affirmative-action identity scam. Would the betrayed idealist
ever recover from the shock?

And to cap it off, he'd learned from Graciella Talltrees that
Joe had a third identity—as a professional gambler.

"Well," Felicity said, stripping the peel from a bruised banana
as we zoomed past the Worcester exits, "are you thinking of Ms.
Talltrees as an informant or a suspect?"

I tried not to gag at the scent of the over-ripe fruit. "I guess
I was thinking of her simply as a source of information."

"Why not as a suspect?" she mumbled around a bite of
banana.

"Why *not*? This is America. Innocent until proven guilty,
right?"

She took another bite. "Okay, I'll buy that. For now. So, what
do you think she was to Lone Wolf, a girlfriend or a tout?"

"A *tout*?"

"You know, someone who promotes something illicit—
illegal gambling, for instance. Who knows what else the vic
was into."

I shrugged. "Girlfriend or tout? I guess that means *love* or
money, huh?" I took myself in memory back to that night at
the bar, the steely anger in Graciella's eyes, the icy control of her
expression, the power behind her punch. "The way she hauled
off and hit him, I'd say it was *love*, at least on her part. Nobody
slugs anyone that hard and that fast for money."

"Ya think so, huh?" Felicity looked dubious. "Well, in either
case, I'd say she's a suspect. Add her to the list."

"What list?"

"The list that starts with your name."

"Oh, *that* list. Right."

◇◇◇

Graciella Talltrees blew cigarette smoke over her shoulder and
away from me. "Yeah, that creepy professor I talked to at your

college told me Carlo was dead. I got off that campus as fast as I could." Seated at the bar in one of the many Native theme cocktail lounges at the casino, she was needle-thin and as jittery as if she were strung together with wire. "That jerk Mangeri caused me enough grief—I don't need to get messed up in a murder."

I sat on one side of the blackjack dealer, with a mounted wolf head snarling down at me from beside the huge beveled mirror. Felicity, sipping from her sweating glass of ginger ale, was on the other side. I was drinking a whisky sour with our new friend while she stuck with Diet Coke and bar pretzels. Once Graciella got over her shock at being asked about Joe/Frankie/Carlo—He of Many Names—by two, as she thought, English professors, she wasn't reluctant to talk to us. As a matter of fact she seemed relieved at the opportunity to get the story off her chest and maybe get some help recovering money he had stolen from her.

The man Graciella knew as Carlo Mangeri had been a regular at the casino for the past few years, she said, spending every weekend at the blackjack tables. He won a lot, lost a lot, was a compulsive gambler. "We'd been on again, off again for a couple of years," she said. "He could be a lot of fun. He'd show up Friday nights and spend the weekends at my place." She held up the empty pretzel bowl, and the waitress refilled it. "He never said where he was the rest of the time."

Then she told us how she had connected Carlo Mangeri and Joe Lone Wolf. On one of her credit cards, she got billed for a cash advance of $10,000 paid into the account of one Joseph Lone Wolf. Furious, she traced Lone Wolf on the Internet and found him at Enfield College, not so far away. The Friday evening I'd seen her at Rudolph's, she'd driven into town and asked for Professor Joseph Lone Wolf around campus. Someone told her they'd just seen him at Rudolph's bar. Her plan was to stroll into the bar, try to identify this unknown Lone Wolf character from among the drinkers, and then decide what steps to take to get her money back. But when she entered the room, cool, calm, and collected, lo and behold, who does she see strutting his stuff at the bar, but the guy she knows as Carlo Mangeri. She made the connection instantly. "It was like when the slots pay off, *boom, boom, boom.* Things just slid into place. He'd stolen one of my credit cards!" She lost her cool, and whamoo! Joe/Carlo was down for the count.

Felicity cleared her throat. "I was right," she said to me, *sotto voce,* "it was *money,* not *love.*"

I curled my lip at her.

"You never asked...er, Carlo...where he was during the week?" Felicity queried. She munched peanuts.

"I figured that was his business." Graciella shrugged. "If he was into something he didn't want to talk about, then I didn't want to know about it. Listen, it wasn't like either of us was in the relationship for the long term. I've got a kid to support, and I don't want my son exposed to the kind of life I lead." She waved an eagle-tattooed arm in an expansive gesture that took in the whole pseudo-glamorous world of dealers, gamblers, false hopes and phony promises. "He's in a private boarding school in New Hampshire—costs me everything I've got. I can't be thinking about marriage or anything like that."

I was moved by the personal disclosure, but Felicity ignored it. "So, what did you think Mangeri was into?" She was starting to sound just a little too much like a cop. I made a slight "down girl" motion with my fingers: *ease up.*

Graciella crunched on a pretzel. "Oh, like another regular gambling venue, maybe, somewhere else."

I raised my eyebrows. "What a fascinating story! It's just like a novel—he had another life!"

"Yeah. Another life. Isn't it funny—it turns out I was right about that." She laughed, harshly. "But being an *English professor* was the last thing I would have expected from Carlo Mangeri."

"His having a second life wouldn't have bothered you?" Felicity asked.

"Hey, no. Take as much as you can get, I say. Whatever floats your boat." A uniformed security guard checked us out. Graciella gave him a thumbs-up. "Things were pretty good between us for a while, and then something happened that he wouldn't talk about. He must've gotten in over his head...must have borrowed where he shouldn't have." She looked deep into her glass. "In these places, ya know, they try to keep the wise guys out, but... That's the first thing I thought when your Professor Hilton said Carlo—Joe, or whatever he called him—had been murdered. I thought the mob must have gotten to him."

Felicity and I looked at each other, wide-eyed. The mob! Nobody, but nobody, in Enfield had thought of the *mob*.

"That's why, when I heard he was dead, I backed right out. No way. Uh, uh. Nothing doin'. I'm not getting involved in anything like that." She was sucking air at the bottom of her second Diet Coke—must have been mainlining caffeine. I lifted a finger to the Latina bartender, who set a fresh drink in front of her.

"How was he killed?" she asked, transferring her straw to the new glass. "Was it a professional hit?"

I turned to Felicity. She shrugged. I looked back to Graciella. "I heard it was a drug overdose. Peyote buttons."

Her whole body jerked upright. "Peyote? What the *hell!* I didn't know you could get that stuff around here. I mean, I'm Hopi, from Arizona. I know magic mushrooms—they're all over the rez down in the Southwest, but here, in New England? So that makes it a different story—the mob doesn't do mescaline. They couldn't have had anything to do with this."

Graciella brooded over her Coke. "So, after I found him in Enfield, I thought I'd never see him here again, and I was trying to figure out how I could get my money back without going to the cops."

"Why not inform the authorities?" Felicity's eyes were slitted. Cop's eyes.

I glared at her. *Tone it down.*

"Yeah, like the heat is going to listen to someone like me. And, besides..." She let it trail off. What was there in Graciella Talltrees' past that made her so reluctant to deal with the police? Her expression hardened. "Then, what does that S.O.B. do but show up at the casino the next weekend with some showy over-the-hill orange-haired slut."

Sally Chenille! I thought, and things began to slot into place for me, too.

"He just wanted to flaunt her at me. Bastard! I got so pissed that when they left, I took off work early and followed them. The slut dropped him off in a parking lot at Enfield College, and he got right into that ugly bus of his and led me directly to his apartment house."

That dark sedan following Joe's VW van from the lot! Graciella Talltrees!

Felicity shifted uneasily on the seat next to our new best friend.

"Really?" I breathed.

"Yeah. So now I knew where he lived, and—"

"Did you go in after him?" Felicity asked, very casual.

She scowled. "What was I gonna do? Throw a hissy fit? Like that would get me my money back! No, I was thinking about maybe finding some guy who could put some…muscle…on him, but it's not as easy as you might think to hire a reliable goon. So, after a couple of weeks, I changed my mind, decided to head back to the college and talk to his boss…like, maybe I could attach his salary or something. And then your chairman tells me…Carlo is dead." A tear splashed in her Diet Coke; Graciella wasn't quite as tough as she wanted us to think.

The bartender tapped her on the wrist and pointed to her own watch—a Mickey Mouse deluxe. Graciella nodded.

"Gotta get back to the table, but first…one thing I don't understand. A smart place like Enfield College? How did Carlo… or whoever he was…get away with passing as Indian?"

Both she and Felicity looked to me for an answer. "I heard that someone on the hiring committee thought it would be offensive to ask him for proof." *Ned, I bet.*

The blackjack dealer snorted. "You know, in spite of this face…" She motioned to her undeniably Native visage…"and even though the casino has an Indian-preference hiring policy, I had to come up with papers to prove I was the real thing. Didn't the college know enough to ask for proof of his official tribal enrollment? Didn't they require him to submit his enrollment number?"

I shrugged. "I doubt the college even knew there was such a thing as 'official tribal enrollment.'" *Someone at Enfield has a lot to answer for*, I thought.

◇◇◇

"So, is she telling the truth?" Felicity asked as we trudged up the ramp of the big, concrete parking garage. My cop friend was pretty happy, having won $500 on the slots on our way out of the casino. I'd lost twenty, my limit—twenty I could have spent on eldercare for Mom; I had no intention of imposing on my friends beyond the end of this week.

"The truth? I thought so," I said, clicking the remote button on my car key. "Her story was convincing."

"But ya know…" Felicity slid into the passenger seat. "Let me play devil's advocate here. She could have killed him easy. She followed him home. She knew where he lived. We have only her word that she didn't barge into his place, confront him, and…" She spread her hands wide.

I checked over my shoulder before backing out of the tight parking space. "Right. And she would have just by chance been carrying a lethal dose of peyote. Which she would then have crammed down his throat. Was there any sign of a struggle?"

"Not that I heard of." Felicity raised her painted eyebrows. "On the other hand, maybe you're right. Maybe Graciella had nothing to do with it. Maybe it *was* the mob, and they did put out a hit on Carlo Mangeri."

"But…peyote buttons again," I said. "Wouldn't they be just a little bit too…esoteric…for the mob?"

It was her turn to shrug. "And why would they kill him? He couldn't pay them if he was dead. Nah. They'd just beat him up."

As we drove out into the wan late afternoon light, a blue-and-grey patrol car passed us, turning slowly onto the entry ramp on its way in to the garage,

"Holy shit!" Felicity ducked down beside me. "That's Boylan in the passenger seat!"

"It is?" Stupidly I craned my neck to see for myself, and looked directly into the startled eyes of Lieutenant Neil Boylan, Massachusetts State Police, Bureau of Criminal Investigation, Homicide.

Before we even got to the main road, they pulled us over, lights flashing, short bursts of siren. "Stay in the car," Felicity said, her face dead white underneath the garish make-up. "And don't tell the bastard anything. We're not going to be able to talk our way out of this."

"I'll talk if I want to," I objected. "We have a right to be here." Then Boylan's irate face filled my window.

He was staring right past me at his errant colleague. "You! Goddammit, Schultz. Pelletier is bad enough. But you? What the hell are *you* doing here?"

Felicity looked straight ahead, mute.

I took a deep breath. "My friend and I are here for a girl's night out. What's the problem?"

My friend gave me a hard elbow nudge to the ribs.

"Ow!"

Boylan's eyes narrowed even further. It was a wonder he could still see out of them. "A night out? It's still afternoon."

"Well," I chirped. "You take your fun when you can get it."

"Shut up, Karen," Felicity muttered in my ear.

Boylan chewed on his lip. "You wouldn't, by any chance, be interfering with an official investigation, would you?"

"Investigation? Of course not."

Felicity's elbow was now permanently planted in my side.

Boylan's belligerent attitude was beginning to make me angry. Why was he here anyhow? Unless he'd talked to Ned Hilton in the hospital, he'd have no way of knowing about Graciella Talltrees. I looked him directly in the eye. "Are you following us? Is this police harassment?"

Felicity, still staring straight ahead, let out an exasperated huff.

But I was thinking fast—what on earth would have sent Boylan to Enfield Regional to talk to Ned in the first place? Could it be he had some evidence pointing to Ned as the killer? Hmm.

"Watch it, Pelletier," Boylan snarled. "That mouth is gonna get you in trouble one of these days." He turned abruptly and walked to the rear of the Subaru. I heard a sharp crack and the tinkle of glass hitting asphalt. Then he was back by my open window, beckoning to the uniformed trooper. "Give her a citation for a broken tail light. And make it snappy. We've got a dealer to interview."

Graciella Talltrees was in for an unpleasant surprise.

"And, Schultz?" Boylan leaned back into the window. "Don't think you've heard the last of this—you and Lombardi. You're in for it, both of you."

My friend's face was now puce, but she didn't say a word.

◇◇◇

We were half way home, and it was full dark, before I said: "I don't think she did it, do you?"

"It doesn't really matter, does it?" Felicity replied. "Boylan knows about her, and she's his responsibility now."

Chapter Twenty-four

All that next week, I waited for the other shoe to drop with Boylan, but neither Felicity nor I heard from him. Nonetheless, his implied threats nagged at me like a budding toothache. And it didn't help that, without even Ned's merely nominal leadership—he was still hospitalized, and colleagues were scrambling to cover his classes—the department was in a state of chaos. On Tuesday, Dean Patel called a lunchtime meeting of the entire English faculty—in his office, a definite assertion of control. The purpose was to browbeat some one, *any* one, of my senior colleagues into assuming the chairmanship for the rest of the year. Junior faculty weren't eligible. Thank God. Sanjay made an eloquent plea for someone to come forward in this time of crisis and take hold of the department. No deal. He offered money. No one bit. Even more enticing, he offered compensatory leave time, but senior faculty just played hot potato with the departmental leadership: *My book is under deadline. I'm already Chair of Women's Studies. I'm on the Committee of Ten. I have a bad cold.* Then, halfway between the roll-up sandwiches, the bullshit excuses, and the mocha brownies, Sanjay threatened to put the department into receivership.

Miles had had enough. "Oh, for Godsake," he exploded, "you people are nothing but a bunch of big babies, solipsistic, narcissistic babies." Abruptly he pushed himself up from his straightback chair, which tumbled over onto the beautiful carpet with a heavy thud. Glaring at the fallen chair in all its cherrywood innocence, Miles breathed heavily. Then, with narrowed eyes, he scanned his colleagues seated around the conference table. Turning to the Dean, he said. "Okay, Patel, I, at least, am a responsible adult. I was chairman for twenty-five years—I think I've more than fulfilled my obligation. But I'll take the chair again. Let's go to Rudolph's and plan out the rest of the semester. I could use a stiff drink." The sigh he breathed was so prolonged it seemed to have begun in 1963. He stalked out, followed by Sanjay Patel, who made no attempt to hide an exasperated roll of his eyes as he looked back into the room.

Friday 10/30

By late Friday afternoon, I was in a state of turmoil. Mom was still staying with Felicity on my teaching days. Charlie was still out of touch. Miles seemed to have made no headway in finding a replacement for Joe. So, after another surprise noontime department meeting and having taught three classes—my own two and Joe's literary Outsiders class—with office hours in there somewhere, all I wanted was to shake the campus dust from my shoes.

On my way to the parking lot, I passed the boxy brick Health Center building just as Ayesha Ahmed pushed open the chrome and glass door. When she saw me she hurried out between a pair of lighted jack-o-lanterns, came down the steps, and clutched my arm. "Professor, are you on your way home?" Her eyes were wide and her dark skin seemed all of a sudden ashen.

"Is something wrong? I can stay, if you need to talk." I really didn't want to. I'd seen Ayesha in class twice, the second time an hour ago in Joe's class. She'd been uncharacteristically subdued both times. Now, having approached me, she swallowed hard. Any effort at maintaining her aplomb had disappeared. "Can I go with you?" she asked in muted tones.

"Go? You mean, go *home*? With me?" I set my heavy briefcase down on the cement walkway, and gave her a serious once over. Hands twisted together so tightly her knuckles were white. Skin pulled tight around her mouth. A tic in her right eye. *Definitely not in good shape.* "Well, certainly, if it would help. But what's the matter? Are you still getting hate mail?"

Ayesha looked both ways on the busy walkway that led through this outer section of campus near the athletic fields. Late autumn twilight was descending, and at that moment, the mock-Victorian sidewalk lamps lighted up simultaneously, casting a pale glow on the faces of dinner-bound students. Peace had fallen on the campus in this in-between hour, classes over, the evening magic ahead. "No. It's not hate mail. I've taken care of that."

I flashed on an image of Ayesha speaking earnestly to someone in the cafeteria one morning. Someone I would never have expected to see her with. And he had had a hangdog look on his face. "It was Garrett Reynolds, wasn't it?"

She waved a dismissive hand. "Yes. Stephanie and Cat put him up to it. They thought it would be funny. But that doesn't matter anymore. I explained a few things to him, he apologized, and it's over." A tear glittered at the inner corner of each dark, slanted eye. "This is something else, and I'd rather not talk here."

And she didn't talk about it at all—or about much of anything—until we were settled at my kitchen table with chunks of fresh ciabatta from Bread & Roses and bowls of leftover beef stew from the refrigerator.

"What you said in class?"

"Yes?"

"About life being real and…what?…earnest?"

"Oh, you mean the Longfellow poem?" We'd been discussing poems of Emily Dickenson and Walt Whitman with an eye to the effects of Outsider status on both the style and substance of their poems. Then I'd given the students copies of a popular nineteenth-century poem, what you might very well call an *Insider* poem. "Life is real! Life is earnest! / And the grave is not its goal; / Dust thou art, to dust returnest, / Was not spoken of the soul." After all the dodgy theoretical relativism Joe had been plying these kids with, I wanted to see how a taste of some old-fashioned absolutism would play. Clearly Ayesha had found it memorable.

"Right." I reached for the grinder and peppered my stew. "Two major Puritan concerns that carried over into nineteenth-century thinking—reality and sincerity. By that time they'd pretty much dropped the Puritan's damnation and predestination. Why do you mention the Longfellow poem?"

"I'm pregnant," she said, not looking at me, spooning up gravy.

"Oh, no!"

"That's as real as it gets, isn't it?"

"Yes, and pretty earnest, too." I balanced my spoon on the bread plate. "May I ask who the father is?"

Ayesha gazed at me solemnly. "You may ask, but I'm not going to say. I'm not telling anyone, not even my parents." She pushed her bowl away. "He can't do anything about it, anyhow."

"Why not? It's as much his responsibility as yours."

She laughed, with a twenty-year-old's sagacity. "Oh, no, it's not. Not now."

A wild thought invaded my suddenly reeling mind, and I recalled that scene in the department hallway, Joe's transgressive touch on Ayesha's arm. I do know that's *not* the way babies are conceived, but his presumption in touching her might indicate a certain familiarity. *Oh, my God! Joe Lone Wolf! No, please tell me—not Joe Lone Wolf!*

But I shut my teeth over the words, and they never got off the tip of my tongue. "What are you going to do?"

"I need some time to think it over."

"Planned Parenthood—"

"No! I'm going to have this baby!"

I opened my mouth, but she squashed my question.

"And keep it!"

"What will your parents say?"

"They'll kill me," she said, matter-of-factly.

"Oh, no!" I reached over the table and grabbed her hands. "We'll go to Dean Johnson. She'll find you a safe place—"

"Professor!" Ayesha was giving me an odd sideways smile. "I don't believe it! Not *you*!" Speaking slowly, as to a child, she explained: "What I mean when I say they'll *kill me*, is that they'll *kill* me, not that they'll kill *me*."

"But I thought…" Better not to say what I thought. "What about *chastity* and *honor* and…all that? Will your parents… disown you?"

"What do you think this is?" she shot back. "The twelfth century? Of course they won't disown me—they'll be furious, but they'll support me. My parents are religious, but they're not extremists. I'm the only one in the family who observes the… sartorial conventions, and that's only since I came to Enfield. It shocked my mother when I put on the *hijab*, but I wanted to see what it felt like to be 'Muslim in America.'" With her forefingers she indicated the quotation marks.

"What does it feel like?"

Ayesha didn't respond for a moment. Then, "I really meant it in class when I said I was questioned by Homeland Security seven times."

"Why?"

"No reason. It's just that, with my head covered, I look like a suicide bomber. Seemingly."

"How awful for you."

She shrugged. "On the other hand, there are some real advantages to wearing the *hijab*. Men don't hassle me on the streets any more. Besides, it's toughened me up. You have to have courage to wear a *hijab* in post-9/11 America."

She lay her spoon down across her bread plate, giving up any pretense of eating, then sipped at the glass of milk she'd asked for. "You have a daughter, don't you, Prof? What would you do if she came home and told you she was going to have an out-of-wedlock baby?"

I laughed, and she gazed up at me, startled.

I cleared my throat; I didn't make a habit of telling students my personal history. "First of all, it wouldn't be an 'out-of-wedlock' baby—it would just be a baby. My…grandchild." *Oh, god, was I that old?* "Of course, I would give Amanda all the love and support she'd need in such a difficult situation." If she ever comes home, self-enlightened or not. "And I could offer her a hell of a lot of first-hand experience."

She frowned at me quizzically. Then her eyes widened. "Really? *You?*"

"Yep. Me."

Her eyes focused on me, glittering. Suddenly I was an object of fascination. "How old were you?"

"Nineteen."

"Oh, wow. At least I'm grown up—I just turned twenty."

◇◇◇

After she promised to go home for the weekend and tell her parents, I drove Ayesha back to campus on my way to pick up my mother in Springfield. In the security light outside the massive dormitory doors, my student looked small and slight. When she'd swiped her key card and opened the door, she turned back to wave at me. I gave the horn a little tap, put the car back in gear, and slowly drove off. I was thinking once again about Ayesha and Joe Lone Wolf and that scene in the hallway when she had cringed from him. What had she told me a few days earlier—that I shouldn't worry about her. That she had family resources? I knew her brothers had been on campus at least once recently to pick her up—Suppose…

Then I mentally slapped myself in the face. Get real, Karen. Stop being so paranoid. After all, this is *not* the twelfth century.

◇◇◇

As I drove past Dickinson Hall after dropping Ayesha at her dorm, the building was completely dark except for light in a single office—two rectangles of illumination in the long wall of shadowed brick. The campus was lively, as always on Friday nights. Students in groups of three or four criss-crossed the commons, cruising for booze, cruising for hook-ups, cruising for drugs. Cruising for the sake of cruising. I pulled the Subaru onto the walkway by the massive front door of the English department's building and turned off the lights; which one of my colleagues would still be working at this hour of night? I counted down from my own office windows. Two. Four. Six. Then the two lighted windows. My god! Someone was in Joe Lone Wolf's office—at 9:57 on a Friday evening. It wasn't unusual for professors to spend late hours at work, but not Joe. Never Joe.

Not even when he was alive.

I just sat there in the car. Who would be in Joe's office? And why? The police had long since removed the barrier tape from the door—I knew because, of course, I'd been in there myself. But that was legitimate—I'd been authorized to look for his grade book and notes.

A young couple passed by, laughing, her hand in the back pocket of his jeans, his hand in the back pocket of hers. Someone hooted from the direction of the Science Building. A slender girl walked alone toward the library. It was Cat Andrews. She was smoking and her head was bobbing—in tune to some iPod beat, no doubt. I sat as far back as I could in the shadow of my seat. I didn't want to be mentioned tomorrow morning on Cat's Facebook page. *Prof P skulking L8 in front of D hall. A tryst? Which male prof was she aw8ing?*

Once Cat had passed, I sat up again and noted that the previously lighted office windows were now dark. I felt ridiculous; it must have been the janitor in there, doing his regular cleaning. But then the front door of Dickinson Hall opened, slowly, and Clark McCutcheon stepped out and paused, glancing casually to the left and to the right. His gaze slithered over my car and moved on. God, I hoped to hell he hadn't seen me, but he'd seemed to take no note of the Subaru. He descended the steps two at a time, a big man with long legs. Then he ambled away in the direction of the parking lot, his hands deep in the capacious pockets of his long rancher coat.

McCutcheon? All I could think of was the afternoon he and I had been in Joe's office together, his intense interest in our late colleague's valuable Native artifacts. A sudden shudder ran through my body. That sleaze! Had he been casing the joint for a little academic burglary? Was he even now strolling away with that exquisite Pueblo Indian storyteller doll in his white man's pocket?

Chapter Twenty-five

Saturday 10/31

In Enfield's academic hallways, Saturday mornings sometimes bustle, but by noon the weekend has set in for real, and no one is around. I got myself into Joe's office with my unauthorized copy of the cookie key. I'd wanted in since last evening, when I'd seen Clark McCutcheon, with his hands in his pockets, leave the building. I'd lain awake wondering if any of the Native artifacts were missing. For some reason, I was fixated on the little story-teller doll—so easy to steal if you had big white-man pockets.

But, no, the doll was still on the shelf, right where it had been when I'd left the office.

Oh, well. Something must be missing. I checked out the walls and the shelves. The eagle-feather war bonnet was in its place. The whimsical kachina dolls. The fierce tomahawk pipe still hung on its brackets between the windows. As far as I could tell, nothing had been taken. Hmm. What then had Clark McCutcheon been doing in here so late in the evening? Simply satisfying his curiosity? I didn't believe it.

In order to get the larger picture, I stood in the center of the room and pivoted slowly around: colorful patterned blankets still on the walls; pottery bowls, glazed and unglazed, displayed just as they had been earlier. An elaborate turquoise and silver pendant spread out on a square of black velvet. The lack of disturbance

in the light coating of dust on the shelves suggested that nothing had even been shifted. Even the rugged old tomahawk on
the shelf by the door remained in its place. I remembered what
Hank had told me about Native weapons, and I picked it up
and hefted it, then whipped my wrist as if I were throwing the
small axe. The motion felt natural, as if I'd been born to it.

But something was different. What could it be?

Then I saw: the mess of books and printouts that had been
littered across Joe's desk and floor was a mess no longer. Stacks
of papers graced the desk in orderly rows, their edges squared
as neatly as if they just emerged from the original quire. The
scattered books had migrated to disciplined piles along the sides
of the room.

Perhaps the janitor had cleaned this up, I thought. But, no,
on closer inspection I could see that the books were organized
in categories he wouldn't know anything about, stacked in disciplinary order and subject order according to their Library of
Congress call numbers and then in alphabetical order according
to author. The printouts, when I checked them, were arranged in
clusters according to subject and website venue. Facebook documents together. MySpace pages, ditto. A particularly tall stack
contained documents relating to the legend of Prince Madoc,
the Father of the White Indians.

Was it Clark who had organized this material? As I'd noticed,
the man was a compulsive neatnik. But, if so—why? What could
he have been looking for here?

And had he found it? If so, he must have taken it. Certainly
nothing here seemed to be of any import. But seeing the Facebook
printouts joggled something in my mind: Joe's oddly close relationship with some of his students. Had he himself been on Facebook?
Did he ever write on anyone's walls? It was worth looking into.

Back in my own office at my computer, I failed to find a
Facebook page for Joe Lone Wolf. Well, of course I did. What
was I thinking; he'd been so Internet-phobic. I decided instead
to go on my own account and access the pages of his students;
perhaps one of them had mentioned something relevant about

him. I checked out his class roster for names. The first, alphabetically, was Cat Andrews—an apt place to begin. But her page and postings said nothing about Professor Lone Wolf. Damn! I clicked on an icon that said *pictures.* Cat asleep in the library. Cat playing air guitar. Cat pigging out on hot dogs. Cat's...bare bottom? Hmm. Cat sitting on a sagging couch somewhere with a couple of students from Joe's Outsiders class—the girl with the waterspout hair and Elmore O'Hara, with the shaved head and goatee. They were all smoking. The stoned expressions on their faces caught my attention. I enlarged the photo, and it expanded not only in clarity and detail but, also, in scope. The cigarettes were hand-rolled spliffs, and two more people were sitting on the long couch with Cat and her friends, one on each end, just as drugged out as the students were.

They were Professors Ned Hilton and Joe Lone Wolf.

◇◇◇

Aha!" Earlene exclaimed. "Hard evidence!" I'd called her at home as soon as I'd realized what Cat's Facebook photo meant. "That's just what we've been looking for!"

"*We? Evidence?*"

"You're on campus now? Listen, I'll be right over."

"But it's Saturday!"

"I know. Meet me in my office in, oh, say, twenty minutes. I'll tell you about it."

"Oka-a-ay...."

"Oh, and e-mail me a copy of that photo, will you, just in case Ms. Catherine Andrews decides to take it down."

◇◇◇

Earlene was not alone when I arrived. A bulky man with a shaved head and a slim dark goatee sat in one of her student chairs, the all-the-comforts-of-home upholstered armchairs that had seen so much student advising. In his Enfield sweatshirt and dark jeans, he seemed at ease there. He was not white. He was not black. His caramel-colored skin, dark eyes, heavy brows, and assertive nose suggested Middle-Eastern ancestry, but I couldn't get any more specific than that.

When I entered he rose and smiled at me, in a manner that was somehow both formal and friendly.

"Karen, I don't know if you've met Fareed Khan yet. He's Enfield's new Director of Security—just started last month."

"No, I haven't." If I'd seen Mr. Khan before, I would have remembered. Believe me.

"I've heard about you, Karen," Fareed said. His accent was pure middle-class, educated American. "From Earlene as well as from others. It's good to meet you finally." His handshake was warm and firm.

"And Sanjay will be here as soon as he can make it."

"Sanjay? On a weekend? Why? What's going on?"

A lot, it seemed. The college administration had suspected for some months now that Joe Lone Wolf's students were far more likely to be involved in drug use than was the norm. Interviews with individual kids had been unsuccessful in eliciting any of the "hard evidence" Earlene had been looking for. When the new Director of Security had arrived on campus this fall, the investigation had heated up.

Then Joe had been killed.

I sat back, stunned. Yet another motive for Joe's murder: he'd been providing drugs to students. Was there anyone left on campus who didn't have a reason to want the man dead? In my mind I scanned the list of suspects—suspects, that is, as Neil Boylan would have seen them.

Number One: well, okay, *me*—as Felicity Schultz had pointed out. I had a good, solid, substantial motive, but wasn't in the habit of committing homicide in the interests of career advancement.

Number Two: hmm? *Ned*, I guessed, for several possible reasons ranging from the departmental to the drug-related—as this new photo clearly showed.

Number Three: well, *Ayesha Ahmed*. Or a member of her family. What *had* been going on between her and Joe? And I hoped to hell that Boylan hadn't found out she was pregnant.

Number Four: *Hank Brody*. Did Boylan know Lone Wolf had threatened to fail the scholarship student?

Number Five: *Graciella Talltrees*. Boylan had obviously gotten on to the blackjack dealer. What had he learned when he'd questioned her at Mohegan Sky?

Number Six: there was no number six. Not really—simply vague speculations about some mob figure or, now, some drug dealer who might have had a beef with Joe.

"Karen, are you with us?" Earlene asked.

Sanjay Patel had entered the room and was studying the Facebook photo. "Jeez-zus Christ!" he exclaimed. "Not only Lone Wolf, but Hilton, too? What in God's name is going down in the English department?"

◇◇◇

"It wasn't like he was *selling* it to us," Cat Andrews protested. We must have gotten her out of bed, because she was in full pajama mode. "Smoking shit was an integral part of our education. He called it 'extracurricular experiential pedagogy.' Formal education is too restrictive, he said, and it was necessary to widen the parameters of consciousness in order to grasp essential experience beyond the mere intellectual."

"In other words," Fareed Khan said, "he wanted to get you high."

"Well, ye-a-a-ah. But it was spiritual experimentation."

"Spiritual, huh? And you all knew it was against the law."

"That was part of the experience—'*Out*-lawing' he called it. 'Transgressive boundary smashing.' It was for our spiritual fortification against the anesthetizing consequences of mundane social conformity. You know, this was all for the Outsiders course. Being an Outsider is good for the spirit."

"And you all knew," Sanjay said, "that using illicit drugs is also against college regulations, and that you risked disciplinary procedures and possible expulsion. And you all did it anyhow?"

"Not everyone. He only wished to initiate a select few, and even then, some wimps chickened out. Like that stuck-up Ayesha Ahmed."

Earlene and I exchanged glances. *Ayesha!*

Cat began to fidget in her chair. It must finally be hitting home that all was not copacetic in la-la land. "Look, am I in trouble here, or something?"

Earlene raised her eyebrows and nodded.

Fareed Khan frowned. "How much trouble you're in depends on whether or not you cooperate in helping us get to the bottom of this."

Cat went white. "Oh, cripes. I don't think I should say another word. Am I under arrest? I want a lawyer. I want my *daddy*."

◇◇◇

When I called Ayesha Ahmed and asked her to meet me in Earlene's office, I was very careful to tell her that this had nothing to do with what we'd discussed the night before. I don't think she quite believed me; when she showed up, her face was ashen and strained. She had Hank Brody with her, and he appeared equally distressed. They stood, hesitant, in the doorway and stared at the roomful of college personnel. "What the heck?" Hank said, his stance one of imminent flight. It must have looked to them like something out of the Spanish Inquisition: two deans and a police officer, as well as one of their current professors.

Earlene rose and walked over to the baffled students, touching each one lightly on the arm. "Hank, how good that you've come, too. I'm certain that you can also help us with our problem."

"*Your* problem?"

She smiled, reassuringly. "Yes, our problem. Neither of you is in any trouble, believe me." She put an arm around Ayesha's shoulders and led her to the chair recently vacated by Cat Andrews.

Hank pulled up a side chair next to Ayesha. He was quite protective of her, confirming my suspicions that these two were tight. They weren't a couple, of course, coming from such very different worlds. But they sure were close friends.

Earlene laid out the problem at hand to the two students. Their eyes met, and they visibly relaxed.

Ayesha was the first to respond. "So you know about Professor Lone Wolf and the drugs."

"Yes," Earlene replied, "we know."

"Awesome!" My Muslim student was suddenly a different person, animated and talkative. "We were afraid to say anything to the authorities, because when Hank told the professor he wouldn't participate, Lone Wolf—er, *Professor* Lone Wolf— threatened to fail him for the course."

That bastard! I thought. Earlene clucked her tongue. Sanjay wrote something in his leather-bound note pad.

Ayesha continued, "and he couldn't afford to fail because—"

I cut in. "Because of his scholarship. Right?"

Both students nodded, solemnly.

Earlene shook her head in commiseration. "Most understandable. But you don't have to worry about that now, Hank."

"No." Hank let out a long breath.

I saw Fareed's eyes narrow, and I froze. Of course. Fareed was a cop. He saw motive here—motive for homicide. But Hank himself seemed oblivious to any threat, and he began to tell us about Joe Lone Wolf's "extracurricular experiential pedagogy." Joe and Ned, with some students, had been doing drugs together on a regular, but voluntary, basis since the beginning of the semester. "But then the professors came up with a truly wacky idea—an 'Anti-Columbus-Day' party."

Wh-a-a-at? But I didn't speak.

Ayesha broke in. "Professor Pelletier, that day you saw me with Professor Lone Wolf in Dickinson Hall, he was insisting that I attend his party. He said dropping peyote together was a legitimate form of protest against the conquest of the Western continent by European invaders. He said that I, as an Outsider to American culture, should understand. That many American Indians ascribed to the traditional peyote religion as an expansion of spirituality, and it would be disrespectful to Native culture if I refused to participate in the ritual. That as a Muslim I had more in common with Native Americans than I did with the white mainstream."

"Yeah, you see…" Hank's words tumbled on top of Ayesha's. "…He wanted to forge an 'Alliance of Outsiders.' Even though I'm white, he choose me to participate because I'm—" he used finger quotes, "'disadvantaged.' He was dead serious about this shit. 'Authenticity, not assimilation,' was his rallying cry."

Fareed Khan was listening intently to Hank, while Sanjay continued to take notes.

"Yeah." Ayesha again. "It was as if he considered all 'Outsiders' to be the same—and to be 'wounded.' I wasn't buying it. I don't feel 'wounded' at all. 'Marginalized,'" maybe, but not *wounded*. I thought he was very condescending, and I told him so."

"So, Ms. Ahmed," the campus cop said, "you didn't go to this…what did you call it? Anti-Columbus Day event?"

She shook her head. "No way. Muslims don't do drugs, and I told him it would be disrespectful of him to insist that I do."

The police captain turned to Hank and asked, "And what about you?"

"Oh, I went, all right. I had to, if I didn't want to fail. But I didn't—"

I tried to lighten things up with a laugh. "You didn't *inhale*, right?" Sanjay and Earlene gave weak grins, but the students were too young to get the joke.

Hank gave me an indignant glare. "Of course, I didn't inhale. And anyhow, it was peyote. You don't *smoke* peyote. But there were a few other students there—four or five. They participated."

Earlene casually reached for a pen. "Can you give me the names?"

He frowned. "I'm no snitch. I'm not going to tell you who my classmates were." He glanced at Ayesha, then looked back at Earlene. "But I will tell you something I overheard the two professors talking about. There was going to be an after-party, and I think it was only for faculty. They expected other professors."

Sanjay dropped his head in his hands and let out a strangled groan. "Professor Hilton was one of those two, wasn't he?"

"How did you know?"

Sanjay didn't respond.

Fareed Khan leaned forward, elbows on his knees. "Now, tell me the truth, Hank, did you use any drugs at that party?"

Hank sat up straight. "No, sir. I did not use drugs in any form at any time at Professor Lone Wolf's party. And, now, I think we've answered enough questions. C'mon, Ayesha, let's get out of here."

"Just a minute, young man." Fareed was up and out of his chair. He wasn't tall, but he was at least twice the body mass of scrawny Hank. "One more little thing. When Professor Lone Wolf was found dead, did you inform the homicide investigators about this party and the 'afterparty'?"

"Are you kidding? And get myself arrested for going in the first place? You see, it was Catch 22. I was damned if I didn't go, and now I'm damned 'cause I did."

◇◇◇

"You know, we're going to have to pass this info about Joe Lone Wolf's involvement with drugs on to the state police investigators," Fareed said, after the students left.

I stifled the impulse to protest—these two vulnerable students didn't need any more hassle.

Sanjay and Earlene looked at each other, sober with the ramifications. A long silence ensued.

Earlene sighed. "Yes, of course we do. But let's keep the students out of it as much as possible."

Fareed opened his mouth, but Sanjay stopped him with a raised hand. "I'll call the staties. I'm Dean of Faculty, and Joe was one of mine."

The security director regarded Sanjay soberly. "Hilton, too, I'm afraid. Has it occurred to anyone else but me that Ned Hilton is in this up to his eyeballs?"

Chapter Twenty-six

"And, so," I told Felicity on my cell phone as I walked back across campus from Earlene's office, "here's yet another possible motive for the homicide. Joe Lone Wolf was supplying Enfield College students with free drugs, and Ned Hilton was involved. I think the new top cop here on campus suspects Ned of being the killer."

"Really?" Felicity replied, and there was a long silence on the other end of the line. Then, "is there anyone at all left on that campus who *didn't* have a motive for wanting Professor Lone Wolf dead?"

I laughed. "You're a funny lady, Schultz."

"Yeah, right. Funny as gangrene. I assume college authorities will be looking into Hilton, but I gotta say he seems like too much of a loser to do something as decisive as commit homicide. You and me have to keep looking into this. So where do you think we should go next?"

"I don't know where you're going, but I'm going back into cyberspace. That's how I found out Joe's true identity, and that's how I got onto the drug connection. Now I have yet another idea. Who knows what else I might be able to learn."

"Watch it, Karen," Felicity said, in that flat, patronizing cop tone that so infuriates me when Charlie uses it. "Someone out there is damn good at covering up his—or her—tracks. No telling what they'll do if you start turning over rocks."

"Don't worry about me," I replied. "I know how to take care of myself."

"I've heard people say that before," Felicity replied. "It's usually the kiss of death."

◇◇◇

Minutes later, with the cold late-afternoon sun streaming through bare branches and into my office windows, I found the Facebook alumni site for the Montana University Graduate English Program. Even though he hadn't actually graduated, this was where Joe… er…Frankie Vitagliano…had done his graduate work. I wasn't looking for anything in particular, simply cruising for stray pieces of information about the man that might lead me to his killer.

Someone had taken a lot of time with this website, and it was beautifully organized. I scrolled through the graduating classes year by year, scanning the accomplishments of newly minted English PhDs: faculty positions at universities from East Podunk U. to UPenn, tenure won, books published.

Nothing from Frank Vitagliano.

I concentrated on the site for the graduate class of a decade or so earlier, when he would have been enrolled at the university. There I found something that really touched me: a memorial website for a PhD student named Sandra Begay, who, tragically, had committed suicide during her final year of courses. Sandra must have been a popular gal, because, on the tenth anniversary of her death, her classmates had bestirred themselves to post tributes, poems, and brief remembrances. One link led to Sandra's own poems and essays, which were lauded by the webmaster as brilliant. When I saw Professor Clark McCutcheon's name listed as the teacher for Sandra's seminar in literary theory, I clicked on the link for her class essay. Sandra Begay's topic was literature, culture and racial theory. The title of the essay was, "Whaddya Mean, 'We,' White Man?"

Oh. My. God.

I began to read, and there on Facebook, in plain sight of any inquisitive Web surfer, and, surprisingly, not password protected,

I found the essay that had made Clark McCutcheon famous. It had been written by a brilliant graduate student, now deceased. I sat back in my desk chair with a thump, astounded. The great man's reputation rested on a plagiarized grad-student paper? Was Joe Lone Wolf not the only fraud, but also Clark McCutcheon?

I pictured Clark, tall, blond, certain of his territorial rights, striding into Joe's office a week earlier, surveying the rows of exquisite Native artifacts just as his forbears had surveyed Native land and villages. In my memory of that day, he seemed to swell until the air was sun-drenched and dry, and he filled the room with his presence. I'd been uneasy about the man then, and this new evidence of his lack of integrity made me sick at heart.

In the academic world, laying a charge of plagiarism against a scholar is an extremely grave move and is never done lightly. Stealing another scholar's words, work, and ideas not only violates the ethical ideals that bind the scholarly world together, it also constitutes theft of intellectual property, leading to career advancement, power, and material gain. I was disgusted by Clark's abuse of professional trust. The ideals of disinterested inquiry, the acquisition of knowledge and the passionate interplay of ideas: did these mean nothing to him?

However, before I would be in a position to make an accusation against McCutcheon, I would have to obtain evidence—*hard* evidence, as Earlene had exulted in earlier this morning with Cat's photo—not simply memory's soft evidence of an essay I had read years earlier.

Where could I find a copy of McCutcheon's essay? There must be one in Joe Lone Wolf's office. If it wasn't there, among the newly orderly piles of papers, I'd head for the library. "Whaddaya Mean, 'We,' White Man?" had been published first in the journal *American Literary History*, and then in a volume of "seminal" essays on the new comparative American literature. It was certain to be somewhere in the periodicals room or in the stacks. When I got my hands on the published essay, I'd compare it word for word with the one on the Montana U. website. Then, if my suspicions were confirmed…what would I do? Call Sanjay or

Avery? But it was still Saturday. Should I wait? After all, plagiarism, while the most blatant form of academic misconduct, is hardly on a par with drug use and murder, both of which the college administrators were dealing with already.

Printing out the website essay as a comparison text, I snatched up my key ring with the passkey I'd copied and sidled out into the deserted corridor. Security lamps illuminated the hallway only dimly, but sunlight still shone through the arched transom over the west door.

Perhaps because the building now seemed devoid of any conscious life, I tip-toed down the hall. Taking a deep breath and letting it out through my teeth in a long hiss, I stopped at Joe's door with the key gripped between my thumb and forefinger, extended my hand, and slid the key into the keyhole. I turned the knob, opened the door as quietly as possible, and stepped inside.

I smelled him before I saw him—that scent of high skies and wide open plains and…maybe…sagebrush? Then I heard him. "What the fucking hell!": Clark McCutcheon's big voice coming from behind the desk.

I let out a screech, my heart thudding in my throat. Dust danced in the slats of light stabbing through the now fully open venetian blinds. I swallowed hard. "You almost scared me to death, McCutcheon."

It looked as if Clark had been riffling through the desk's deep file drawer. Still seated, he gazed at me with slitted blue eyes. I could hear the effort it cost him to modulate his voice. "Karen, what are you doing here?"

My heart was still pounding. "What are *you* doing here?"

"I asked first. And close that door behind you."

"I don't think so." I was uncomfortable being here alone with him. I'd suspected Clark of lusting for Joe's Native artifacts, and if he had been standing over by Joe's display shelves, handling the dead man's Indian treasures—the jewelry and pottery, the tomahawks and little dolls—I wouldn't be thinking the unspeakable thought that was beginning to invade my mind. If I had found the shelves looted, and the war bonnet and baskets packed up and ready to be appropriated by an academic grave robber, I would have been appalled but not surprised. But the Native goods in their neat rows were intact. Nothing seemed to have been disturbed. Obviously it was not the precious Indian objects that Clark was after. Why was he here, then, in Joe's office—behind Joe's desk? I backed toward the door as unobtrusively as possible.

Earlier I had seen the professionally sorted and classified stacks of books and papers, the evidence of an evening's search through the printouts, Xeroxes, and books that had previously cluttered the room. Now Clark seemed to have been systematically sorting through the personal files in Joe's desk drawers. It must be papers he was looking for. But what papers? And why?

The late Indian-summer sun shone straight through the blind slats, now and, right there, at that moment, all the pieces fell together: Clark McCutcheon had killed Joe Lone Wolf. Joe must have found the source of the famous "Whiteness" essay on the Montana U website and confronted Clark with it. Clark's high standing in the profession was based on that essay. His opportunity to be awarded Enfield College's prestigious Palaver Chair was based on it. Had Joe threatened him with exposure? I recalled that evening at Rudolph's bar, when the two had been huddled together in the corner. Was that what had been going on? Had Clark responded to Joe's threats by eliminating Joe?

Standing there in the dead professor's office, I knew it wasn't the wisest thing in the world for me to be shut up alone with this man. I sidled closer to the door.

"You don't think so, huh?" McCutcheon barked. "I said 'close the door.' Do it! Now!"

When I saw the gun in Clark's hand I stopped stock still. The small, shiny nickel-plated automatic was pointed directly at me. Clark stepped out from behind the desk, his stance that of a man who knows how to use a gun, holding a gun he intends to use. "Well, I DO think so. Shut that door and get away from it."

"You don't want to do this," I said, with as much bravado as I could muster. A lot of good that open door a mere two yards away would do me, this quiet afternoon with no one in the building and a gun aimed in my direction.

"You're right, I don't." His long white-blond hair was in tight braids today, pulled forward, one hanging over each shoulder. He shook his head, and the braids shifted back and forth across the shoulders of his fringed deerskin jacket. "Such a waste of fine womanhood." His *tsk, tsk* of regret sounded sincere. "But, you *know*, don't you? I saw it just now in your expression." I couldn't tell from his sky-blue eyes exactly what his intentions were toward me. Then he shook his head as an annoyed stallion shakes off flies. "Goddammit, woman, why couldn't you leave well enough alone?"

"You *really* don't want to do this," I repeated, gesturing toward the gun. My mind raced, looking for a way out. "That would be ill-considered. The police aren't stupid. Think about how hard they'd pursue a second homicide investigation." The half-open door behind me offered no escape; a bullet could fly faster than I could run.

"And, besides…" I tilted my head seductively, widened my gaze. Maybe I could delude him into thinking I'd make some kind of sexual *quid pro quo* deal. I knew he was…interested in me; he'd told me often enough.

But his eyes were arctic blue now, cold, killer's eyes. "Nothing escapes me, Karen, I told you that before." He shook his head slowly. "And I can see your mind working. I've killed one man. He was blackmailing me, the fool. And I can't afford to dally around with you." His white teeth flashed, but there was no humor in the grin. "No matter how much fun it might be."

The sunlight was slashing through the blinds now, straight from the west. Facing the windows, I could see the dancing dust motes thicken in the bright air. "Corpse dust," I thought, though I didn't know what that meant or where I'd heard the term. The light just about blinded me, but every object in the room was illuminated. Eagle feathers gleamed. Kachina dolls shone. Light flashed off a silver squash-blossom necklace. All these beautiful artifacts seemed alive, infused with spirit, and there I stood, paralyzed. Helpless.

Faced with a gun, what could I do? I was without a weapon. My brain was frozen. I'd tried my seductive wiles in vain. Certain death was only moments away.

To die like this, with Charlie and Amanda, the two people I loved most, half a world away....To leave my poor mom alone and grieving....To abandon my students when I still had so much to teach them....No. No. I couldn't allow it to happen. Desperate with despair, I felt my hold on rational thought lift and diffuse itself into the swirling air

the pulse in my ears quickened
    its beat my spirit loosened
        its ties with this time and
            this place I was in the light
                a dancing mote in the light
then suddenly a single ray of brightness concentrated itself within the dancing dust was it the pounding of my heart or did I hear the low steady beat of drums louder now and louder voices from the darkness of the past chanting

And then the hovering arrow-shaft of radiance whizzed across the room, striking the battered stone-headed hatchet on the shelf by the door with its illumination.

On the shelf, just out of reach.

Hank's story joggled my mind. Joe Lone Wolf had told his students that the homely little tomahawk by the door held more spirit than a Shakespeare sonnet.

Clark spoke again. "Anyhow, I wouldn't believe any seductive come-ons, Karen—not from you," he scoffed. "You just drip with integrity." He made "integrity" sound like an STD. "Now get over there and shut that door." He motioned briskly with the gun, then quickly trained it back on me.

In that room filled with Joe Lone Wolf's spirit-infused relics of an ancient culture, I shrugged. "Okay," I said. "If you insist." Taking two steps in the direction of the door, I snatched up the small plain tomahawk from the shelf, spun on my toes, raised my arm high, flexed my wrist, and, as if I'd been doing it for centuries, whipped the ancient little throwing axe straight at Clark McCutcheon's head.

Chapter Twenty-seven

The following Friday

"I think I must have been hallucinating," I told the group of friends gathered around the table in Rudolph's private back room. "It was as if I were surrounded by a tribe of phantom warriors. I must have been in a waking dream. What else could it have been?"

We were out for a celebratory dinner. Felicity had arranged the party. Mom was here, shepherded by my former student, Sophia Warzek, whom I'd hired to live with us and care for Mom while Sophia worked on her MFA thesis. Greg and Irina were present, and Earlene, unexpectedly with Fareed Khan in tow. Hmm. Even Jill had come, up from New York with Eloise, her little red-headed imp of a daughter. Miles and his formidable wife, Dolores, arrived late, rather sweetly uncertain about their welcome. The wine was on the department, he said, and proceeded to order the best in the house.

Amanda was present only in spirit; she had called, as promised, from Kathmandu, and, weary of world travel, was on her way home. She was the only one I'd told about our Native ancestry, but I hadn't yet told her about my ordeal with McCutcheon.

◇◇◇

The past week, since I'd clobbered Clark McCutcheon, had indeed been an ordeal. I was on sick leave, recovering from shock.

The shock of almost killing a man. The shock of almost having been killed myself. The brand-new PhD who'd been hired to cover Joe's classes had been assigned my classes as well. I objected; I was perfectly capable of teaching. Just because I couldn't eat, and couldn't sleep, couldn't stop shivering, and couldn't stop crying whenever I heard music, there was no need to think I was in anything approaching a state of crisis. Was there?

People treated me as if I were made of porcelain. Sophia took good care of Mom. Together they baked a different variety of scone for me every day. Greg brought mystery novels. Monica held all my calls. Earlene cooked wonderful meals; she was into Mexican cuisine at the moment. I was, to say the least, well cared for.

◇◇◇

After all the bone and all the blood and all the sirens; after the official questioning, the shaky answers, the appearance of a savvy college attorney; after the treatment for shock, the medication, the psychological evaluation, I finally had been released from both police and medical custody. Before taking me home, Earlene accompanied me to my office to retrieve my purse and briefcase. There, holding place of honor on the desk, was my black-and-white-speckled tenure box, its documents intact. The attached memo from the director of custodial services read:

> *Professor Pelletier, we apologize for misplacing your file box. Ricardo, the new custodian for Dickinson Hall, misunderstood the order to pick up a box for storage from another professor's office. We hope this mistake hasn't caused you any inconvenience.*

Inconvenience? No. I would say not. Not inconvenience. Major life trauma would be more like it.

◇◇◇

In any case, here we were, my friends and I, celebrating the submission of my tenure case to the English department, celebrating the solution of Joe Lone Wolf's murder, celebrating—what?—the spiritual epiphany that had strengthened my warrior arm. I'd slammed McCutcheon good with that tomahawk, the butt of it, thank God, not the blade. It had whacked him in the left temple and knocked him cold. A copiously spreading pool of blood at first convinced me that I'd killed him. When Lieutenant Boylan showed up at the scene, he'd said, with his usual personal and political insensitivity, "Geez, what the hell you tryin' to do—*scalp* the man?"

But McCutcheon would live to go to trial, Felicity assured me, even though the case against him wasn't quite rock-solid. Spaced out on pain killers, he'd confessed from his hospital bed that he'd supplied peyote for the anti-Columbus Day after-party, but had added a side treat for Joe of a dried poisonous mushroom—Destroying Angel—one cap of which was lethal. As he had told me, Joe was blackmailing him, threatening to publicly expose his plagiarism and thus scuttle his career. And since Joe was prepared to make the transition to a new persona, Clark didn't have anything to hold over his head. Joe could simply vanish at will.

"But," I asked Felicity, "Will a confession obtained under the influence of palliative drugs hold up in court?

With my testimony and that of the students who would testify that McCutcheon was at the party, Felicity said, the D.A. would make damn sure it did.

◇◇◇

As the appetizers were delivered, the student server placing a small turquoise plate of ceviche in front of me, my friends listened to my tale of mystical warriors with various degrees of amusement and concern. The amusement ticked me off. Spearing a perfect, coral-hued shrimp, I continued, "I'm a rational twenty-first-century scholar. I don't believe in the supernatural. It *must* have been a hallucination. But…" I finished up, my voice wavering. "It was such a powerful experience. Somehow it changed me."

"Sure you didn't partake of the magical mushroom yourself?" Greg asked, taking a bread stick from the basket and winking at me.

Jill frowned at him. She snitched a marinated scallop from my plate. "*How* did it change you?" She bit the scallop in half and shared it with Eloise. "Other than that you became a red-hot tomahawk-throwing mama?"

I hesitated—I'd had a second glass of wine—then answered. "There was *that*. But otherwise…" I felt my shoulders shrug of their own volition beneath my denim jacket. "Otherwise—well, I seem to have come to my senses. Being tenured at Enfield is no longer the most important thing in my life."

Miles Jewell clapped his hands over his ears. "I didn't hear that."

"No?" Jill gaped at me with mock consternation.

"Yeah—can you believe it? If I don't get tenure, then I don't get tenure. Enfield's loss." I glanced over at Miles with faux bravado.

◇◇◇

I truly meant what I said, but I was being somewhat meretricious in saying it. Midweek, Avery had come to visit, bringing a dozen white roses and a first edition of Sylvia Plath's *Ariel*. "About tenure…" he said, biting into a ginger scone. At his request, Sophia and Mom had gone for a walk. He took a sip of tea. "Don't fret about it. Cooler heads than Hilton's are evaluating your extremely impressive case."

"Oh?" What else was there to say?

"You understand me, I know," he concluded, setting down his half-empty cup and rising from the couch. Everything the man did was graceful, including inserting his arms into the sleeves of his wool topcoat. "And," he continued with a half-smile, pointing a finger at me, "remember, this conversation never happened."

◇◇◇

I could make a life for myself away from Enfield, I thought, if I'd had to. As long as I had Charlie and Amanda, I'd survive. I let my gaze light briefly on each face: my old colleagues—Earlene, Greg, Jill—and, Felicity, my new friend. I would have missed them if I'd had to leave. But Charlie was the one essential. From the Iraqi hinterlands he'd finally returned to Baghdad, and he'd called me, four times, listening quietly while I sobbed. But it had been three days since I'd heard from him, and I didn't understand why.

Felicity, awkward among all these academics, shifted in her seat and checked her watch. She probably couldn't wait to get away from the shop talk. I'd expected Lombardi to join us, but he hadn't. I hoped he and Felicity weren't still on the outs.

◇◇◇

I lifted my glass of Cabernet and drank. Through the arched door to the main dining room, I could see the restaurant begin to fill with its usual Friday evening crowd. Ayesha entered the room along with a stylishly dressed older woman, whose dark hair was uncovered. The woman's arm was around Ayesha's shoulders, and she was smiling. Must be Ayesha's mom. They sat at a large, round table, their heads together, laughing at some private joke.

I stood up; I couldn't help it. Either I'm an incurable Nosey Nancy, or I care deeply about the lives of my students. Same thing, probably. "Back in a minute," I said.

Ayesha, in a festive peppermint pink robe with a sequined bodice, saw me coming and whispered into her mother's ear. Mrs. Ahmed glanced up, smiled, and then patted the seat next to her. I sat, with Ayesha on my other side. Both women smelled of jasmine.

"I've heard so much, Professor, about how you help Ayesha." The older woman's English was lilting and a bit formal. "You will be first one I tell. My daughter is to be married soon. We are here tonight to celebrate."

"Is that so?" I looked at Ayesha with questioning eyes.

"Yes," my student said, glancing modestly away from my direct gaze. "We'll have the wedding during winter break. I hope you'll be able to come."

"Yes, of course," I said, a million questions assaulting my mind.

Two dark-skinned young men entered the dining room, one in jeans and a leather jacket, the other wearing a beige linen tunic and an ornate medallion. Mrs. Ahmed raised her hand, and they headed in our direction. I glanced from one man to the other, hoping my scrutiny wasn't too obvious. Which one was Ayesha's husband-to-be? Both were handsome, and each carried himself with impressive confidence. Whichever one it was, this must be the father of her unborn child.

"Congratulations, Ayesha," I said, squeezing her hand, fondly. I must admit, however, I felt cheated. When Ayesha became a married woman and a mother, I'd lose my pet student, and she only in her sophomore year.

Mrs. Ahmed went on, "These are my sons, Professor."

I nodded at them. Her *sons*, I thought. It must be the custom in their culture to accept the groom completely into the family. But which one *was* he? The men sat together, across the table, the guy in the leather jacket reaching out to shake my hand. Neither sat next to Ayesha. Perhaps another custom? I was beginning to feel very provincial.

"And now my husband arrives, as you can see." A tall, dark, older man, impeccably dressed in a gray pin-striped Western suit, walked toward us. He looked every inch the diplomat Ayesha had told me he was. And then it struck me why Ayesha had been so nonchalant about Lieutenant Boylan's suspicions of her. She was a member of a diplomatic family; could it be that she had diplomatic immunity?

I leaned over in her direction, gesturing at the two young men, and asked, "Which one is the lucky man?"

She gazed first at one, then at the other, and her eyes sparkled. At first I thought it was a sparkle of joy, but a second glance convinced me that, for some reason, my student was deeply amused. But, why?

Now Hank Brody had somehow gotten into the mix, trailing Mr. Ahmed by a few feet. Hank must have a job at Rudolph's now, I thought; probably as a part-time maitre d'. He looked surprisingly good, dressed in a sport jacket, shirt and tie. His jeans were ironed. And—could it be?—he'd even had a haircut; his dreads were now short and shiny; Hank must have really wanted the job. That boy worked entirely too hard. I'd have to speak to Earlene about him. But, nonetheless, Hank looked happy—if a little…what?…dazed?

Then Ayesha jumped up from her seat, threw her arms around Hank, and hugged him tight. "Behold," she said, grinning at me, "the bridegroom cometh."

◇◇◇

"Joe Lone Wolf may have been a liar and an opportunist," I said to my friends, as the server came around again with the coffee pot. "But, you know, it's strange, I don't think he was a total fraud. He seemed to have loved his work and cared deeply about what he taught his students. He couldn't say a pleasant word to his colleagues, but he seems to have opened whole new worlds for those kids." It was almost ten p.m., and I was waiting for my slice of chocolate espresso layer cake. Coffee *and* espresso cake: there'd be no sleep for me tonight. But, what the hell.

"How can you say that?" Greg asked, scowling. "He was completely bogus."

I'd gotten to the mellow stage of the evening. "I'm not sure about that. I think it's not so much that he was a fraud, but that he lived within…a self-constructed identity fantasy. I think that by the end, he must have felt his spirit being eaten away by falsity."

Miles squinted at me. "You know, I'm afraid the department is somewhat to blame, here. We never really saw Lone Wolf—we simply imposed on him an image of what we thought he was supposed to be. We never even checked into his bona fides, as we would have with anyone else. We wanted an Indian, and he said he was an Indian, so we saw an Indian."

"Indians?" My mother, who'd been drowsing throughout the evening, suddenly looked up at Miles, and spoke. But Miles continued before she could go on. "I believe that in so doing," he said, carefully enunciating his words, "we were practicing an egregious form of racism." He began to pour more wine, but Dolores pulled his glass away. The old academic warrior sat there a moment with the green bottle tilted. Then he set it back on the table.

Mom said, "It's a different time now—we're proud to be Indians."

Everyone looked at her uncomprehendingly.

"Indeed we are, Mom," I said, smiling at her. Connie had finally called. She'd gotten the job as Lowell WalMart manager, would be flying home from Arkansas tomorrow, and would pick our mother up on the way back from Bradley Field. I told my sister that Mom had done well with me and asked her if I could take Mom again for the six-week break between semesters. That would ease her transition to the new job, I said, and help ease my loneliness with Charlie gone. And, by the way, would she like to bring her family for Christmas? Amanda would be home and she adored her cousin, Courtney, and I could make a real old-fashioned *tortière* for dinner. Connie said she'd think about it.

Earlene breached the awkward conversational gap. "And what about Ned?"

I turned to her. "What about him?"

"He seemed to bear the whole guilty history of white oppression on his narrow shoulders. He *meant* well—it's just that he was so damn…reductive and sanctimonious."

Fareed spoke up. "And when McCutcheon found out Hilton was mistakenly favoring a lily-white charlatan for the only tenured department position, he told Ned about Joe's true identity."

Miles grasped his head with both hands. "I didn't know that. So—Hilton put his professional credibility on the line to support the minority tenure candidate, only to find out Lone Wolf was bogus? The poor sap."

Greg jumped in. "Not bogus, Jewell." He winked at me, again. "Joe lived within a self-constructed identity fantasy."

"Humph," Miles said, "no wonder Hilton freaked out. He'd taken Joe on as a holy cause. And then that blackjack dealer showing up with *her* story…Hilton was always a bit…tenuous of sanity. I wonder if he'll be able to come back to work next semester?"

Nobody seemed to care much. The party was winding down, my mom was back in her daze, and Felicity was becoming increasingly restless, watching the clock, pacing, muttering into her cell phone. Poor thing, I thought, she must be uncomfortable—time for her to get home to that baby.

When I'd been out talking to Ayesha, someone had appropriated my seat, so I was now sitting with my back to the door. Belatedly, Sergeant Lombardi joined the party, taking the seat upon which Felicity had piled her coat and bag. She gave him a questioning look, and he nodded.

Taking a second bite of espresso cake, I felt what little was left of my energy evaporate. "I'm so looped," I said, putting down my fork, "I don't even know if I can drive home."

There was some sort of mild commotion behind me, but I was too tired to turn around. Everyone was looking at me with big grins on their faces.

"What?" I asked. "None of you ever drank a little too much?"

Behind me, I heard a familiar deep, warm laugh, and I suddenly stopped breathing. Could it be? No, not possible. I jumped up and spun around. Oh. My. God. "Charlie!" I screeched, bursting into tears. The love of my life swept me up and held me tight in his strong embrace.

Emergency family leave. Somehow, Lieutenant Charles Piotrowski, United States National Guard, stationed in Iraq, had managed to get himself home for two weeks emergency family leave.